CONTRACT OF DEFIANCE

SPECTRAS ARISE
BOOK 1

TAMMY SALYER

CONTRACT OF DEFIANCE

CONTRACT OF DEFIANCE: SPECTRAS ARISE, BOOK 1

eBook ISBN: 9780985319212

Paperback ISBN: 978-1-954113-01-5

Cover design by Miblart.

INTRODUCTION

Hello and thank you for being here! Should you enjoy the words on these pages (and I hope you do!), I encourage you to join my Book Club and visit me at:

www.tammysalyer.com

I occasionally send newsletters to my Book Club with new releases, special offers, and other bits of news. As a special thanks to new members, please enjoy a handful of novellas and short stories from my many and sundry universes FOR FREE.

ONE

Maybe running for my life during a firefight with a squad of Corps soldiers isn't the best time to be having second thoughts about my occupation, but I have to ask myself, why the hell did I become an arms smuggler? I could have been an engineer!

David vaults over a discarded tool caddy like a champion hurdler and I follow on his heels, clipping one foot on a drill and pinwheeling my arms to keep my balance without missing a step. This is a race where the loser dies.

The rest of our crew already has the holodisc, so now it's just a question of distracting the Corps until they can get safely back to the *Temptation* and off Obal 3. We can handle that. Our body armor doesn't provide as much protection as newer-issue Corps gear, but at least it's lighter, and we're starting to lose the two squads on our heels. We had enough time to deploy decoys around the station before being detected, and their shots aren't coming anywhere near us.

Still in the lead, David slams through a swinging door to his right. As I veer through, a round flies past my ear, whistling like a miniature surface-to-air missile and knocking the door from its hinges. That was close! *Most* of their shots aren't coming near us anyway.

The launch docks are just ahead and we propel toward them. David slams the heavy blast door behind me as I tumble in, barely making it through before the squad fans out behind us and fills the gap with bullets. Shielded by the blast door, he jams a wad of E-10 wax into the lock system, hoping to fry it and buy us some time, and we keep moving. Two rights, two lefts, then down a flight of stairs to subdock three and we'll be at our escape shuttle. Almost there.

Almost.

A door to our left blows open and automatic fire stutters down the passage. Regular rounds. They must have realized seeker rounds were useless. I'm suddenly spun sideways as a round grazes my ribs, but the low impact does no damage to the armor. We make it into the concealment of the stairwell door that leads to our shuttle's dock. Locked! Smoke hangs in the air, burning my lungs with each ragged breath as I lean out of sight. David frantically scans the corridor but can't see through the haze.

"Bypass it. I'll keep them busy."

He fires down the corridor as I pry the face off the locking system and rip wires free until I can short it out. It hisses as the bolt slides free.

"Shit!" David yells.

Warm, sticky blood speckles my face. I jerk my head back and see it pouring from his left shoulder. He's pressing one hand over the wound, and I can't tell how serious the damage is. If the bullet struck bone, he has major problems.

Pulling him toward me, I try to get us both through the door, but he resists.

"It's open, come on!" I yell.

He lets go of his shoulder and pushes me backward with his good hand—hard. His eyes are squinted and his face pale, but the message in his expression is clear. *Get out of here!*

"What are you doing?!"

"Keep going. Don't stop. Get to the shuttle and get out of here," he says.

"No, David, I'm not leaving you!"

"Get back to the crew and finish the job. And, little sis, whatever you do, don't let Rajcik out of your sight."

Before I can stop him, he throws his carbine into the corridor and yells, "Don't shoot! I'm unarmed!" He gives me a final push through the door and slams it shut, the sound like a coffin lid.

For a split second, I'm stunned, unable to believe he'd do this. Surrendering to a squad of Corps soldiers is a death sentence for deserters like us. A muffled voice outside commands, "Hands behind your head! Move forward slowly!"

They know there are two of us, and they'll be coming through the door in seconds. The only chance David has is if I can get help. The shuttle should be docked outside, and if I'm going to go, it has to be now. I take the stairs two at time, jumping over the rail when I'm still about two meters from the deck. Landing hard thanks to the body armor, I crumple to one knee but ignore the sting and keep running.

My mind is filled with one stuttering mantra: get to the shuttle and rendezvous with the crew. I'm working on reflex now but I'm torn. Part of me wants to double back and ambush the squad holding David, but one against ten is asking to be shredded, and the rest of me says today is not a good day to die. It's the crew or nothing.

Bursting into the docking bay, I sprint all the way through. Where's the shuttle? The only thing in the cavernous bay is a modified and very used ISPS—Intersystem Propulsion Shuttle—sitting in the middle with its loading ramp open. Am I in the wrong bay? I keep running, not wanting to make myself a target to anyone that might be in the ship. If I get to the control room on the other side of the bay, I can stop and check my VDU.

I get to the blast door and start working on a lock bypass, but it begins sliding open before I finish. Fueled by pure reflex, I hit the man coming through in the throat with the stock of my AK-80 pulse carbine. Caught by surprise, he collapses backward, gagging and going limp when his head hits the floor. As I hop over him to get inside, the left side of my neck suddenly burns with liquid fire, as if I'm being branded, and the bullet pings against the wall in front of me. The shot probably would have gone through my skull if I hadn't been jumping when it hit me. Spinning ninety degrees, I land on my side and start firing back at the soldiers streaming across the bay. They quickly duck and cover behind scattered equipment. Climbing over the man I knocked out, I note with some regret that he's no soldier, but at the moment, I have other concerns. Once inside the cover of the control room, I try to drag him in so I can close the damn door, but his body is too heavy.

The squad closes on me fast and a soldier springs through the doorway before I can get the man moved. I fire one-handed, aiming for his vulnerable neck, and he goes down like a felled tree, blood spraying the walls and me. He must have thought I'd exited through the rear door or he wouldn't have charged through like that. His mistake.

Everything falls quiet outside. I lean against the wall next to the doorway, listening and waiting. I can almost hear them breathing, and now I have two bodies to get out of the way if I'm going to be able to close the control room door. What are my options? I could dive for the second exit, but I'll be exposed. If I wait for them to move in, they'll have plenty of time to call backup and surround me. My options, clearly, are shit.

There's no more time to think it through. Scooting backward, I risk a glance through the reinforced porthole into the bay. There's movement out there, a couple of people coming down the ISPS's ramp. They keep low, moving carefully, trying to avoid being seen. What are they doing? Doesn't matter—they may be just the diversion I need to get the soldiers off my back while I haul ass to the escape shuttle. If they'd just make some noise.

There are two of them. The bigger one is built like a champion fighter, and tall enough to have to hunch when standing beneath the ship. The other is about David's height, with dark brown hair and a several days of beard growth. They move with too much practiced stealth toward the front end of the bay to be civilians. Former Corps maybe? As they disappear from my line of sight, I want to scream in frustration.

"Put down that weapon!" It's one of the soldiers, but he's not talking to me.

Another voice rings out. "We don't want any trouble. Our mechanic is in the control room. We just want to get him out. No trouble."

"This is a Corps-controlled hangar. Put your weapon down and show yourself."

This is the moment and I lunge for the rear door. But the day just gets worse and worse as a soldier tackles me from behind. My ribs take both our weight as we hit the floor and I grit my teeth against a scream of pain. The soldier gets his feet planted and yanks me up by both arms, forcing me to drop my carbine. Fighting back, I kick against the wall and throw him off-balance. He staggers backward, loosening his hold enough for me to jerk one hand free. I spin sideways, snatching at his sidearm as I do. It comes clear of the holster, and I shoot him right below his armpit where the body armor is thinner to allow for articulation. A look of anguished surprise freezes across his features. My other arm, still entwined with his, twists painfully as he falls, pulling me back to the floor. I yank it free and jump up, immediately taking a shot mid-torso by another soldier. The range is so close that it feels as if my entire chest collapses as it blows me back into the second doorway. Gasping, trying to force my lungs to suck in air, I watch helplessly as he aims, preparing to blow my head off.

A rifle report echoes across the dock, and the soldier is thrown into the wall behind me. The shot was well aimed, tearing through his neck, and he crumples lifeless to the floor.

Tendrils of acrid smoke from the volume of shots fired waver through the room as I lie bleeding, my lungs struggling to expand. Lurching to the wall, I lean into it, listening. Footsteps approach quickly and cautiously. There's no time to think, only to react. I check the soldier's pistol and then my own. Empty, dammit! I holster mine and scan the room, but the bluish smoke conceals any other weapons. Pulling an NKT bolo from my equipment vest, I lower into a crouch beside the doorway. Black dots shoot across my vision, making it hard to concentrate, and my legs shake, wanting to spill out from under me. Yeah, engineering would have been a better choice.

The black barrel of a rifle materializes, framed in the doorway. Trying to get the drop on the gunman, I lunge, staying low, and thrust the blade up, aiming for his vitals. But I'm too shaky. The blade barely nicks his thigh. As I pull back, prepping for another attempt, a galaxy of stars explodes through my head.

TWO

No blackness is as dark or deep as unconsciousness, and rising out of the murk takes as much effort as waking the dead. Slowly, as if time has been stretched, I float back toward awareness, the still layers of my torpor gradually being disturbed by the suck and whoosh of an air exchanger.

After a while, nausea creeps in and rudely yanks my addled consciousness out of its insensate serenity. Not the kind of immediate nausea you feel right before throwing up, but the penetrating queasiness of vertigo. A familiar feeling. Having suffered other concussions, it's easy to pin the cause on the bludgeoning my skull took right before I checked out.

It takes considerable effort to focus. Where am I and how the hell did I get here? Why am I not dead? Images flash behind my eyes. Soldiers, David, the dock control room . . . it comes back to me in pieces, starting from the blackout and rewinding to when my team had been discovered in the data warehouse on Obal 3. We were there to collect a holodisc with intel for our next job, the big one that will finally give David and me enough capital to get as far away from the Admin as a ship can go. When the security squad closed in, we ran, trying to draw them off so our crew could get away. The lingering cacophony of the firefight echoes in my head, making the transition into this subdued atmosphere incongruous, like the feeling of shrapnel wrapped in velvet.

A dull ache slowly shrink-wraps my body from my cheekbones to the arches of my feet, becoming unbearable within a few minutes. Jesus, I feel sick, and stiff. I try to reach up and rub my eyes, but my arms are immobile, clamped to whatever I'm lying on. The realization that I am completely and irrevocably screwed crashes over me like a jet of freezing water and I finally jolt fully awake.

Lights pierce my optic nerves and spear directly into my bruised brain. A flicker at the edge of my consciousness threatens to tug me back down, my mind unwilling to accept the harsh brightness or my uncertain fate. Craning my neck in each direction causes the skin to tug painfully where the bullet grazed me. I'm strapped to a gurney, in a room about five-by-three meters. Cupboards and medical equipment line the walls and the air has that sterile bite that dries the mucus in your sinuses, like a sensory deprivation cell. Which means I'm not in a hospital but on a ship. The med supplies lack any insignia or labels, so not military. Could be transport or cargo. Maybe I haven't been pinched by the Corps, but I'm not sure. They sometimes hire civilian contractors, but not usually for prisoner transport. Then whose ship is it? Could be the ISPS that was docked in the bay of the control room I'd ended up in. But why?

No one has come in to check on me, but a large two-way mirror dominates the wall to my left and there's a security and observation camera hanging from the ceiling.

"Anyone there?" I try to shout, but my throat is dry, lined with felt. How long have I been here? Lifting my head makes my stomach jolt and brain feel like a rotting cantaloupe. There's an IV stuck in the bend of my left elbow. Someone has taken my clothes and dressed me in a sleeveless, shin-length gray robe, which allows me a good look at the multicolored explosion of bruises running along my arms. My aching ribs force me to lie back down, and a groan wants to crawl out of me, but I won't give whoever's watching the satisfaction. Trying to wiggle my wrists from side to side to test the tightness of the restraints is useless. They're made of a thick banding material, and there's no way I can tear through them. At least they aren't chafing the skin off my arms.

The doors slide open with a grating-metal sound and I jerk my head to look, the wound in my neck stinging and making me hiss in pain. *Here we go, Aly. Wake up and get on top of this.*

A striking woman, easily a head taller than me, with a spider-web patchwork of tiny lines around her eyes, strides toward me, her gaze dark and level. She's dressed in a sleeveless top and baggy cargo pants made of a vinyl-cotton hybrid similar to the fabric of military uniforms, and wears a snug ambidextrous-draw shoulder holster complete with two pistols. She looks as if she knows how to draw them fast enough to matter. Behind her is a man that I think I recognize as the scruffy, ex-military type from the hangar. He also carries a pistol, this one on a belt. Same cargo pants and a black utility jacket over a washed-out gray T-shirt. Simple, nondescript clothing. And, most importantly, not Corps. They watch me coolly. I stare back at them with the same consideration.

The woman starts us off: "I'm Captain Eleanor Vitruzzi, and you're a passenger on my ship." I don't miss the inflection she puts on the word *passenger*. She means *prisoner*. "This is Strahan, the one who nearly deflated your skull. Consider yourself lucky, after what you did to our mechanic." Her posture is relaxed and in control, but her eyes betray tension. Anger, maybe curiosity.

"You're probably disoriented right now because of the tissue regeneration stimulants and painkillers you're on. They should wear off in a few hours." She analyzes a monitor near my right shoulder and checks my IV drip as she speaks. "Your ribs look like you got hit by a cannonball, but nothing is broken. And the wound on your neck is superficial. In fact, you're incredibly lucky." She pauses, letting me absorb the information, and then continues, "Now why don't you tell us the rest of the story."

This is not the way I want this to go. I want out of these restraints and I want my guns. Neither of which is likely, so I start by trying to negotiate with something small.

"Look." I clear my throat. "I don't know you and I don't know why I'm here. But I assure you, I have no problem with you, and as far as I know, you don't have one with me. So let's be civil. Take off these restraints and tell me what I'm doing here." My voice gains momentum after the first few words. I've always been a quick healer.

Vitruzzi looks at me with skepticism for a moment, and Strahan's scowl deepens. Surprisingly, she starts unbuckling the restraints.

"Captain!" Strahan challenges, but Vitruzzi frees both of my wrists.

She stares directly into my eyes and says, "She's right, Karl. No reason to think she's a threat to us. She's unarmed, and we are civilized people." Softening her tone slightly, she finishes, "This can't be comfortable and you need to get some blood moving if you're going to recover."

Strahan takes a step back and rests his hand on the grip of his pistol, ready for anything. I have to be careful what I do here, and what I say. I don't want to set these people off, but I have a few questions of my own.

I sit up as slowly and carefully as I can, more because of the sickening complaint from my ribs than any fear of alarming them. "So who are you? Admin? Where are we and what do you want with me?"

Vitruzzi takes another few seconds to look me over before she answers. "We're in flight, three days from Obal 3."

She continues to talk, but my mind is spinning. We've been flying for three days! I barely hear the rest of what she says before I'm on my feet, yelling, "I've got to get back there!"

"Hold it! Sit down." The tone of command.

I comply as my head seems to fill with concrete, threatening to pull me face-first into the hard floor, and shifting gray veils materialize in front of my eyes. With an effort, I continue, "Look, my name is Aly Erikson and you've got to take me back to Obal 3. My brother and my crew are there, and I need to find out what happened to them."

Neither of them comments, just look at me. Anger suddenly tears through the tight fabric occluding my brain, making my next words rough and raw. "Why the fuck did you kidnap me? I haven't done anything to you!"

Strahan's eyes narrow further, but Vitruzzi seems unperturbed. It's almost as if she's holding back a chuckle. What's the joke? If my head wasn't so fogged up I'd be more on top of things. What am I missing?

"To tell you the truth, we brought you on board for your own safety."

Urgency cleaves through my body like a plasma torch. I need to find Rajcik and the rest of the team. At this point, I don't even know if they made it off Obal 3. If they did, they may know where David is. These thoughts pulse in time with the pain in my head, blocking everything else out. The last glimpse I had of David's face, pale and severe as he surrendered so I could get away, floods my mind. Hold on, brother. *I'm going to find you.*

She continues, this time with a hard edge to her voice, "If you think nearly killing an unarmed man is nothing, you have a disturbing lack of empathy for others."

The memory of a face comes to mind. "The blond guy . . ."

"That's right. His name is Bodie Murdock. He's a damn fine technician and a member of my crew. Lucky for you, he's going to make it."

"I can explain that. I didn't mean to hit him that hard. I was trying to get away from the Corps, and when he came out of the control room—it was just reflex."

"You almost killed him." Strahan's voice is granite.

I didn't want to hurt the guy, but it was instinct, and something tells me Strahan would have done the same thing under the circumstances. Maybe already had. I'm thinking of the soldier who'd been about to shoot me in the control room, and the rifle shot that had come out of nowhere, ripping his throat out. It had to have been someone from the ISPS who'd saved my life. Maybe intentionally, maybe not.

Vitruzzi continues, "So let's talk about what's fair. We saved your ass on Obal 3. You can just think of it as a neighborly gesture among people with common interests. And now we're going to give you a chance to make it up to us."

This just got more complicated. I force myself to stay still, though every muscle in my body is ready to fight. I could jump them, steal their ship and fly it back to Obal 3—in my dreams. In my shape, I'd be dead before I got to the door. One thing, at least, is clear. They're not Admin, and if they haven't turned me in yet, they probably aren't planning to.

But what had they been doing on Obal 3 in the first place? It's a small planet, mainly an outpost used by the Admin for launching security operations in that quadrant. The only reason for citizens to be there is if they're under contract with the Admin. And the kind of citizens contracted by the Admin are the law-abiding kind, which leaves out kidnappers and people who shoot Capital Military Corps soldiers.

Vitruzzi watches me closely as I piece all this together. She seems to have relaxed a little, but Strahan looks as if he might be considering what I'd taste like spitted and roasted. His build is medium, neither bulky nor lithe. He could be a wrestler or a runner, but the rigid set of his shoulders and chronic, brooding scowl that carves deep lines across his forehead indicates his default setting is pissed off and dangerous. There's no mistaking it —I can see by the way he holds himself that he's ex-Corps. His at-the-ready stance and casual awareness of everything in the room makes it as obvious as if he were still wearing a uniform. It's hard to know what kind of switch might be flipped if he decides he doesn't like what I say.

She continues, "So here's the deal. We heard a security transmission that your crew was smuggling something from the data warehouse. It sounds like they got off world, but you were left behind. Why? Were you running a diversion?"

"I don't know what you're talking about." Why make it easy for them?

Her eyes don't leave my face, and her expression remains very calm. "It doesn't matter. The thing that does matter is that we have you, and your crew has the structural and security holodisc for the Fortress."

One of my eyes twitches, but I clamp down on my surprise. How the hell does she know that?

"Now, here's where you get to answer some questions. What's your team planning on doing with them?"

This is not what I want to be happening right now. As I lean forward to hide the emotions rampaging across my face, my ribs moan in protest. I'm not telling them a damn thing.

"I'm losing patience," Strahan warns.

What do they want? A cut? There's no way in hell Rajcik will give them a percentage, not even in trade for me. At this point, the crew may even think David and I have both been arrested and have already started making their way to the Fortress to complete the job. If that's the case, my leverage here amounts to nothing. If this situation could be worse, I don't know how.

Completely without warning, Strahan's grip locks around the neck of my smock, pulling me to my feet. My head spins, but I still have the reflexes to strike out and try to dislodge his grip. The exertion and pain are too much. My knees give out, spilling me on the floor, half out of the smock. Waves of nausea leave me huddled, shivering on the cold tile. Warm, fresh blood from my neck drips down my shoulder.

"Karl, let her go!" Vitruzzi's voice is sharp, but not angry, not out of control. She is definitely in charge here. He lets go, and I see his booted feet backing up through my half-open eyes. My head is reeling, yet my senses are hyperacute and strangely disconnected, as if I'm watching everything around me through a high-rez telescope. Grains of dust and debris the size of sand seem to be miniature planets set in the dimples of his boot leather, their details as clear as my own name. I can even smell the smoky residue of the firefight. Is it coming from my hair? I have to get off this floor. Summoning more will than strength, I pull myself up, holding on to the gurney to stay upright.

"If you ever touch me again, you're a dead man. Get me?" Of

course my threat is hollow; we can all see what kind of shape I'm in. But my silence isn't doing me any good, so I'll dangle them a little rope. "Look, you're right. I'm a smuggler working with János Rajcik. We deal mostly in arms, and you probably know as well as I that we could lift enough from the Fortress to live a long, comfortable life." I look for any sense of recognition in their faces. Anyone in the system working in law enforcement or crime will know Rajcik's reputation, but their faces remain stony. Either they're very good at hiding their thoughts, or they're completely clueless. If they haven't heard of Rajcik, they're small time.

Vitruzzi asks, "Why didn't you fly out with the rest of your team?"

She must be trying to suss out my value to my comrades. It's no use evading her questions. I have nowhere to go, and considering the fact that we're most likely a couple of astronomical units from the nearest planet's orbit, neither do they. All we have right now is time and distance, one too short, the other too long and getting longer. Somehow, I have to persuade them to let me go. I'll tell them as much of my story as possible. If I'm lucky, they'll have a little sympathy. Really lucky.

"My brother and I were drawing off fire, making for a short-range shuttle stashed in . . ." And I remember. The shuttle wasn't where we'd thought it would be. Their eyes stay on me, and I shake off my confusion and continue, "We got pinned down by Corps and David was arrested. I escaped and ended up in your dock's control room. And then you," I look pointedly at Strahan, "killed the remainder of the squad." I pause, giving him a chance to elaborate on that point, but he doesn't.

"So here I am. I'm cut off from my team and you're harboring a fugitive, which probably isn't the smartest move you've ever made. If you're looking for a percentage of our take, I can't promise you anything. We only stole the holodisc, nothing that can be split."

It's a risk to tell them this much, but what difference does it make? Vitruzzi made it clear: I'm their prisoner. I have nothing to bargain with, so they can do whatever they want to me. If they were going to kill me, they wouldn't have gone through the trouble to fix me up. I have a feeling that these people aren't cutthroat smugglers willing to spill blood out of convenience. I hope like hell I'm right.

A look passes between them, but I can't tell what they're thinking. Finally, Vitruzzi turns back to me. "All right Erikson, we're going to be in the sky for a few days. Maybe you'll think of something else you want to tell us before we get where we're going."

"Which is?"

"Spectra 6."

I mentally flip through navigation charts in my mind to figure out how far that is from Obal 3. It has to be a week at least. Alarms shriek in my head, but I manage to keep my tone at least semireasonable. "Wait. You don't understand. My brother's been arrested and I have to try to rescue him. There's still a chance! Look, take me back, let me rendezvous with my crew, and I might be able to get you in on the deal. We can work something out so it won't be a waste of your time. But your chances for making any bank on this get worse with every kilometer that passes between me and my team."

The corners of her mouth drop into a frown. "It would be suicide to take you back to Obal 3. By now they'll have the planet locked up like a holding cell and every Corps search-and-destroy team in the quadrant will be looking for your crew." She crosses her arms resolutely. "Face it, you're better off here than anywhere else right now. Why do you assume we want a cut, anyway?"

She's testing me, and I almost laugh at the absurdity of the question. But I don't have the energy to haggle anymore. "Why else would I be here?"

She stares at me blankly, long enough for me to figure out that my question has pissed her off.

She walks to the cabinets and comes back carrying tissue glue and cleaning solution. "We're not pirates, Erikson. My crew and I have a contract with the Admin, and some of us are citizens. But we're not going to turn you in. Which you've already figured out." She hands me the solution and some gauze and motions for me to clean off my neck. The bleeding has stopped on its own, which is a good sign. "All we want is the holodisc."

Strahan finally relaxes. The verdict is in: I'm not nearly as threatening in my weakened, bruised, and spinning state as I want to be. Reaching into the breast pocket of his jacket, he pulls out a small box of cigarettes and shakes one loose.

They seem sincere, but what could they possibly want the holodisc for? Vitruzzi has one thing right: the disc contains all the plans for the Fortress—a space station designed by the Admin as both a containment and development site for its covert research, mostly in biological warfare, the kind that regular people would shudder to think about. Nuclear and chemical munitions development is its secondary purpose. Its location, and until now, its infrastructure, are only known to the scientists and soldiers who operate there, and the few leaders in the Admin's hierarchy who keep the station funded. Most citizens don't even know it exists. It's the Admin's bogeyman, the nightmare leviathan of an advanced military industry.

And Vitruzzi, this down-and-out captain of an obsolete and ramshackle transport ship, wants me to believe that I was kidnapped for a copy of the holodisc? That I'll happily hand it over as a thanks for saving my skin? This has to be the joke she was trying not to laugh about earlier.

I hold her eye, waiting for the punch line, but her expression is somber. Letting my glance jump to Strahan's face, the amusement I expect to see isn't there either. Nothing. They're serious.

"So that's it, huh? A copy of the holodisc? And if I arrange it, you'll let me go?" She doesn't nod. She doesn't need to. I can't think of a reason for anyone besides my crew to want that disc. It's worth next to nothing on the black market because no one besides us is crazy enough to get anywhere near the Fortress, much less smuggle weapons from it. I won't bother asking Vitruzzi what she wants with the disc. If I were her, I wouldn't tell me anyway.

Trying to sound convincing, I continue, "Yeah. I think we can work that out." Which is about as likely as me growing wings and learning to breathe nitrogen. Even if I could contact Rajcik and the team, there's no way in frozen hell that he'll ever, *ever*, let anyone else have a copy of the disc. The deal he made with T'Kai to get his hands on it was practically signed in blood. But what else can I say?

Which brings up a more important question: How do they know about the disc and our intent to steal it in the first place? Rajcik has been on the Admin's top-ten most wanted list for years, and if Kurosawa T'Kai, the Admin's director of the Ministry of Science and Engineering, is ever tied to those plans being leaked to him, T'Kai will be tried and fried before the sun sets. Everyone involved knows the risks, and no one else should know about the disc. *No one.* So, either T'Kai had changed plans and betrayed us, or . . . what?

I bring my attention back to the present problem. "When can I contact my people?"

"We'll be on Spectra 6 in about four days . . ."

Impatiently, I cut in, "We need to get back to the Obals *now.* There's no time to lose."

"Not going to happen. Spectra 6 is the only place with the kind of equipment we need to send encrypted communications across citizen-controlled satellites. Once we get there and you get in touch with your people, we'll decide how to proceed. When will they make their move on the Fortress?"

If I tell her it will be soon, it might speed up her willingness to get back to the Obals. But she'll see right through me if I lie. "My best guess is that we'll . . . they'll be ready in a couple of weeks. That'll be too soon for the Admin to make major changes to the Fortress's security protocols, even if they find out we have the details. Which, according to the contact who provided them, they won't." I watch them carefully as I say this, trying to catch any hint that might reveal how much they know. But they're too good at this game; their faces are as smooth and expressionless as a missile housing.

"So we have some time. Where were you supposed to rendezvous with your team?"

She gets right to the point, but I'm tired of answering questions. "Look, Vitruzzi, I've been incredibly cooperative, considering the circumstances, and I'm done until you give me something in return." I'm pissing in the wind, but I'm exhausted, angry, and have a sinking feeling the whole shitstorm is just a prelude to a catastrophe. "What about giving me back my clothes and weapons? At least my gear."

Strahan lets out a sarcastic grunt and drops his cigarette butt into a sealed trash canister. Vitruzzi decides to be more accommodating. "Sure. Karl, let Desto and the rest of the crew know we've got a guest on board." Strahan exits and she turns her hard gaze back on me. "I'm going to let you out of here, Erikson, because I know that you know there's nowhere to run, and we're your only chance of finding your brother and your crew. We've got an arrangement here, and as long as you keep as level about it as you are right now, we'll all come out of this with what we want. But the minute you fuck up, no one on this ship will hesitate to send your ass into cold space."

THREE

An hour later, my weapons are still MIA, but I manage to twist myself into my returned clothing. It hurts in spectacular ways and makes sweat pop out on my forehead, harshly reminding me of the beating the Corps squad dealt me. As Vitruzzi fills the gash on my neck with tissue glue, she hands me a mirror and I see my contused face for the first time. Pulling my shoulder-length auburn hair back with one hand reveals ghoulish streaks of green, red, and black bruises shrouding the side Strahan had thumped with the butt of his rifle from hairline almost to the tip of my slightly pointed chin. The eye on that side opens a little more than halfway; Vitruzzi did a good job of keeping the swelling down, and I count myself lucky not to have a fractured skull. I've seen uglier, but not much.

She works efficiently, not wasting movement. She's done this before. When I ask her if she's a doctor, her reply is a curt nod. Captain of a transport ship and doctor— everything about Vitruzzi dispenses authority. I've already sized her up in my mind, a habit from years of never trusting anyone who's breathing. She's muscular, a little taller than me, and dexterous. Her efficient movements betray no weakness or hesitancy. Something about her eyes tells me she's seen a great deal of the darkness of the human psyche but is still resolutely humane. She lives a hard life, relying on order and control to make sense of it.

When I was still Corps, I met a handful of non-comms, and even fewer officers, with the same presence of leadership. Her type is a rarity though, especially out here on the fringes. It makes me wonder what brought her here, and why she's resorting to petty extortion when she could be working in a cush hospital on one of the Obals or running a department in one of the Ministries. As I size her up, I realize two things. She's dead set on getting that disc, and it'll be a brutal fight if I don't hold up my end of the deal.

When she's done, we walk out of the infirmary together and run into Strahan standing outside. Wordlessly, his familiar scowl still firmly set, he follows us to the galley.

I glance through the window of the first door we pass, posted INF 1. Sleeping on the gurney inside is a shaggy-headed blond man with a full beard, wearing a smock similar to the one I'd worn earlier. I recognize him as the man I'd knocked out to get inside the dock control room. His neck and chest are encased in a stiff metal brace with an attached mouthpiece covering the lower half of his face. The device looks as if it would be worn by an underwater diver.

In the Corps, I'd been a Tech 1 Sergeant and a navigator on mass deployment troop carriers. The ISPS is much smaller than the ships I'd been assigned to and I examine it curiously as we make our way forward. The Admin originally commissioned these to be Corps micro-ops combat ships, usually as backup fighters. They travel light and fast, but with enough room and storage for a squad of about ten to live on for a couple of months without resupplying. This one's been refurbished for use as a transport vessel, probably for low-volume supplies. It's a fairly old model, and has seen rough use. Scars appear here and there where the metal has been welded and patched, indicating damage, most likely from small arms.

As we ascend a metal staircase beyond the infirmary rooms, I hear three or four new voices. I can't make out what they're saying until Vitruzzi presses the opening sequence on the control pad to the galley door. It slides open and three heads swivel toward us.

"Everyone, our guest, Aly Erikson. Desto," she nods toward the other man I'd seen with Strahan on the dock. "Show her where things are." Turning to me, she says, "Erikson, I have a feeling you're smart enough not to make trouble, but that's not a lesson I'm going to learn the hard way. Strahan will be your shadow while you're on board. Where you go outside your own bunk, he goes." Without sparing a second for my protests, she leaves the galley.

They all stare at me and I stare back. Music wafts into the room from an invisible source, its tinny sound and basic beat creating an urgent backdrop to the room's uncomfortable tension. The words are hard to hear, something . . . *reckless . . . feckless . . . Rudie can't fail.* I recognize the song, a flawlessly preserved relic from Earth. The band had been called the Clash.

A smallish woman with hair so short it stands on end is the first to speak. She glides up to me, her eyes slipping over my features—hairline, eyes, nose, cheeks, mouth, neck—probing every centimeter of my skin as if reading a data log. With a friendly grin, hand outstretched, she says, "I'm Venus. I fly this rig. I fly it, and Bodie fixes it. He should be okay, just so you know. No permanent damage the captain says. And just so you know, any enemy of the Admin is a friend of mine." Energy seems to pour out of her palm into mine as if I'm holding a live wire.

"Dr. Kellen Vilbrandt." This comes from a wiry man sitting at the table, sizing me up with a veiled expression. He's young looking, with a long, pale face and black hair. Something about his feigned casualness puts me on edge. That name: Vilbrandt. It causes a faint spark of recognition. Should I know this guy? My brain is still too addled, I can't remember. If I do know him, I hope it comes to me before I need it to.

Desto steps in front of me so closely that his massive build blocks everything else from my sight. With a boxing glove-sized hand, he takes mine and shakes it. "*Mr.* Bomani Desto." He spins "mister" with a touch of sarcasm, making fun of Vilbrandt. "If there's anything you need while on board, you just let me know. Making you comfortable is my *specialty*." Judging by the tightness of his grip, sheer power is another. I can't miss the lewd suggestion in his introduction. A man with his strength doesn't have to be polite.

My mouth decides to fire before engaging my brain. "You must be the brains of the crew."

Instead of being insulted by my sarcasm, a low-pitched chuckle radiates from his throat, and he says, "You're all right."

Without letting go of my hand, he pulls me relentlessly toward the wall of cupboards making up the galley storage.

"In here is everything we have to eat. Most of it is pure slop, but nutritious slop. Not much needs cooking, which means not much to clean. We like to keep things simple on the *Sphynx*." He turns to face me, and suddenly his expression is savagely serious. "We like simple *very* much. Meaning, we aren't going to have any more problems with you, right?" The threat tears through his campy exterior, and I know he won't hesitate to break me in half if I give him a reason.

Staring hard into his unflinching eyes, I acknowledge his question with a slight nod, extract my hand from his grip and step up to the nearest cupboard to examine what's inside. It's not in my interest to give anyone here the impression that I'm harmless or easily intimidated. Regardless of the deal Vitruzzi and I struck, I have more important things to think about then making nice with a bunch of strangers.

I feel more than hear him walk away. Damn he's quiet. Now I see how he and Strahan had gotten the drop on the Corps squad. Grabbing a nutrient bar that might be palatable, I walk back over to the galley table and have a seat, hoping the solid food will settle my shaky limbs. The pressure of chewing creates a reverberating beat in my head, but I'm ravenous and eat it fast.

They don't talk much while I eat, and their quiet observation of me should make me uncomfortable, but I'm too distracted by Venus. She's fidgety, frenetically animated, and stays in constant motion: picking things up and putting them down, wiping off counters, sometimes bobbing her head up and down with the music and staring off into space. Her incessant activity draws my glances again and again.

"Don't let Venus bother you. She can't help it." Desto leans toward me, grinning at my discomfort.

The ceaseless activity makes me feel as if I might jump out of my skin. Trying to stay calm, I start a conversation. "So Venus, you're the pilot? You seem a little young to be flying a . . . transport ship. Where did you learn?"

Thankfully, she stops drawing random figures in the air with one finger and looks at me. "I started out flying a mining shuttle between my moon and Spectra 5. I have natural abilities that make me very good at flying ships."

I take the bait. "What are those?"

"Well, you know Spectra 5 was where the Admin used to have a curienite mine. I was born with a mutation in my brain from the stuff. My folks mined it their whole lives, so it was built up in their systems. Like poison, you know. Except, it didn't work like poison. It changed my brain. I just have naturally faster reactions, um, to, well, everything."

Vilbrandt interrupts, "Basically, her synaptic connections exceed most people's by a power of ten. It's as if she's always in fight-or-flight mode. Her sympathetic nervous system is constantly stimulated because her mind works too quickly to filter or counteract sensory input. It's somewhat complicated to explain." He looks around at us with an expression that suggests he's speaking to a roomful of idiots, and continues, "She also has an adrenal-inhibiting response to offset the cortisol that would naturally build up in someone with her physiology, which keeps her from just burning out. It's amazing, actually."

We all look at him the way children examine a fascinating bug. "What kind of doctor are you?" I ask.

"I was a biological engineer."

Venus says with a cheerful grin, "I'm harder to catch. Which makes me an excellent pilot."

"Makes it harder for you to chill out and let us relax, is what," Desto says, grinning at her as if she were a favorite sister.

"That's very interesting," I comment. "Having mutations, I mean, adaptations like yours seem like the kind of thing the Admin would exploit. I'm surprised you're not locked up in some lab."

"Oh, they took all kinds of samples of my DNA and even some brain tissue when I was still a kid. But I guess they figured, you know, why let all this talent go to waste?"

I wonder how many human guinea pigs the Admin has tortured trying to copy her phenomenal biology.

"I have a perfect flying record. Been doing it since I was fourteen. Never crashed anything that still had energy to fly." She grins proudly and pours water from a glass into a pitcher, then back in the glass.

The atmosphere in the room seems to be thawing some and I dredge up a small grin in return. Finished with my nutrition bar, I'm ready for another and help myself. Strahan hasn't sat down, instead opting to lean stiffly against the door we'd entered through, the same expression stamped on his face. He still looks as if he wants to toss me straight out the nearest hatch into thin—nothing.

After sitting down to enjoy, if that's the right word, my second bar and a glass of water, I watch the rest of the crew carefully, cataloguing my impressions of them. Desto and Venus ease into familiar conversation as if they'd been flying together for a while, but Strahan keeps his sullen distance. Kellen also says very little, and I notice the others don't try and engage him. I get the impression that he's not totally at home here, maybe a new crewmember. Our eyes meet several times. He's watching me as much as I'm watching them.

In a few minutes, Desto draws Strahan into the conversation. "You know, Karl, you didn't have to smash her head in. You're supposed to hit the pretty ones lower so you don't mess up their looks." He winks at me.

Strahan remains silent.

Desto doesn't let it go. "Erikson, you know, we're about three more days from Agate Beach. You got your own bunk, but if you get lonely, I'll make sure you know how to find me. No need for anyone around here to get cold at night. Just take a look at Karl over there—that's what happens to a body that doesn't get enough love."

This elicits a sneering smirk from Strahan that serves as a silent warning no one can mistake. *Shut up, Desto.*

I'm not so easy to embarrass. "You know, Desto, if I get that lonely I think I'd be better off finding something battery powered to keep me company. You don't look like you've had much companionship lately. Must be rough being cooped up on this ship with no one else from your species."

He laughs so hard the dishes in the cupboards rattle and Venus joins him. Kellen's lips only curl into a ghost of a grin, as if his mind is on other matters. Still laughing, Desto gets up, slaps me good naturedly on the back, nearly causing me to choke on my food, and heads toward the opposite galley door. "Venus, you and I better get back up to the flight deck."

"Erikson, it's a pleasure to meet you. I hope you find your stay with us . . . accommodating." Kellen's eyes latch into mine, forcing me to pay attention. His comment is strange; what does he mean? I don't respond, and with a nod, he leaves too. That leaves Strahan and me.

"Come on. V—the captain—says you're healthy enough to leave the infirmary. I'll take you to your bunk."

He leads the way out of the galley door and for the first time I notice that he carries his right leg stiffly, limping slightly. So, I'd hit him after all. No wonder he's so unpleasant. He waits for me to get through and then points me toward a corridor lined by the crew quarter doors. We're nearly at the end before he tells me to stop. Punching a code into the keypad opens the metal doors to what will be my bunk. One half-meter step up separates the corridor floor from the cabin.

Lights come on. "This is it: bed, sink with a couple liters of water, can. If you need anything else, ask me, and I'll ask the captain."

I nod, irritated at being treated as a prisoner. But if I weren't here, I'd probably be dead. For the moment, like it or not, I'm completely at their mercy, and our agreement makes us business partners. It doesn't do me any good to continue provoking anyone. Trying to dispel some of the animosity, I say, "Thanks. I realize things could have gone much worse for me."

Oblivious to my sincerity, he leans into the room and points out another keypad inside. "Just punch in lima-nine to turn the lights on and off. I'm locking the door. You can't open it, so don't try."

Fine, we're not playing nice. "And I'm sorry about your leg." I don't try to soften the sarcasm in my voice.

For the first time, a hint of a grin turns up the corners of his mouth. "Well, I guess I'm lucky. Ten centimeters up and to the left, and Desto would have a lot more to laugh about." He thrusts his chin forward, signaling me to go inside.

The gas-filled ceiling glows a murky white as his footsteps recede down the corridor, illuminating my newest cell-slash-room. There's a narrow bunk to my left, embedded in a niche between sets of drawers below and shelves above. All empty. Another smaller door to the rear leads into the head with a nonbreakable metal mirror, a sink with a bottle of water hooked up to the tap, and a toilet. The identical setup to every Corps crew quarters I've ever lived in. After removing my boots, I stretch out on the bunk.

Despite days of unconsciousness, I'm now more tired than groggy. The drugs Vitruzzi had been giving me are finally wearing off, and I have some time to sort out everything that's happened since jumping out of my last nightmare into this one. How am I going to find David and convince Rajcik to deal with Vitruzzi? Does she think she'll be able to trade me for the disc? I'm enough of a realist to know that that may not be enough of a bargain for Rajcik. His loyalty isn't to people, it's to profits. Even though we've smuggled and sold enough illicit munitions together over the last six years to outfit a private army, I wouldn't bet my life on his loyalty. And what had David said right before being arrested? Don't let Rajcik out of my sight. What did he mean?

When I followed David, two years my senior, into the Admin Corps Military Academy, I thought the life of a soldier would be a thousand times better than my other option: civil service. Our mother abandoned the family when I was three, leaving me a burden on our dad—*David's* dad. The old man never believed I was his. The only impact our mother had on my life was teaching me what it felt like to not matter. I thought the Corps would make me part of something real and noble, that I'd be protecting the perfect and faultless order of The Political and Capital Administration of the Advanced Worlds. Like all fourteen-year-olds, I was naïve.

By twenty, I'd seen more combat than I could take. The Algol triple-star system was supposed to be peaceful and prosperous, with humanity happily ensconced in the orderly and beneficent arms of the Administration. If that were the case, why had I been ordered to arrest or neutralize more Admin-condemned non-citizens than I wanted to count? The people we targeted didn't seem like much of a threat to orderly society to me; most of them didn't even have weapons beyond whatever crude, handmade junk they could piece together for their own protection.

I began to ask questions of my CO, and when he wouldn't answer, I asked people further up the chain. The more questions I asked, the harder it became to get answers. David warned me to keep quiet or I'd be arrested, or worse, for disobedience. But he knew I couldn't. He saw the same shit go down as I did and had no more ability to stomach it than I did. It was only a matter of time before the hammer fell and I was extinguished from the Corps like a smothered candle.

Then the Rebellion hit. David and I helped take over our combat craft, crashed it on a moon off Obal 8 called Dramma Sdutti, and, like hundreds of other soldiers who weren't caught and exterminated, disappeared from the Admin and the Corps.

When we met Rajcik, he instantly knew us for what we were. Deserters were all over the system for a while, before the Admin rounded most of them back up. He recognized the advantages of having people from our backgrounds on his crew, mine as interstellar ship navigator and David as an infantry platoon leader. We were smart, knew weapons, and had a detailed library of knowledge about Corps tactics and operations.

We joined him, not out of greed, but out of a shared disgust and enmity for the Admin and its clean, orderly, monstrous totalitarianism. Rajcik operates from a core that's fueled by pure hate, planning every heist and operation with the intent to damage the Admin as much as possible. After what I'd been commanded to do as a soldier, I can relate to that.

These thoughts occupy my brain while I lie stretched on my bunk, aching along every streak of the rainbow of bruises covering my body. The darkness and the quiet bring a sense of lucidity again. Despite starting to feel more like myself, uncertainty and fear for David still gnaw at my guts like a rodent. I get up again and try the door. Strahan hadn't let me see the code he had input in the keypad to open it, but I try a couple random sequences for the hell of it. No luck, but there's nowhere for me to go anyway. All I can do is lie here and think about how I'm going to find my brother. If he's alive.

FOUR

I'm suddenly awake. I don't know how long I've been asleep, hadn't even noticed myself doze off, and I'm disoriented. By reflex I roll off my bunk, reaching for the pistol that should be taped to the bottom, but my fist hits a drawer instead. My door is sliding open, though it's too dark to see anything but a man's shadow. Before he gets more than halfway into the room, I shoot off the floor, ignoring the protest from my ribs, grasp his wrist, and using the momentum of my lunge, twist his arm behind his back, slamming him against the wall.

"What the fuck are you doing in here?" I keep my voice low so that no one can hear me except the intruder.

"Relax! It's K-Kellen! Vilbrandt! Jesus, you're breaking my arm!"

"What are you doing here?" I hiss again, pushing his limp hand farther up his back so that it's nestled between his shoulder blades.

"I just want to talk to you! That's all, just talk, please!"

His voice is a strangled screech and his body is taut with pain. If I push a fraction more, his shoulder will pop out of its socket like wet driftwood snapped in half. Instead, I loosen the pressure just slightly. He draws a relieved breath.

"What about?"

He cranes his head around so he can look at me with one wide brown eye. "Do you know who I am?"

"Why would I?" But I remember the feeling I'd had a when I'd met him. Why is he familiar?

"You don't recognize me? I'm Dr. Vilbrandt. I used to work for Director T'Kai."

And it hits me. "You're the head of human subjects R&D in the medical branch of Science and Engineering. Or you were. The newscasts said you were sent to prison for selling information to smugglers."

"Yes, that's right. But I wasn't selling information, that was a lie T'Kai created when I discovered *he* was leaking information. To you. Can you . . . would you let go of me?"

"You're lying!" I give his arm another shove to encourage him to tell the truth.

"Oww, Christ!" He sucks in a tortured breath. "Where do you think Vitruzzi found out about the disc?"

Surprised, I pause. Could Vilbrandt actually have found out what T'Kai was up to? Or is he a plant, sent by T'Kai to round up my crew because he'd gotten cold feet? If that's the case, everyone on this ship is in on it.

Sweat begins to drip down his neck and, at this point, I don't think he'll be able to use the arm for a couple of days. His voice is desperate. "Please, please, Erikson. It's true. I don't have any proof, but just hear me out."

The door is open and I could run for it. But where would I go? He hardly seems fast or strong enough to be a threat, so I'll give him a chance. "If you do *anything* I don't like, I'll kill you. I think you know I can do it." Turning on the lights, I release him and take a step back.

He turns around slowly, smart enough to keep his hands where I can see them, and reaches up with his undamaged arm to rub his injured shoulder. His lips are pressed into pain-tightened slits, his eyes equally narrow. There's a smear of blood behind him on the wall where his lips impacted when I jumped him.

"I worked for T'Kai—"

"You said that."

"Yes. I did. A month ago, he asked me to meet him at the Ministry of Engineering to retrieve a sequence of data. All of our testing data on human subjects are stored there."

Human subjects data. He's talking about experimentation. Research on the effects of new weapons—chemical, biological, nano, all of it. There's no proof that this kind of thing occurs, the Admin is careful. But anyone who's been in prison or the underground long enough has heard the stories.

"As head of R&D, I am, *was*, supposed to be informed of all data being accessed, even by T'Kai. I wasn't made aware of any retrieval authorizations given to him, specifically for the Fortress, but he needed my access signature to query the system. When I insisted on seeing his authorization, he threatened me. I remitted to his authority, and didn't say another word about it. But I went back later and used his access code to see the logs of what he pulled. That's when I discovered he created the disc that went to your crew."

He looks young, too young to be as high in the Admin echelons as he is. Which means he's very smart, and talented in manipulation. Listening to the way he talks, his precise phrasing, his clipped syllables, and the sneering disdain in his voice for T'Kai illuminates an ego that is anything but small. His type is dangerous, mostly to themselves because they have a hard time believing anyone could outsmart them. He, and what he stands for, makes the spit in my mouth taste sour and my fingers twitch to slap him.

"You just happened to have T'Kai's access code?"

"It came in handy, didn't it?" There's a new menace to his voice that sends cold pinpricks of suspicion up and down my spine. He must notice my reaction and moderates his tone. "I mean, I thought it would, so I acquired it. Perhaps it wasn't ethical, but someone in your line of work should understand."

His somber eyes are wide with deep, dark circles beneath them as if he hasn't been getting a lot of sleep. He has an angle, but he's taking his time in revealing it. Impatience makes the blood throb dully behind my eyes. Saying nothing, I wait for him to continue.

"When he realized what I knew, he had me arrested. I was locked in a holding cell on Obal 10 while he made up all those lies, slandering me, ruining my career. I was given no trial, no lawyer, no defense. He saw to that. Then he had me shipped to the Fortress, trying to wipe out my existence. But I escaped."

I chuckle, the sound more a threat than amusement. I'm beginning to regret not breaking his arm and giving him the chance to shovel me such crap. The Fortress isn't a facility people escape from. Especially soft, spineless scientist-types like him.

"You escaped the Fortress. Are you some kind of magician?"

"I worked there for years. Given the liability the Admin would face if someone with my in-depth knowledge of the station's research activities were holding a grudge, I concluded some time ago that I should create my own insurance should the Fortress ever become something other than my laboratory."

He's not going to tell me exactly how he escaped, if he really did, but I have no trouble seeing the picture he's painting. Even the Admin's own don't trust each other. Despite the impossibility of his story, there's a ball of disquiet growing in my stomach. If T'Kai knew we were compromised, why didn't he change the rendezvous? Maybe he *did* get cold feet on the deal. For all I know, he could have tipped off the security on Obal 3 himself. If we'd been caught, he already had a convenient scapegoat locked away to pin the leak on, and any trail leading back to him would have been wiped clean. Which could mean Vilbrandt's story about being framed is true.

"Once I was free, I headed out here to the Spectras where no one would know me. I needed time to figure out a way to clear myself and send T'Kai where he belongs. Then I met Vitruzzi and Strahan. I overheard them talking to people about the Fortress, trying to find out where it was."

"Why?"

"Didn't Vitruzzi tell you this? Apparently friends of theirs were arrested for stealing energy and imprisoned there. Vitruzzi wants a copy of the disc because they're going to attempt a rescue." He chuckles as if the idea amuses him.

It's as if a light is switched on, illuminating all the answers I'd been missing. I was right about Vitruzzi. She has a good gig out here as a legally contracted transport ship. She's not the criminal type, and she's sure as hell too smart to try and break into the most highly secured installation in the system for some petty thievery. But when you throw people she knows into the mix, people who are friends and allies, it makes sense.

Vilbrandt's story is too simple, too full of coincidence. I know he's lying, or at least not telling me everything, and it sets my nerves on edge. "So you just walk over to Vitruzzi and tell her you know where it is? And about the disc? Do I look stupid to you?"

He takes a seat on the bunk, still cradling his shoulder. "But that *is* what happened. I knew that helping them get the disc would help me clear myself, you see? With a copy, I can turn myself in and prove that T'Kai is responsible for it being leaked in the first place. It's the only evidence that could possibly carry any weight."

"And she brought you aboard?"

"Exactly. Once Vitruzzi understood the advantages of having both the disc and someone who knows the Fortress from the inside, she would have done almost anything to have me join her crew. She's very desperate to save her friends. I'm sure you're aware of the theories about what happens to human subjects in the Fortress."

"They aren't theories." It's a statement, not a question. "And you were in charge of that."

His expression doesn't change; there's no remorse in his eyes. "I didn't choose to be, I simply went where I was assigned, where our government thinks I'm best suited. My own Hobson's choice, if you like."

The urge to slap him returns, stronger, but I rein it in.

"I explained the smuggling operation your team planned as I knew it. Vitruzzi is a legal transporter of Admin armaments and arranged a pick-up on Obal 3 the same day. She'd intended to set up a meeting with your crew to negotiate for a copy of the disc, but things turned out differently."

I listen carefully and have to admit that, laid out like this, the pieces of his story are cohesive, maybe even plausible. Except the part about him escaping the Fortress. "I already told Vitruzzi I'd get a copy for her. So what do you want?"

"It's simple. I know what your team is planning to steal, and I want to be involved."

"I thought you wanted to get your career back."

I don't miss how quickly he buries the exasperation my remark provokes. "I may or may not be able to prove T'Kai's involvement, and I could still end up on an examining table with my insides liquefied by some very unpleasant disease for trying. Money is starting to sound much better to me than revenge. And if you cut me in, introduce me to your boss, perhaps we can cut T'Kai out. And I'll still have my revenge."

This man, a scientist who had probably ordered more than a few instances of the same kind of research he just described, thinks he can convince me to do something every nerve in my body tells me not to. A visceral knot of resistance tightens in my guts and I don't bother to hide the threat in my voice. "What is it exactly that you think you know?"

His expression doesn't change from that same wide-eyed vulnerability, but there's a shift in his attitude, something subtle. My nerves go on full alert again, as if I'm not talking to a man but a poisonous viper. "The Nova, Erikson. I know about *that*."

The spit in my mouth takes on the consistency and taste of oil run through a diesel engine. How does he know so much? Keeping my voice neutral takes some discipline. "Why should Rajcik cut you in? It would be easier to just kill you."

His voice drops to a sharp, sinister edge, and his expression is vulpine. "I've been there. I'm a living map and I can get you in and out of the Fortress faster than any schematic. You must realize, as senior biogenetics researcher, I had full security and administrative clearance. And the time to create back doors." He gives me a look of impossible hubris. "I can go anywhere I want in the Fortress and no one will ever know."

I gaze at him levelly. "Bullshit."

"What good would I be doing myself by lying? Why else would I be trying to get back? T'Kai's worst mistake was not killing me when he had the chance. And perhaps there are other gems on the Fortress your boss can appreciate. There's no reason not to help each other."

You're a retrograde, sociopathic, Admin rat. That's plenty reason. I'm not convinced, but if what he says is true, his participation could be the difference between my crew's success and failure. Rajcik could see it that way too.

"Think about this, Erikson." His eyes leave my face and begin wandering around the room, as if our conversation is of very little interest to him. The practiced casualness in his voice keeps my attention. "I saw how you handled the security squad in the dock on Obal 3, and you were able to fire one of their weapons. The only way you could do that is you were also Corps, with an active DNA signature tag. A deserter? One of the lucky ones whose records were destroyed during the Rebellion? And your brother also. Am I right?"

I let the silence answer for me, his shrewdness surprising. He may be more dangerous than I realize.

"You know stealing Corps property is a capital offense. And if you are deserters, the Admin is within its rights to sentence you as they see fit. Your brother is a prime candidate to become an R&D test subject. I'd almost bet my life he's already on his way to the Fortress."

He lets that sink in, craftily aware of the kind of effect the idea has on me. I hadn't let myself think that it might be a possibility, but hearing it spoken sends a shockwave through my body that nearly makes me stagger.

His eyes scan my face the way a fly crawls on a wall. "I'm probably the best chance you have to save his life."

"How the fuck did you get in here?"

We both jump at the grating sound of Strahan's voice. He's standing in the doorway, eyes burning furiously, holding a pistol in his right hand.

"Captain Vitruzzi gave me the code." Vilbrandt quickly rises from my bunk and takes a step backward, away from the menacing edge of Strahan's gaze. "I thought I could illuminate the situation for Erikson, help her see how important her cooperation is." The vulnerable, slightly scared expression returns to his face, as if it's a mask he slips on when needed.

Strahan looks as if he might be contemplating shooting him anyway. "Captain wants us all in the galley. *Now.*"

Vilbrandt surreptitiously glances at me, his look beseeching. *Keep this between us.*

I will . . . for now.

FIVE

As we enter the galley, Venus rushes toward me with her impossibly frenzied energy. Instinctively, I reach for my Sinbad, which isn't there, uncertain what the girl's intentions are.

Instead of jumping me, she says, "Hiya. How are you feeling?"

Her friendliness is more unexpected than a fight would be. "Like a planet landed on me."

Vitruzzi motions me to the table. Handing me a bottle containing half a dozen white pills to dull the lingering, but finally fading, soreness, she says, "Erikson, this is Murdock." To her left stands the blond man from the control room.

Uncomfortable with the casual introduction to a man I'd nearly killed, if not by accident at least by necessity, I nod meekly. He's taller and stouter than I'd realized on Obal 3. Stiff bandages still enshroud his neck, but the metal apparatus is gone. One of his lips is swollen, probably from landing on his face when he'd fallen. He lets me stand here for a few seconds without saying anything but then cocks one side of his mouth back in what I take to be a grin. His keen blue eyes light up, the crow's feet beside them deep, reaching back toward his temples.

"'Meet ya." He is clearly straining to force the words from his battered throat.

Self-consciously, I find myself trying to explain, "Uh, look, I'm sorry about . . . that. I was in trouble and it was, um, just the circumstances."

"No hard feelings," he manages to whisper. His voice sounds like sandpaper scraping along wood, barely there. It's obvious that speaking causes him some pain.

"Hey, what's a smashed trachea among friends?" Venus trills, giggling. There's something not right about the kid.

Vitruzzi intervenes, "Everyone listen up. I received a message from Patrick this morning. He set up a trade with smugglers on R'Kadia for a supply of solar seeds, and we're going to make the exchange. We need as many as we can lay our hands on for the trip to the Fortress. We'll be within range of R'Kadia in an hour, and should be down in two. The man in charge is named Fitzsimmon. Not a pretty . . . "

Sirens shriek inside my head, drowning out Vitruzzi. I don't have time—David doesn't have time—for us to be making pit stops all over the system! Stay cool, Aly. Vitruzzi is captain here and if she's like most officers I know, she doesn't like to be questioned. Let her talk and then try and get her to change her mind when the crew isn't around.

"We'll land about fifteen klicks from their complex and take the Rover from there. I'll drive. Desto and Karl, you'll come." She looks at me. "Erikson, I want you to help us."

My eyebrows aren't the only ones that rise in surprise. All heads turn toward me. Did I hear her right?

"We're a gun short with Bodie still recuperating, and we need a replacement."

"V, you can't be serious!" Strahan nearly shouts. "We can't give her a gun! You want to give her a chance to shoot one of us?"

Vilbrandt sits bolt upright in his seat and asks, "Do you really think that is a wise move, Captain? She *is* nothing but a criminal." He knows that if something happens to me, he'll never get a chance to join Rajcik.

I keep my mouth shut, hoping the situation sorts itself out.

Her words are like blunt objects, pummeling them. "When did you get the impression that this is up for discussion?"

The muscles in Strahan's jaw clench hard, about to pop through his cheeks, and Vilbrandt slumps in childish capitulation.

She continues, "The operation runs out of an old mine. The Administration abandoned the site, but the men we're dealing with use the remaining structures to run a smuggling op. They bring in and sell whatever they can, and it turns out they have about as many solar seeds as we can use right now. They're dangerous, but they're the only people within a month's travel with energy for sale, and they're willing to deal. I don't trust them and I want to make sure we have enough firepower with us to convince them we're not an easy mark. That means you, Erikson."

"Do I have a choice?" I'm sure it's a purely rhetorical question.

"No. Desto, get the Rover ready. Make sure the grenade launcher is full. Strahan, show Erikson where the rest of her gear is."

"Captain, can I have a word with you?" Strahan isn't ready to let this issue go. I'm not sure I am either, but if it means not being locked up, it might be worth it.

Her reply is curt and absolute. "No. Anyone else have a problem with this? No? Good." She looks the crew over, ready to squash any disagreements with pure rage. "And Karl, our guest won't be needing a shadow after this."

Vitruzzi exits and everyone else disperses to attend to their duties. Without looking at me, Strahan stomps out toward the crew quarters. I follow him, keeping my footsteps light to avoid attracting his attention. I don't need to bring any more shit down on my own head than I have to. Stopping in front of my door once more, he turns toward a storage locker in the opposite wall. Another keypad is mounted beside it.

"The code is alpha, zed, omega, two, one, zed, same as your bunk," he grunts, and stalks off, jaw still clenched.

It's been a while since I've provoked this kind of raw hostility in anyone. Shrugging, I start sorting out my gear.

BODY ARMOR, EQUIPMENT vest, AK-80 pulse carbine, Sinbad pistol in my left side holster, Mini-Derg laser concealed within a boot-sheath; the only thing missing is my NKT bolo. I strap everything on in efficient movements honed from the hundreds of times I've done it before, as if slipping into a second skin. The familiarity of my gear makes me feel more in control of an otherwise uncontrollable situation, and I'm pleasantly surprised at finding they'd picked up my carbine from the dock control room floor. The carbine has saved my ass too many times to count and I think of it as a lucky rabbit's foot. The sights are calibrated and the stock is specially molded so the weapon fits like an extension of my body. It would have been easy to spot—the only weapon present that wasn't military issue.

It's been twenty minutes and we should be hitting R'Kadia's orbit soon. They'd given me my gear, but my magazines are all empty. It's time to catch up with Vitruzzi. Heading back up the corridor, I run across Desto and get directions to the flight deck.

I approach the cockpit quietly out of habit and catch Strahan and Vitruzzi in conversation.

"She's a liability, V. You know that. The longer she's aboard, the more likely it is the Admin'll pinch us and everything we've worked for will be over. We don't need her on R'Kadia. It's not worth the risk. We have no idea what she'll do."

"Relax. She needs us right now as much as we need her. And she knows it."

"Yeah? We could lose our citizenship, our contracts, the *Sphynx*. We don't need the disc to get Zeta and Doug and the rest. We've got Vilbrandt and he's just as useful. I don't trust her. And I think you're wrong—we don't need her."

"Karl, you don't trust anyone who hasn't taken a bullet for you, so why should she be any different? Besides, I trust Vilbrandt even less. He worked for the Admin, after all."

"So did we . . . once."

There's a pause, and then Vitruzzi takes a deep, resigned breath. "Point taken. But our chances are doubled with both the disc and Vilbrandt's cooperation. You know I'm right. I'm not giving up on Doug and Zeta and I'll be surprised if you are."

"But we don't have . . ."

It's time to stop eavesdropping. Scuffing my boot on the metal floor just loud enough to be heard, I step through the hatch into the flight deck. They both turn toward me, slightly surprised at my intrusion. Immediately, Strahan brushes past me toward the exit. I give him plenty of room to pass.

The cockpit is smallish, just enough space for the navigator's seat and the pilot's controls. Nobody sits at them now; we're on auto. The ceiling is low, and two jump seats line the walls to either side of the cockpit's rear, stowed in the recesses built to hold them.

"Got a second?" I ask.

"Yes. I wanted to speak with you anyway."

Leaning against the stowed jump seats, I try to seem relaxed. I want things to go smoothly, just this once. "I haven't thanked you for the way you patched me up. I'd be in bad shape right now if you hadn't, so thanks for that."

She nods, impatient for me to get to the point.

"But we have a problem. Is this side trip to R'Kadia absolutely necessary? The longer we stall, the harder it's going to be to regroup with my team and get you what you want. My brother's life is on the line."

"You really think he's still alive?"

"Maybe not, but my first priority is to find out."

She ponders my words for a moment, measuring how determined I am. "Vilbrandt told you about our missing friends? Doug and his crew?"

I nod.

"Did he tell you why the Admin arrested them?"

"Theft. Stealing energy." She's deviating from the point, but I have no leverage to stop her. Gritting my teeth, I wait for her to continue.

"They're not civilians, but they're not criminals either. We all live in an independent settlement on Spectra 6. We don't bother the Admin and they don't give a damn about us. But it isn't easy, and sometimes we have to be creative in finding the basics we need to survive. Three weeks ago Doug and a crew of four, all good people, tried to jack some solar seeds from an Admin warehouse on Obal 8, and got caught."

"I thought you said they aren't criminals."

"Don't argue semantics with me, Erikson. You know as well as I do that the Admin doesn't have the right to hoard the system's seeds. People on the outer planets need them, citizens or not."

I let it rest, not wanting to provoke her.

"We have no alternative. We need the seeds for energy, both at home and for the *Sphynx*. We won't get far without them. Spectra 6 may not be close to Admin oversight, but it's not plush with resources either." She steps over to the navigator console and inputs the course-sequencing diagram. "If you're worried about how long it will take, we're only going about ten hours off our course. Look at this chart." Pointing to a moon orbiting Spectra 5 in the system's Delta quadrant, she continues, "Here's R'Kadia. And we're headed to Spectra 6, right here. It's on the way, just a quick detour. If you help us get these seeds, you'll get your ride back into the Obals and we can finish our other business. If not . . ." She allows the statement to hang.

She's using me, but if I were Vitruzzi, I'd play the same cards. Her friends and my brother, both in Admin custody, both probably being held at the Fortress. What wouldn't I do to try and rescue David? Doesn't matter, the similarities between us end there. Vitruzzi isn't trying to come out rich in this deal, she just wants to do what she can for her friends.

Facing the fact that I'm not going to change her mind, I bring up another issue. "How much do you trust Vilbrandt?"

She regards me cannily before answering, "I don't. I know he's trying to make a deal with you, but it doesn't matter, does it? Listen to me carefully, though. If you and he try to double-cross us or get any of my crew hurt, you'll be dead before you ever see the Fortress, or your brother."

There's no mistaking the promise in her words. This is the second time she's threatened me, and the message is coming through loud and clear. Her loyalty to her crew is fierce. "David is my brother. I'm not going to do anything to jeopardize whatever chance he still has."

"We have an understanding then."

Can an alliance formed out of desperation and distrust end any way but badly? We'll soon find out. "One more thing, I'm low on ammo. Do you have any 5.7 millimeter rounds, about three magazines, and . . ."

"Go to the cargo bay. Desto can sort you out."

SIX

Desto isn't in the main cargo bay, but there's a wide blast door at the rear that's partially open. Curious, I approach quietly and peer inside. Just left of the door sit several rows of missile transport tubes chained securely to the wall. A glance at their stenciled labels confirms: this is serious firepower. AU5 Glower missiles, perfectly suited for striking planetary targets from orbit, and farther down the row, RFX Murphys, which wouldn't be out of place in a full-blown fleet action. Beyond them, an entire wall is dedicated to ammo bins, holding rounds and magazines for about everything I've ever used. Another wall houses neatly stacked crates stenciled with the names of different weaponry components and military-issue equipment. It's an ammo vault. How and why do they—?

"Glad to see you found your way down here." My head jerks back in surprise toward where Desto works, his back to me. Impressive— my entry had been completely silent. I've known people who have developed that sixth sense, that internal radar that never quite shuts off, usually soldiers or survivors with a good deal of combat behind them. What's Desto's story?

"It's not that big a ship. But by the arsenal you have here, I'd think I was aboard a fleet cruiser."

With an amused grunt, he says, "Just tools in our toolbox. So what do you need, sweetheart?" Uh-huh. No answers here, I guess.

"Just some 5.7."

The bemused grin never leaves his face. "For that little AK-80 of yours, right? Yeah, we've got some right over here," he says, moving farther along a stack and taking out a regulation, standard-issue crate of Corps ammo.

I feel a twinge of annoyance at his dismissive reference to the carbine I carry. "It's light, handy, lets me move fast, and it's never jammed on me in a fight. Plus, I can carry more ammo."

He smiles, not missing the opportunity to crack a joke at my expense. "Miss often, do you?" Before I can respond, he continues, "You should try one of *my* toys sometime." He steps past me to some lockers closer to the door opposite the missiles and pulls out a large, dark-colored rifle scabbard.

"Thresher M-2209," he says, slipping the scabbard off and hefting out the heavy weapon with ease.

Holy shit. I haven't seen one of those since early in my Corps training. A squad-level weapon, used to supply more punch when standard rifles and carbines wouldn't do. Not long after I'd joined, it was dropped in favor of lighter, smaller-caliber weapons with smart ammunition. Just remembering its brutal recoil makes my shoulder ache.

"Now," he continues, "unless you hit them in the head or heart, it might take two or three rounds with 5.7 millimeter to put somebody down. With the 7.9 in the '209, here," he sights down the barrel affectionately, "one round is all you need."

"Old fashioned, isn't it? Christ, the grip is made of wood! And the ammo is heavy as hell."

"Yeah, it's nothing like caseless, but this baby can't be spoofed or jammed, either. And body armor doesn't help. At best, your insides are still going to be pounded into salsa. As for the weight . . ."

"Right. Of course." What was I thinking? This guy could probably hold one in each hand without much trouble.

He hands it to me. Well used but definitely not abused. Examining the wooden fore grip closely, I notice something else. What I at first thought was the standard checkering to give the shooter a better hold is actually an intricate carving of planetary scenes, starscapes, ships, and people. A tapestry of his life?

"Is this—?"

Vitruzzi's voice rings over the intercom: "Approaching atmosphere. We should be entering in five minutes. We'll hit dirt in less than an hour. Everyone who's going, meet me at the Rover. Out."

"Better get your ammo loaded up." Desto takes the Thresher and slings it across his back. "Anything else?"

"Yeah," I answer, snapping back to practical reality. "I need something to replace my bolo."

He looks around thoughtfully. "I have a Torcher that would fit in your vest."

"Not the same as a knife, and I'm not crazy about lasers."

"Something we agree on." He snaps a knife off his own harness and tosses it to me. "Here you go. I've got another one."

Business concluded, we walk out into the cargo bay to finish prepping the Rover, the *Sphynx*'s auxiliary land transport. The bay is about twice the size of the weapons vault, room enough for plenty of cargo. There are stairs leading up from either side to the crew quarters and galley level, ending at a landing that runs the circumference of the bay. In the middle of the floor, a hatch to its short-range shuttle is surrounded by yellow paint to mark its border. A few crates and boxes lay around, but the space is mostly empty. The Rover sits to one side, secured to the deck by heavy cables. It's a four-wheeled all terrain vehicle, covered by a bubble made of clear, bullet-resistant plating. The metal upper frame provides adequate strength to withstand a rollover but is sparse enough that the passengers have a 360-degree view outside. Four interior bucket seats are arranged back to back, two facing forward and two backward. Gray material covers them, worn and thin, and in some places torn away, revealing solid metal plates underneath that were probably built to withstand an external blast. Attached in the front and rear are a set of cargo racks that look sturdy, designed to carry a lot of weight.

Strahan enters the bay and, passing me without a glance, opens one side of the Rover's hatch. It swings up on a set of center-mounted hinges on the top bar like a giant clam. After loading two rifles into racks attached to the seat frames, he secures a smallish crate to the cargo rack.

"Can I help with anything?"

"Just stay out of my way."

And just like that, my patience gives. "What's your problem, Strahan? Did I steal your lunch money in another life or something?"

He drops the cam strap securing the cargo and focuses on me for the first time. "I think you're dangerous, Erikson. People like you will do anything for profit. I think Vitruzzi made a mistake bringing you on board, and I'm not going to give you a chance to prove me right."

Icy cold fury rushes through my veins. His comment hits me somewhere deep inside, a visceral strike with the force of a tank. Sucking breath through my clenched teeth, I face him woodenly. "Don't think for a second that you know me, Strahan. You don't know anything about me."

"Just stay where I can see you. I'm not getting stabbed again." His tone, still level, is dismissive.

Vitruzzi and Desto approach and Strahan jumps aboard the Rover. Desto nudges me and says with an impish grin, "Don't worry. That's how he shows he cares."

"Get ready. We should be down in about ten minutes," Vitruzzi says, and turns to me. "Here, put this on." She hands me a small, white breathing apparatus, and points toward my nostrils. "It'll filter out things you don't want in your lungs. You'll feel light-headed at first because the air is mostly oxygen, but you'll get used to it. Just remember to breath through your nose as much as you can."

I press the flexible device into my nostrils, and the walls and floors begin to vibrate furiously as we penetrate R'Kadia's atmosphere. On most military ships, it's best to be strapped into something for this part, but no one seems worried. My stomach does a lazy flip-flop as we begin decelerating, and I brace myself for the sudden shock that usually occurs when breaking through the troposphere. The vibration increases for a few seconds, making the shipping crates rattle, but then, just as suddenly as it had started, the bumpiness ends and we're sailing smoothly through the air, like fish through water. Whatever else they'd done to this craft, modifying their atmospheric thrust compensation could be the most impressive.

Venus's high-pitched, girlish voice floats out from the intercom: "Setting us down in five, Captain. Looks like a nice day outside, no weather issues. Temp is thirty-four degrees C."

As the ship maneuvers through rising air currents from the ground, we all take our seats in the Rover, Vitruzzi at the wheel next to Strahan, Desto and I beside each other in the back. Once we're on the ground, she remote-opens the cargo bay door and then we're out, rolling over rough sandy terrain.

I've never been to this moon. It's bright out, but I don't see any of the Algol stars illuminating the landscape. It must be approaching night here. Brownish-green plants dot the landscape, but not many, and they are all short and dry looking. Not a very habitable planet, but the air is relatively clear. We cruise along quickly, eating up kilometers, as the *Sphynx* shrinks behind us.

Vitruzzi speaks into the com unit, telling Bodie and Venus to be online for a quick retrieval. Her actions are sure and direct, not nervous, but alert, ready for anything. I turn around in my seat to look ahead. We've gone about halfway and are quickly approaching the entrance to a canyon with steep sloping walls.

Desto suddenly tenses up next to me and I turn around quickly to see what has set him on edge. There's a flash of light, as if from a solar panel, behind us on a hilltop to the east.

"Vitruzzi," Desto warns.

"I know, they're signaling each other. There's another one up there." She points ahead toward the western cliff.

"They must not be using radio. They're signaling each other so we can't pick up what they're saying," Strahan says.

"Only people who have something to hide are worried about other people hearing them." Desto sounds angry.

Vitruzzi slows the Rover, trying to buy us some time to prepare for whatever might be coming at us.

I scan the horizon before us, spotting another signal flash on the western wall above us. Almost directly beneath it, a spur of crumbling rock creates a sharp corner. The canyon walls narrow and begin a short curve west just past the spur. I have an idea.

"Vitruzzi, if we can get the drop on them, they'll have to rethink whatever ambush they might be planning."

"Do you have any suggestions?"

"Those rocks up ahead. The signalers above won't be able to see us when we're right next to it, and the eastern wall will block the group behind us. They won't know it if we stop. Someone can scale the slope and overtake that signal station right above it. If we do it fast, they'll never know we're coming."

Vitruzzi backs off the Rover's accelerator a fraction more, thinking it through. Desto chimes in, "I'd be happy to crash their party."

"All right, let's try it. If they're planning to attack us, they'll do it outside the mine where there's less chance for crossfire and better cover. If we can snag them up, they may lose their nerve, or at least buy us more time. Desto, get ready to jump out when I stop. Stay low, use the cover in those boulders. Radio us when you have things under control. But don't take any chances. If it's too hot, get back to the Rover and we'll make a break for it. Try and beat them back to the ship. Ready?" Retreat is Vitruzzi's last option. They must need these seeds pretty badly.

In a moment, we're passing the spur. I watch the signal station fade out of view behind us as the walls conceal our position. Vitruzzi slows just enough for Desto to open the clamshell and leap out, becoming quickly obscured by dust kicked up from the tires. We catch brief glances of his ascent as he scrambles up the steep slope: a hand, a foot. He's stealthy, not dislodging a single rock. As he nears the top, he moves farther around the corner, toward the mine entrance, until we lose sight of him altogether. Vitruzzi brings us to a stop a few meters past the spur and we wait in stillness. Only a couple of minutes pass, but the tension makes time warp and extend.

There's no sign of Desto for several long seconds, and then the radio on the Rover crackles to life. "*Sphynx* crew, do you copy?" An unfamiliar voice.

"This is Captain Vitruzzi. Who do I have?"

"Suarez. Your friend asked me to extend you a welcome to our mine. Fitzsimmon is waiting for you. Just keep heading to the entrance." The radio transmission wasn't perfect, but his voice doesn't convey much warmth or welcome.

"Let me speak to my guy."

A pause. "Hey, Captain. Looks like we've got some new friends." Desto lets out a satisfied-with-himself chuckle. "It's handled. Me and these guys will meet you in the mine. Out."

Vitruzzi starts driving forward again. The maneuver worked, but my stomach still clenches in a tense knot. These people have something planned, and it's pretty clear it's not something we're going to like. Another sixty meters and I can see where the mine begins. The canyon narrows and leads to a derelict but still functional barricade marking the entrance to a dark tunnel. As we roll toward it, I hear a small engine off to our left. It's Desto and the men from the signaling station coming down a graded road in another ATV. As we meet at the entrance, we can see three men in the cab with him. Desto's flash-suppressed pistol is out, trained, more or less, on the driver's skull.

Desto is on the radio again. "Captain, the mine is deep, it's about three klicks in to their HQ. Follow us. Out."

Switching on a set of lights, Vitruzzi pulls in behind Desto's hijacked ATV, staying close to present less of a target. Soon, we pull into a wider, dimly lit area with a steel and concrete cargo elevator marking the end of the tunnel.

"Karl, I want you and Erikson behind me. Keep your eyes open." Vitruzzi and Strahan push each side of the Rover's shell up and we all climb out.

"Captain Vitruzzi. Did you bring what we arranged?" A stooped man with septic green eyes and teeth that match approaches, squinting suspiciously. He's armed with a slung rifle and a pistol holstered in a chest harness. Another man, similarly armed, walks beside him. They're exactly what I'd expected from carrion smugglers of this sort; the type that's always looking for ways to steal what could easily be bought for cheap. They don't distinguish between entities like the Admin who have the resources to cover their losses, and honest people who are forced to make dangerous deals just to get by. For men like Fitzsimmon, the goal is profit, no matter who it hurts.

The men Desto had corralled move up next to Fitzsimmon. With a look of contempt, he motions them aside. Desto stands beside me.

"I have it. Let's see the seeds."

"They're underground. We'll go get them together."

"No. Bring them out here or we're gone."

He grunts derisively, not willing to give any ground. The cave is littered with cargo, most of it in bins or under tarps, and I can't make out what anything is in the gloom. There are too many hiding places. Hot and cold pinpricks jig down my spine, a hypersensitivity that assures me we're moments from open hostility. The depth of the mine and distance between us and the *Sphynx* cuts off communication and any help the rest of the crew can provide. Vitruzzi and Strahan face off with Fitzsimmon, poised to draw their weapons.

Her next words astonish me. "Desto, get back in the Rover and keep watch up here. Karl, Erikson, let's go." She faces Fitzsimmon. "We'll come down and get the goods. The money stays up here. After we have the seeds loaded on our ATV, you'll get your price."

She must have a lot of faith in Desto to leave him up here alone. She must also be crazy to separate us like this. What choice do I have but to go along? Strahan stares unblinking and unafraid at the men before us. Confident, but wary.

Fitzsimmon turns and opens the elevator. A massive blast door rumbles upward, exposing a wire-caged platform. One of the men from Desto's group slides the cage open and he and another man move inside. Desto steps inside the Rover and shuts the hatch. Fitzsimmon waits for us to get on the elevator, closing the door behind us.

The elevator is spacious, with plenty of room for six of us. The descent takes close to a minute and the hard stone walls passing by outside the elevator cage radiate deep, earthen cold that increases the farther we descend. One yellow light hangs from the wire mesh, turning the condensation from our breath into golden vapor. The floor is plate steel, made to haul heavy equipment and earth.

"I have to say, it's your lucky day—you needing solar seeds and we just happen to have some." Fitzsimmon stares straight ahead as he's talking, trying to divert our attention and keep us off guard. "Acquired them from a crew whose ship crashed on the other side of the moon. They were happy to give 'em up since that bird was scrap. Only needed a tiny bit of convincing. Who says crime doesn't pay?" Scavenger. He and his group had probably murdered the wrecked crew and taken everything they could. He turns to us and flashes a seedy grin, clearly thinking of us as his next opportunity.

The elevator hits bottom. Another thick blast door rises and we're looking into a large room, about forty meters deep, with concrete walls and heavy steel and concrete struts bracing against the earth. An alternate shaft enters the chamber ten meters above the floor on the far end. There may once have been a ledge running the perimeter of the upper story, but it has long since fallen apart or been used for scrap. Fitszimmon steps out of the lift, Vitruzzi right behind him. I follow with Strahan at my right elbow, and feel the other two men breathing on the back of my neck.

As we walk forward, Fitzsimmon tells us that the crates up ahead hold our seeds. I know it's a lie. He's trying to get us out into the open where we lose the advantage and can't escape behind the blast door into the elevator. Furtively, I look around, trying to see what other surprises are in store for us. This room is well lit, at least better than the tunnel above. There's movement above us, coming from the second-story entrance. Crates are jammed into the opening, but my battle sense tells me there's someone behind them, covering the room from the better vantage point. Envisioning the ambush they have planned is as easy as if I were watching it on a video screen. My nerves start firing, raw adrenalin squirting into my muscles. After I clear my throat to catch Strahan's attention, he gives me a sidelong glance and I hold out a finger in front of my stomach, shifting my eyes up to the opening. His chin drops almost imperceptibly, acknowledging the situation, and I breathe more easily. I'm here with professionals. Good, maybe we have a chance.

A crackle explodes from Vitruzzi's radio, like a fission bomb, blasting the silent tension into pieces. "Captain, they fucked us! Get out of there!" Desto's voice is sharp, sudden, absolute. *It is on!*

SEVEN

My elbow smashes into the nose of the man behind me too fast for him to react. He flies backward off his feet. Going with the momentum, I fall on top of him and roll to the side. Pistol already out, I shoot him in the head then dive for a concrete support to my left that holds the roof in place. Rapid firing cascades into the cavern from above, and Vitruzzi is crouched behind a stack of crates about seven meters to my right, returning fire. I look behind me and the other man is lying on his face, not moving, blood pooling beneath him. Did Vitruzzi shoot him, or was it crossfire? Strahan grapples in the middle of the floor with Fitzsimmon. He's completely in the open, but Vitruzzi is keeping the man above from getting a clean shot at him, and I join the barrage with my carbine.

The elevator motor rumbles, signaling that we're about to have more company. Shit! This party is getting out of hand. The blast door begins to gape and I press my back against the support beam, firing a barrage under the door. Screams and blood flood out, followed by two heavy thuds. Suddenly two surprised and agonized faces stare at me from under the door and I aim carefully, finishing them off before they can fire a single shot.

Turning back, I see Strahan crouching over Fitzsimmon's lifeless body, firing his pistol toward the upper entry. He's in the open, completely exposed, and the return fire isn't abating. There must be at least two shooters up there. I glance at Vitruzzi; her magazine has to be close to dry. She suddenly drops with her back to the crates and grabs at her ammunition vest. Got to make a move. "Vitruzzi, Strahan, make for the elevator! I've got it!" I yell.

She breaks immediately and I flinch as a bullet ricochets from the corner of the beam I'm hiding behind, less than a fist's width above my head. Shrapnel stings my hands and tiny beads of blood well up, but I keep firing—can't let those bastards get a clear shot.

"Strahan!" Vitruzzi yells in alarm. I look over in time to see him dive behind the crates where she had been hiding, blood mixing with the grit on the dirty floor beneath him. He twists awkwardly onto one knee and continues firing. Vitruzzi is behind me with good cover in the elevator, loading a second magazine. The display counter on the carbine's stock reads three shots from dry. I pop off two and grab a new magazine, reloading it before the final shot so I don't have to chamber a round. No one fires, and no targets are visible. Whoever is up there has the luxury of waiting us out. They have better cover and a better vantage point. If we move, Strahan and I will be easy targets, but we have to get to that elevator.

I'm crouched on the ground, my back to the beam. I can see Vitruzzi's barrel and one eye from her cover in the elevator. I look over at Strahan. His jaw is clenched, eyes narrowed to slits.

"Strahan," I call. "Where are you hit?"

"My goddamn leg!"

"Can you walk?"

He tries to bring his foot underneath him but gives it up with a gasp. His glance is furious. No fear there. Making a decision, I turn back to Vitruzzi and signal for her to open fire at the shooters, pointing at myself, then at Strahan, and lastly back toward the elevator. She nods and brings her gun around.

Rifle blasts echo throughout the chamber. Rocketing from behind the beam and staying low, I lunge for Strahan. Firing his pistol with his left hand, he swings his right arm over my shoulder. I spring upward as hard as I can with almost his full weight on my shoulders. Christ, he's heavy! Doesn't matter, moving forward. I can feel him lurching with his good leg, trying to improve our speed. We're not fast enough—a bullet hits me in the back, smashing into my body armor like a sledgehammer, instantly propelling us forward a few meters. My lungs go limp as the impact pushes all the air out of me. This can't keep happening. But we're in the elevator! I stumble over one of the dead men's legs and Strahan and I hit the floor. The blast doors shut with agonizing slowness as bullets skid off the ground outside. Finally, the doors seal.

Wheezing, I'm finally able to suck in air and re-inflate my lungs. Vitruzzi is on the radio. "Desto! Do you copy? What's your status? Over."

"Captain, they've shut me in the Rover. Broke the latch from the outside. I can't open it, but I'm alone up here."

"We're in the elevator. We should be up in less than two minutes. Do not shoot when the doors open! Out."

"Strahan, how are you doing?" Blood saturates his right pant leg above the ankle and his face is ashen. Two bright red spots flame over his cheeks, making his eyes glint like gemstones. "I'm going to take a look at this, all right?" Gingerly pulling up his pant leg, I see a clean hole going all the way through the bottom of his calf. He watches me, sweat beading up on his brow. "I don't see any bone. Looks like you got lucky." Ripping a sleeve from his shirt to bandage the wound, I tie it extra tight to aid in supporting his weight. We're not out of this yet. "What do you think now, huh? Still think I'm dangerous?" I'm just trying to distract him, not really paying attention to what I'm saying. But his response grabs my attention.

"I think we're even." His burning eyes catch mine and hold them for a split second.

The elevator stops and Vitruzzi hits the button to open the blast doors. We wait. Nothing happens.

"Shit." She hits it harder. Nada. "They must have rigged it. Desto, do you still have control of the Rover?"

"Yeah, I just can't get out." He's angry, an irate animal caught in a cage.

"All right, I want you to launch a rumbler."

"V, no grenade is getting through that blast door."

"I know. Hit the wall to your left. Hit it is many times as you have to. Smash through it."

"Copy."

"Okay, get down. There could be some debris."

Strahan pulls his knees up, wincing, and Vitruzzi and I crouch against the far brace, covering our faces with our arms just as we feel a blast. Dust fills the shaft. Another blast, and another, the sound pummeling my eardrums like a hammer. The elevator light is burst by a flying rock. I pray that the impact doesn't damage the elevator cables. It's a long way to the bottom.

"Captain! There's a hole, climb through!"

I open my eyes but can't see anything except a disquieting red glow coming from below. They must have the doors open down there, but they won't be able to shoot up the shaft this far—unless they have a pulse launcher. Vitruzzi slides the cage door open, grunting as she struggles to get the warped rollers to give. There's just enough space between it and the blast door for her to fit. Squeezing through, she climbs around the cage until she's next to the jagged opening.

"I'm going to try the controls from outside. If they still work, I'll open the blast door for you. If not . . . Karl?"

"I'll manage," he says, and pulls himself up using the elevator wall.

Maneuvering through the crater in the tunnel wall, she disappears. Moments later, the door rumbles open and I take Strahan's arm again. "Let's go."

The tunnel is nearly dark. Vitruzzi runs to the Rover and begins working at the driver's side latch with a knife pulled from her ammo vest. Desto crouches inside, poised and ready to shove it open as soon as the latch breaks free. As Strahan and I limp forward, beams of light bounce along the walls, speeding down the tunnel toward us.

"Wait!" he yells, jerking me to a halt. "Over there."

Two metal containers marked "Solar Focusing Amalgam" sit beside one of the rough stone walls. A tarp lies crumpled on the ground next to them, blown off by the concussion from the grenades. Exactly what we came here for.

"Those bastards," I manage to pant. "Come on, we can't carry them." We make it to the Rover as Desto finally kicks open the hatch.

"Vitruzzi, the seeds are over there! We can still get them."

Her forehead wrinkles for a half second, gauging the situation, wondering how much time we have. Then she says, "Desto, bring the Rover! Come on, Erikson."

Strahan lets go of my shoulders and takes aim down the tunnel. Whoever's coming is moving fast, but I can't hear anything, only see the lights approaching. Vitruzzi and I get to the crates and work together to quickly load them on the Rover's cargo racks.

"Let's move!" She jumps in, scrambling over Desto to the passenger seat, and I'm right behind her. Desto passes Strahan, slowing down enough for us to haul him over the side. Vitruzzi and I pull the hatch closed but it won't latch, so I hold onto it using the closing strap. Desto presses hard on the accelerator, forcing us into a spin, and then the Rover lurches straight ahead. A four-wheeler comes into view from the tunnel entrance, cruising at top speed. The next instant, I'm thrown into Strahan as Desto turns sharply, losing my grip on the hatch. It flies upward, smacks against the other side, and slams back down with a thud. I manage to grasp it again, and wrap it tightly around my fist as I hold my breath, just waiting for a blast to hit us. Then Vitruzzi says, "Take this you fucks." A hollow thump comes from beneath us, and the tunnel is filled with dazzling brightness as the four-wheeler explodes.

"Got him!"

We speed through the smoky blaze, momentarily riding up on debris. In seconds, we break through the tunnel entrance and back into the open air. Twilight has hit and the sky above us is a mix of purple and red clouds, shifting like the superheated plasma of super-nova remnants. It's not until Strahan shifts beneath me that I realize I'm still sitting half on top of him. I pull myself back into my seat. Finally, the *Sphynx* comes into sight.

Venus pilots us off the moon the instant we roll into the cargo hold and seal the hatch.

"Whew! That was the shit, wasn't it?!" Desto jumps off the Rover, grinning like a deranged butcher. Still sitting, I lean back and take in the ceiling, letting the fact that we survived sink into both my senses and muscles before I trust myself to stand.

"Damn woman, you know how to keep a firefight from getting dull, don't you?" It takes me a minute to realize he's talking to me, and I drop my eyes to see his outstretched hand ready to help me out.

Still winded, I say flatly, "You're nuts."

He laughs, grasping my hand and pulling me out. With a wink, he says to Strahan, "She's as smart as she looks. Come on, let's get you to the infirmary." The two of them start off.

"You should come too, get that hand cleaned up," Vitruzzi says, staring at me keenly. What is she thinking? I'm a complete stranger, a dangerous stranger who had nearly killed one of her crew, and yet she'd taken a major risk on me, gambling I would come through for them when the shit hit the fan. And I had. Where does that leave us now?

Without a hint of mockery, she says, "Thank you, Erikson."

Standing in INF 1, I wince with every cement fragment I pluck from my knuckles. Vitruzzi cuts through Strahan's pant leg as he sucks down a cigarette like a jonesing opium addict, teeth embedded in the filter, smoke pouring simultaneously from the end of the butt and out through his flared nostrils.

As Vitruzzi runs a scanner above Strahan's wound, a to-scale three-dimensional image appears in the air. It takes me a minute of staring before I can make sense of what I'm seeing.

"Cybernetic tissue?"

Strahan replies around the cigarette, "Yeah. Lost the real one from the knee down when I was still in the Corps. Proximity grenade. That, and these." He waves the last three fingers of his right hand at me.

Vitruzzi speaks with the distracted tone of a teacher as she works on the wound. "Most of the leg is still natural tissue, only the nerves and bones are synthetic. Titanium fibula, tibia, and tarsals, and semi-conducting fibers tracing the neural pathways. His muscles and blood vessels re-grew easily once the structure was replaced. We haven't been able to perfect the neurological system yet, but the synth-nerve fibers are a functional replacement." She returns her attention to Strahan. "The bullet went through, but it made a mess. I can suture things back together and put you in regeneration brace, but you'll be hobbling for a few days."

Finished cleaning the scrapes on my hands, I have nothing left here to do and move toward the exit, expecting them to say or do something to stop me. But only their eyes follow me out.

Now what?

Now, I wait.

Once in my bunk, autopilot takes command, and I follow the same, almost ritualistic, pattern I always do. Throwing a rag I'd found across the cabin's bench, I begin tearing down my weapons and laying them out, uniformly, methodically, piece by piece until the bench is covered with a smorgasbord of black metal. I attack the pieces using a cleaning kit from my belt, scraping each of them clean until they gleam like living embers. Knowing my weapons function smoothly and flawlessly, that they'll be reliable when I need them, gives me the extra edge of confidence that can mean the difference between living and dying. Soon, the smell of gun oil infuses the pandemonium of thoughts whirling through my head, transporting me back to Obal 3. All I can think about is David, guessing how much danger he's in, weighing his chances.

Common sense tells me to accept the probability that he's dead already, but I don't believe it. *I can't.* Capturing smugglers alive is Admin SOP. The Soldier's Rebellion had left a mess behind that they're still trying to clean up, and deserters control many of the system's black market operations and smuggling rings. With the destruction of the Capital Military Corps' central personnel database and part of the backup, the Admin lost the ability to reference or track the identities of soldiers who'd deserted or who had simply been lost, their ships obliterated in the uprising. It was a blow that nearly crippled them . . . for a while. Thousands of deserters like David and I simply disappeared from existence, anonymous and untraceable. In order to clean up the system and regain control, the Admin's best option is live capture and interrogation. All information is potentially valuable. Because of this, I let myself believe David is still alive. But for how long? Five days have already passed.

Picking up the bolt of my AK-80 pulse carbine and scrubbing the carbon residue vigorously from its short barrel, I try to imagine what would have happened after David surrendered. He threw out his weapons and went quietly. They'd have had no reason to kill him. But citizens and non-cits carrying weapons get them a guarantee of a quick trial and judgment, followed by an inevitable capital sentence.

The mechanical process of cleaning and checking my weapons keeps me occupied while I let my mind wander freely. My own version of meditation. Unique, yeah, but it keeps me from bugging out. Next to the AK sits my Sinbad auto-pistol, already cleaned and reassembled, and the Mini-Derg XM2 laser that lives strapped to my right calf. The only piece that can be disassembled and replaced on this small but expendable weapon is the battery. As I press the cold metal into the holster, my mind jumps to thoughts of the Fortress itself.

Designed and built in secret, the Admin never intended the space station to be exposed; yet they still prepared for the possibility. Instead of locating it on a planet or moon, it was designed to be mobile, keeping it virtually untraceable. I've never seen it, never met anyone who claims to have been on it until Vilbrandt, but I've heard the stories, and I'm a firm believer that every myth contains some truth. My years in the Corps are enough proof that any government with unlimited power is a government with a reason to hurt people. Sometimes they don't even need a reason. My naiveté died the first time they commanded me to take aim and fire at an innocent.

Hot tears of fear and frustration seep into my eyes. Blinking against them, I slam my fist against the bench and force myself to just STOP thinking. I'll go crazy if I let myself imagine what might be happening to David, but Vilbrandt, with his sidling innuendoes about the types of research done on the Fortress, hadn't made it any easier. Soon I'll be back in contact with Rajcik and won't have time to sit around being tortured by my corrosive thoughts. I hope.

If Vitruzzi's guess is right and Rajcik and the crew made it free and clear with those plans, they're already preparing for the assault on the Fortress. David and I should have rendezvoused with them three days after the mission, two days ago, so Rajcik has probably already written us off. But if I can contact him and make some kind of arrangement to get Vitruzzi the disc, there may still be time to find my brother.

Resuming my ritual, I wipe the AK's bolt spring down with the rag and a drop of oil, mentally weighing the likelihood that Rajcik will be willing to deal with Vitruzzi. Maybe he doesn't need David and me for this job, but then, we've operated as a team for six years. He knows he can rely on us when the shooting starts—and there will be a lot of shooting—and he may be counting on the same level of mutual reliance to increase the odds for success. On the other hand, when have I ever seen Rajcik make a deal that could put a payoff in jeopardy? Never. Our lives might not mean a damn thing to him, and Vitruzzi and her crew can write their friends off for good.

These thoughts continue chasing each other in a maddening circle until I hear footsteps echoing up the metal walkway. I prefer the silence, and slivers of disappointment and irritation cut through me. Reluctantly, I raise my head to see Strahan standing in my doorway.

"You need any help with those?"

"What—are we friends now?"

With a dark frown, he spins around to leave, but then hesitates. Turning halfway back, he says, "You know Erikson, maybe I was wrong about you."

"Maybe you were."

"At least I'm willing to admit it." Abruptly, he stomp-limps away.

Clicking the carbine's barrel into place, I try to ignore an unexpected tinge of regret.

EIGHT

My weapons can't get any cleaner and my thoughts can't get any grimmer. I'm completely helpless, at the mercy of Vitruzzi and her crew, and it's infuriating. With nothing to do but wait for time to pass until we reach Spectra 6, I decide to make my way to the galley. The Sinbad is hidden beneath my bunk, the carbine lies on the bench, and the Derg is attached to my calf. Normally the gun is hidden inside the baggy material of my pants, but this time I attach the holster to the outside. I'm not leaving the weapons locked up where they'll be useless if I need them in a hurry.

I run into Vilbrandt at the staircase leading up to galley level. The stairs are so narrow I have no choice but to wait for him at the bottom. That's part of it. The other part is that the thought of brushing against him makes my skin feel slimy.

"Congratulations on your successful mission." A red glow seeps through a vent beside him as he reaches my level, casting a mesh shadow over his face that gives his pale features a sallow, sickly glow.

The memory of his protestations when Vitruzzi had announced my enlistment on the mission makes my teeth clench. "What kind of shit were you trying to pull with Vitruzzi?"

Of course he knows what I mean. He's a quick one. "You're important to me, Erikson." His tone is sibilant and calm. "If anything happens to you, I stay poor *and* a fugitive. I'd rather you not risk your life for these . . . people, if you don't absolutely have to." His eyebrows arch, and he ends his sentence on an upward note. The message is clear: he doesn't think there's *any* reason I should risk my life for Vitruzzi's crew. Prick.

I want to throw him off guard and ruin that smug calm of his. "She knows you're trying to deal."

"She's an intelligent woman. I think she has more of a criminal mind than she lets on. Why wouldn't I try to make a deal with you? I have nothing to lose, and everything to gain."

His callousness makes me feel as if I'm biting tinfoil. How many people are this cold, this disconnected from normal human emotions? I'm beginning to see why T'Kai was so quick to try and have him erased. It's unnerving to be around someone this unapologetically avaricious.

"I told you I couldn't guarantee anything."

His smile is a squashed worm writhing on a hot sidewalk. "Just introduce me to Rajcik. I'm quite certain he will see the benefit of involving me in this enterprise."

"We'll see." His slippery gaze follows me up the stairs as I maneuver past him.

DESTO AND BODIE SIT in the galley drinking bottles of what looks like flat, warm beer. The fermentation process in space is an imprecise science. Constantly changing pressure and inconsistent matter in both the air and water make for interesting, and usually questionable, brews. Alcohol of any kind is as illegal as weapons are on the governed planets, and plants as marginally useful as hops don't often warrant room in artificial growing environments. There's something to be said for the people who continue trying to develop the beverage.

They nod to me as I enter, much of their earlier coolness seeming to have thawed. Helping out on R'Kadia has earned me some good credit. This newfound trust, or at least indifference, could come in handy.

Rummaging through the cabinets in hopes of finding something, *anything* more appetizing than travel-packaged nutrition bars turns out to be a pipe dream. I haven't eaten more than a few bites of food since waking up almost twenty-four hours ago, yet my appetite has been minimal. Must be a side effect of the drugs and whatever Vitruzzi had been pumping into me through the IV. Surviving a firefight usually makes me ravenous, and my insides feel as hollow as a balloon.

As Desto and Bodie, whose voice now resembles large stones rolling along a streambed, talk, I sit with them and jump in with an observation, "The amount of seeds we got could turn a solid profit. There are a least fifty kilos there."

"We don't need them for cash," Desto says. "We just use them to keep the power on and the *Sphynx* flying."

"Right, sure," I nod, pretending to consider the statement, but I have other ideas. "Have you thought about what you're going to offer Rajcik for the holodisc?"

Desto gives me a flat look, his expression completely blank.

"I'm just asking."

"Aren't you enough?"

"Let me get this straight. The options are my crew either hands over a copy of the disc, or you'll kill me?" I pause, hoping to read something in their expressions that says that's not what they intend. Bodie's clear blue eyes squint slightly, as if the idea makes him uneasy—all the proof I need. "You're not going to do that, so it's not really much of an incentive for Rajcik, is it? I'll be straight with you, he would kill me himself if he thought it would help his cause."

"What cause is that?" asks Bodie.

"He hates the Admin and he'll do whatever he can to sabotage it, as long as it's profitable."

Vitruzzi walks in, Strahan limping doggedly behind her. The brace he wears is a sophisticated piece of medical equipment. Not much bigger than a boot, it fully encloses the lower leg and creates a hydro chamber that combines with sensors. These attach to the surrounding tissue and detect the optimal nutrient and chemical necessities of the wounded area. While running continual tissue scans, it releases biochemical components directly into the bloodstream to expedite healing. In the Corps, I'd seen them used to repair soldiers' broken bones in less than four weeks, and flesh wounds even more quickly. It's surprising to see such a useful and expensive piece of equipment outside of an Admin medical station. Then again, it's surprising to meet a doctor out here who knows how to use one.

Vitruzzi must have overhead us. "So your boss has an agenda. In that case, suppose you tell us what he plans to steal from the Fortress?"

"That's not part of our deal."

An angry vein begins pulsing in her forehead, a warning that she's losing patience, but her voice is steady. "Erikson, you did a good job back there and we might not have made it without you." She glances at Strahan, who eases into a chair next to me. "But I'm not going into this deal without knowing *all* the details. I didn't press the issue before because I wanted to be sure you weren't bullshitting us. But I've heard of Rajcik, I know some of the things he's accused of. If we're going to deal with him, I have to know what he's planning. This isn't negotiable."

Damn. The fun just keeps getting better and better. "Weapons. High-tech munitions."

"There are lots of illicit arms all over the place. What does the Admin care if you steal a few more?" Strahan asks.

Bodie follows up with his own question, "And why steal weapons from the Fortress? I can name ten different locations that you could break into with a fraction of the effort that would take."

My eyes shift to Vitruzzi whose eyebrows are now creased together, the vein pulsing like an accusation. If she hasn't already guessed our plan, she's about to.

They would have some good points if we were just after a nominal return. But Rajcik wants to strike deeper. He wants to show the Admin how vulnerable they are, prove that their most well-protected facility is still no match for him. It's a personal vendetta, a primal, gut-stick fight that he's bringing to their doorstep.

Sighing, I take the plunge. "The Fortress is the only place you can find a weapon like this. It's experimental, secret. The only reason we know about it is T'Kai got greedy, and it was the best carrot he could dangle to get Rajcik involved. It's called the Richter Mini-Nova. The technology is new, but it's the same concept as a chain reaction fusion bomb."

Bodie whistles, almost appreciatively. "Someone could do a lot of damage with a bomb like that."

"Or kill a lot of people." Strahan's voice is icy. "Whom exactly would you sell something like that to?"

"Back to the Admin. They won't want it out in the system. Can you imagine the kind of backlash there would be if citizens knew they are designing weapons like this?"

"And what if they don't buy it?"

This is the part this crew won't like. "They will definitely pay after we threaten to detonate it if they don't."

Alarmed, Bodie sits up straight in his chair. "That's crazy! You'll kill thousands of people!"

Keeping my gaze steady, I scan the room, drawing them all in so that they'll listen carefully. "Millions, actually. The experimental aspect of the device uses antimatter. If it's detonated above, say, a city like Tunis, it'll be completely wiped out, and most of the continent with it. They've finally perfected a way to end worlds, to obliterate everything."

The look on Strahan's face, all of their faces, is a livid mix of horror, disgust, and loathing. A natural reaction, really.

"But you have to understand, we would never *actually* detonate it. I may be a smuggler, but I'm not a psychopath. Neither is Rajcik. The Admin will pay, they won't risk that many lives."

"You're out of your mind if you think you can get away with this. No one will recognize your bodies after they catch you," Vitruzzi says.

The same thoughts had occurred to me when Rajcik first brought up the idea. It's a risk, the biggest risk conceivable. "If we can break into the Fortress, we can handle the Admin. It's worth it."

"So you're suicidal and crazy," says Desto.

"Maybe, but if they build something like this, they should be prepared to deal with the possibility of it getting into the wrong hands. Rajcik's just using their own tools against them. Why should something with that much destructive potential even exist? Maybe the Admin isn't quite as benevolent as it makes itself out to be." My impromptu speech surprises me. *Don't forget,* I tell myself, *you're just in this for the money. When you start taking sides, you start losing the initiative.*

Strahan leans back in his chair, his lips twisted into a sarcastic grin. "That's just beautiful, Erikson. You work for a man who wiped out a squad of thirty soldiers to escape from Keum Libre, a prison he no doubt deserved to be in, and help him steal a bomb that could potentially wipe out the population of a planet. And you make out that it's the Admin's fault? That's rich."

Bodie stares at the table, his face sagging in dismay. Desto and Vitruzzi mirror each other's disbelief. Ignoring Strahan, I keep my mouth shut. I knew they wouldn't want to hear this.

Finally Vitruzzi asks, "And if they call your bluff? What will you do with a weapon like that? Put it in storage? Wait for a good buyer? You can't think something like that would be safe anywhere. Except where it is right now."

Her tone isn't patronizing, but my temper is starting to burn anyway. "You think leaving it at the Fortress is safe? Have you thought about why the Admin is building it in the first place? How they plan to use it?"

"None of this shit matters right now. V, Erikson and her insane plans are not our problem. We need to figure out what it will take to get that disc from Rajcik so we can help Mason and the rest." Everyone listens to Desto, the deep bass of his voice flooding the room. My earlier comment about bargaining chips must have hit a chord with him, and I'm starting to think he's had his own taste of the criminal world.

After a moment to consider, Vitruzzi straightens up, her eyes never leaving my face. "All right, Erikson. Your plans for the Fortress are your business. I just hope you know what you're doing." She punctuates this comment with a glare that says this isn't over. "So tell me, what do you think we should offer Rajcik for that disc?"

"Nothing. He won't give them up." Their faces register, not surprise exactly, more like exasperation. "I know that's not what you want to hear, and you don't have a damn thing to lose if you toss me out the cargo hatch right now. But if there is a chance, I'm it. I've known Rajcik for a long time. He trusts me, as far as anyone can trust anyone." This is a major exaggeration of Rajcik's confidence in me, but they don't need to know that. "He might listen to what I have to say and be persuaded. As long as there's something to persuade with."

"As in?" Strahan asks, but Vitruzzi answers for me.

"He needs energy just like anyone else, right?"

I nod in agreement. "Those seeds would probably draw his attention long enough to at least think about the trade you're proposing."

Venus's voice sounds off over the intercom. "Captain, thirty minutes to touchdown. Brady's on the link for you."

Vitruzzi walks to the intercom and presses the speaker. "I'll be there in a second." Turning back to face the table she states, "We're home. Erikson, we've got a com boost that will link you to wherever you need. That will be the first order of business when we land." With those words, she leaves.

NINE

Venus engages the *Sphynx*'s backup thrusters, gliding us to our landing zone with the precision and lightness of a machine-operated feather. The landing gear slides into deployment with a mechanical hum, and in a few seconds we're settled firmly on the earth. The kid is amazing.

My hands want to twitch while we wait for the loading doors to open, and I clench them into tight fists. They don't need to see how on edge I am about facing a group of strangers on this unfamiliar planet.

Alone.

I've been working as part of a team my entire life, first in the Corps, then with Rajcik's crew. Knowing you're the only one who can save your brother's life, the only family you have, is more than pressure, it's gut-wrenching dread. He needs me. For the first time since I followed my big brother into the Corps, I'm alone in the universe, with no one to rely on but myself.

As the ramp lowers, I take a long look around. We're inside an enormous mine, another dried-up Admin operation, yet the place is alive with activity. Giant fixtures rigged to the ceiling wash everything in a brutal white incandescence. People and ships pack the space, everyone and everything involved in different activities. I realize immediately that this colony of non-citizens is big, and organized.

Nothing throughout the cavern appears disorderly or random. A crew to the right of the *Sphynx* is working together to operate a giant crane. Attached to its loading chains is another ship, this one a small shuttle that is probably used for intra-atmosphere transport. Another group at the end of the cave carries supplies in and out of an enclosed area. Judging by the carts loaded with bags of chemical fertilizers some of them push, they're working in a greenhouse or growing room. The space is filled with everything from earthmoving equipment, to generators, to stacks of building material—all the tools a colony needs to build and maintain an independent infrastructure. There are more supplies and equipment than you see in typical settlements on most of the uncivilized planets by a power of ten.

How much does the Admin know about them? From what I can see, their operation is advanced and self-sufficient, at least enough so to draw unwanted Admin attention. Not everything in this cavern could have been legally obtained, and a well-organized enclave of non-cits, no matter how anonymous or noncombative, is usually considered a threat. At least a hundred people are at work in this mine alone. Who knows how big this place is or what else they've got going on?

The ramp hits the dirt and the *Sphynx*'s crew quickly disembarks. A middle-aged man waits at the base, and I stand at the top of the ramp watching as he exchanges greetings with everyone. Vitruzzi waits next to me. Glancing in my direction and cutting her eyes toward the door, she invites me off.

We step onto the gritty floor and she and the man embrace, arms wrapping tightly around each. They hold onto each other for several tender seconds, their affection overshadowing everything around them. Up to now, her attitude had been cold, efficient, and impersonal, deep-freezing any thoughts I might have had about her inner motivations, the things that drive her to take the kind of chances she has in the last few days. This glimpse into her real life, the life not involved in kidnapping and smuggling, finally drives home how important her friends are to her, and how much she's willing to risk to help them.

After a few seconds, she extracts herself from the man's hug. "Patrick, this is Aly Erikson."

His face is deeply lined by hardship and years of work. A stark white scar runs from his right temple down his cheek, neatly parting the salt-and-pepper stubble covering his jaw, and branches into two lines next to his mouth, one stopping at his top lip and the other ending at the angle of his chin. It's a stern face but not cruel. He jabs his hand toward me.

"Patrick Brady."

His attitude is as gruff as his handshake. I return the gesture but say nothing. The strength in his grip reminds me of how on my own I am. I feel as if I'm standing on a chair with a noose around my neck.

His eyes linger on me for a moment, sizing me up before dropping my hand. I look at Vitruzzi. Time to send the message.

"Patrick, I'll meet you later," she says. "We'll be in the com room for a while."

"Yeah. Bring her by when you're finished. We have things to discuss." Dismissing me, he runs his hand down Vitruzzi's wavy black hair to her shoulder, leaning forward to kiss her. The rest of the crew is already gone, attending to other things. Brady steps back and Vitruzzi turns to me.

"This way."

We walk through the chamber to a lift on the northern wall of the cavern. The ride up lasts a few seconds and we enter a room housing an impressive collection of satellite and radio communication equipment. I settle into a chair in front of a large video display, while her hands move over the controls, activating the necessary channels.

"All communications are scrambled, dissected, and bounced over multiple com nodes throughout the system. We'll have to direct the message to a contact on Obal 8 who will put it back together and transmit to wherever you tell him. The shorter the message, the better, but say what you have to." Her dark eyes bore into mine to emphasize her next statement. "A lot of people are depending on this."

David is one of them. Looking into the video feed, I take a few seconds to think about what to say, then switch it on. "*Temptation* this is Erikson. Situation stable. Need mission status and new rendezvous location. Out." I bite back the urge to press for information about David. It's not likely Rajcik knows anything, but it's hard not to ask. Turning around, I say, "Short and sweet. Just tell your contact on Obal 8 to transmit to uplink 548 in Delta Alpha. If he encodes it, send the key to uplink twelve, same quadrant. Rajcik will get the message."

She types the directions into the satcom computer and inputs the transmission code. "For what it's worth."

Deep lines materialize around her mouth and eyes, only pronounced when she thinks no one notices, when she forgets people are looking to her to be in charge. The lines are like a map of her burdens, but they also reveal the inner strength with which she manages them. Right now, we have a lot in common. Too much. We're both afraid people we care for are going to die at the hands of an enemy who, reason tells us, should be anything but. She leans back in her chair, her focus on people millions of miles away. I recognize the difficult position she's in, wanting to do what's best for her crew, people who depend on her, and having to rely on me, a smuggler, a criminal, someone who shouldn't be trusted no matter how much she needs to. I wish we were on the same side, as real allies instead of collaborating out of necessity.

"Now what?" The sound of my voice brings her back to the here and now.

"We wait," she says, the lines smoothing back into calm authority. "Hungry?"

"Yeah. And I could use a shower."

TEN MINUTES LATER we're aboard the Rover and leaving the cave through a long, well-lit tunnel. Emerging into the brightness of midmorning, I can see the outlines of three small moons fading to ghostly circles high above, and the hot ball of Algol A. Spectra 6 doesn't appear to be much different than any of the other outer planets I'd been too, at least in terms of climate. Dry and hot, with negligible life-supporting material thanks to its proximity to the star. The Spectras that were once rich in minerals or ore lack much else that makes them appealing or livable to people. Once the Admin took what it could from them, they were abandoned. People still manage to populate some of them, but the living is harsh and tenuous. Those who come out to the Spectras have learned to forget, if they ever knew, about nice things—things like fresh food, civil structure, and law enforcement. Like packs of hyenas, those who live here have to become half-savage and dangerous in order to survive.

For all the harshness of the landscape, the settlement is good sized. A multitude of housing structures, mostly assembled from scraps of metal and discarded junk, rise out of the coarse and sandy ground like ancient relics, cleverly built into the strange and abundant rock formations that cover the surface so that they almost seem organic, growing naturally from the earth. Though most of the materials are probably scavenged, nothing about the settlement seems accidental or derelict. It appears there have been people here for a long time, making use of whatever they found, and making the best of it. With the scarcity of anything besides rock and dust as far as I can see, I can't help but wonder about the people living here and what it is that makes them tick.

A quick ride takes us to one of the dwellings, a sand-colored structure with an arched roof peppered with photovoltaics, and she leads me inside. The building is round and the front entrance opens into a main room with a kitchen and table and chairs. Dusty skylights nestled between the solar panels shed enough light on the interior to see clearly. It's cooler in here, well insulated. The walls are probably filled with dirt and a fan system circulates the air inside. All in all, it's surprisingly comfortable, another indication of a relatively advanced long-term settlement. These people are well beyond simply trying to survive out here. Brady is waiting for us, and I sit at the table across from him.

"You've got friends here, Erikson, so it wouldn't be a bad idea to try and trust us." Brady's statement is abrupt and unexpected. He stares at me as if I'm something he might have scraped off the bottom of his shoe. Vitruzzi sits next to him, very still, her back rigid.

Looks as if that shower's going to have to wait. Cursing silently, I keep my features still and impassive. Why can't anything be simple?

I shift a little in my chair, trying not to explode with frustration, and wait for someone to start telling me what Brady is talking about. I could demand answers, but it wouldn't do any good. They have the advantage here and the only thing I have is a complete lack of options and patience. Both are excruciating.

Shoving a cup with some orange liquid and a plate of food across the table toward me, Brady continues, "Eleanor has told me about you, Erikson, and I did a little digging, too. You're ex-Corps, like Desto and Karl—special tactical operations. It surprises me that someone in spec-ops would end up in your shoes. Usually, once those dogs get the taste for blood, they never lose it."

Is he trying to make me angry? I sit motionless in my seat, holding his eyes with mine. He's long past pretending to be friendly.

"But then, you haven't have you? Just changed flavors." There's a harsh, bitter edge to his voice, and suddenly I understand. He mentioned I was ex-Corps, like Desto and Strahan, but *not* like him. The scar on his face, his obvious hatred for spec-ops soldiers—he's a non-cit of course. Born and raised on a desolate rock in the outer planets with cancer-causing dust in the air. Treated like a machine or worse by some Admin resource extraction franchise—used, abused, then tossed when it became too expensive to keep him working or the mine dried up.

Then what? Did he fight back? Did he become a problem the Admin needed to deal with? Yeah, it makes sense that he'd hate me, or at least, hate what I was. Corps special operations squadrons are in charge of eradicating insurgent threats throughout the system. The long arm of the law. My unit's mission is, *was*, to police the massive and scattered non-cit populations of sixteen Obal and Spectra planets and well over a hundred moons within the Algol system. And police them hard.

The ship David and I had been stationed on, PCA *Thor's Hammer*, operated as an enforcement craft. Mostly we were put down on what the Admin termed "insurgent enclaves" to deep six all rebellious activity. We were trained to be efficient, and that's exactly what we were. Like all good soldiers, we weren't supposed to think about what we did. We just followed orders, and the orders were always the same: exterminate all threats, no questions.

Long-suppressed memories of those firefights begin to float up from beneath the swamp rocks I'd buried them under in my mind, as if they are the noxious contents of a broken sewer line bubbling to the surface. Soldiers with pulse rifles, grenades, missiles, and armored land cruisers deployed from orbiting long-range warships, fighting against people in rags with a few handguns and maybe some homemade dynamite. My stomach clenches as I recall the methodical ruthlessness with which we utterly squashed all the petty resistance they'd tried to mount. The way we'd killed every man, woman, and child on those planets so no one would live to tell about what had happened to them. Just folks who wanted to live without Admin interference, on their own terms. People like Brady.

His grim face is set as he watches me process these thoughts. Staring at his unflinching eyes, I remain speechless and my anger evaporates, leaving a cold and empty void. Why wouldn't he hate me? I represent all the atrocities that soldiers like me had done to people like him.

The room is hushed and tense. Finally, Vitruzzi breaks the silence, "Erikson, we want to offer Rajcik a trade. He gets twenty kilos of solar seeds for a copy of the disc."

Her all-business tone lets me escape Brady's accusing gaze. "Seems like a good idea," I comment glibly. They don't have anything else that Rajcik would care in the least about.

"And his crew and some of us team up in a rescue mission for your brother and our friends."

I take a drink of liquid Brady gave me and nearly choke on it. Coughing, I ask, "You're kidding me, right?"

No. She's not kidding. Not joking, not pulling my leg, not having a laugh at my expense. She's serious. Another glance at Brady confirms that they are both serious.

Enunciating my words as clearly as I can, I promise them, "That . . . is . . . NOT . . . an option."

"Why not, Erikson? We up our odds with every able-bodied fighter we have. You know it. If Rajcik is as clever as we've heard, he'll know it."

"Did you forget what I was doing when you *kidnapped* me?" I use the word deliberately, trying to incite enough hostility that they'll drop the idea completely. "I was smuggling. Smuggling plans to steal a weapon so dangerous it could destroy an *entire planet*. And you want to team up? Maybe I have some screws loose, but you people are completely nuts."

Pausing, I read their faces, looking for an indication that they realize their idea is ludicrous. "Besides, Rajcik isn't the group-effort type. He probably won't even be willing to trade for the seeds."

Vitruzzi's expression doesn't change from the same calm focus. Maybe I persuaded her that she's pushing her luck with her proposal, or maybe not, but I'm willing to bet she doesn't like what I said. Brady's pinched stare has gone from sour dislike to outright detestation. He leans forward slowly, putting all four legs of his chair back on the ground and gets up stiffly from the table, as if he's about to walk the plank.

Superficially, it seems like a smart move to pool our resources. I've seen how tightly Vitruzzi and her crew work together, and it's apparent that they can handle themselves in a tough situation. And as much as I hate to admit it, confirmation that Desto and Strahan both share my military background makes me trust, if not them, at least their abilities. If all we had to do was break through the Fortress's security, let ourselves in, grab David and their friends, and get the hell out, I might even be willing to go along with her idea. But this isn't just a rescue mission. There's a monumental payoff involved, and if I know János Rajcik, anyone or anything that tries to remap his intended course of action will be eliminated.

Disgusted, Brady turns his back and walks to the kitchen. Vitruzzi waits calmly, trying to will me to reconsider. She doesn't know how stubborn I am. Or how dangerous Rajcik is.

Finally, she says, "Have it your way, Erikson." She stands up, concluding the discussion. "Meet me at the hangar at 1600 and we'll see if Rajcik has responded."

"So what am I supposed to do until then?"

"Whatever you want. I'll take you over to Venus's and you can get that shower. Come on."

As I pass in front of Brady, he reaches out and grabs me by the arm. I tense up and face him, ready for whatever might be coming, but the look on his face isn't what I expect. I see weariness and resignation just under the surface of his weathered skin. His anger is still there, but subdued. We look at each other for a drawn out second and then he lets go. The message is clear: *Don't be a fool.*

Venus's dwelling is similar to Brady's, just a bit smaller and wildly untidy. No one is home when Vitruzzi drops me off, but she assures me Venus will be around soon. Inside, electronic consoles, maps, unidentifiable parts, and machine schematics are strewn everywhere. An engine of some sort lays disassembled on part of the floor, pieces of it and other mechanical equipment dumped helter-skelter all around it like an asteroid field. It's difficult to tell what's supposed to be furniture and what's just taking up space.

The room is dim, and after a short search, I'm able to locate the controls for a ceiling panel. Activating it rotates the panels toward the brightest part of the sky and catches the light, reflecting it back inside, but the room doesn't look any better.

It probably wouldn't be difficult to steal a land transport and run. But where would I go, and what good would it do me? As far as I know, the only communication link-up on this planet is here in this little settlement and I don't think I could manage to steal an interstellar craft and fly it by myself. Could I get Vilbrandt to help me? I dismiss that thought immediately. Even if he knows anything about flying, I don't trust him any farther than I can throw him and definitely don't want to be in a situation where I'm forced to rely on him.

Forget it. The best thing for me to do right now is wait, no matter how difficult it is.

A narrow door leads into the bathroom. The shower is a round metal cylinder that requires an upward step of about half a meter to get inside, the lower portion a catchment and filtration system to either recycle the water or direct it to another use. Stripping down and leaving my clothes on the floor, I carefully balance the 'Bad on the top of the stall. Pushing the single round button on the wall dumps enough water on my head to get my hair and body wet. The temperature is lukewarm, probably regulated to stay exactly that. Finding a soapy gel in a tube on the floor, I lather up. It feels good to be in a shower with real water. Ships don't carry much more than the essentials for the crew's basic needs. Showering is done using a dry enzymatic powder that breaks down, rather than rinses off, all the dirt and grime on your skin, and is then scrubbed off with a microfiber towel or blasted off with an air blower. Washing in space is a little like being in a sandstorm.

When I'm finished, I push the button twice more and rinse off. I don't have a towel, so I stand inside for a few more moments to drip dry.

I'd like to take a look at my bruises to see how much discoloration remains, but the mirror is nearly hidden by image captures. People, animals, landscapes, ships—everything imaginable is pinned to the wall, pictures on top of pictures until all I can see of some are the corners, the rest buried underneath layers. I stare at them, thinking that they're a perfect representation of how I perceive Venus. Scattered, filled with bits of information that is so profuse and disconnected that even she can't make it make sense. Or maybe it does make sense to her, but I'm at a loss.

A sliver of mirror remains, enough to see just my eyes. At thirteen, my first boyfriend had told me that they were the shape of elm leaves.

He said it trying to sound smart and seductive, awkward coming from an adolescent boy, especially since neither of us had ever seen a real elm tree. Years later, I ran across a model of one in an Earth relics museum and discovered that the boy hadn't been wrong. My eyes do slant to severe points at each corner. But they are blue instead of green.

"Sorry, I don't have any towels. The air is so warm, usually you dry off right away anyway."

I whirl, caught completely by surprise. "You shouldn't sneak up on me like that!"

"Oh, okay." Her focus is on a small video display unit in her hands, totally unaware that she'd startled me, or of the fact that I'm still half naked. I've been on ships long enough, where the only privacy is in your head, that it doesn't really bother me. It's the way she seems so detached that makes me nervous. Not in a distracted way, but as if she's wired into a different frequency than most people altogether. Without a glance up, she motions toward my pistol, still on top of the shower stall. "Don't forget that." Then wanders back into the main room. I finish dressing and join her.

She's cleared a small table of its clutter. On top lies the same tray of food that Brady had given me. At the time, I hadn't been in the mood to eat, but now I feel hunger gnawing away at my stomach. I sit down on top of a crate and lift a square sandwich to my lips. Real bread! Venus sits opposite me and remains engrossed in watching the handheld VDU. Her feet tap a rhythm on the floor that would make a tap dancer tired in seconds. I have to take deep, calm breaths to cope with the incessant motion.

Suddenly, she looks up and levels her plutonium green eyes on me, disconcertingly like a cat's in a dark room. "Did you know I lost my family because of the Admin? In a mining . . . accident." She sneers the word, making it a curse. "My little sister and my parents. My brother died before that, from the chemicals that got into our food, our water, everything. The same chemicals that made me a freak killed him. Strange, isn't it?" I don't know if she wants me to answer, but I'm glad I ate so fast. I'm losing my appetite.

"I wasn't there when it happened. I might have saved them if I had been. But it was already too late when I found out. I should have died too, but it happened at night and I don't sleep much."

I'm not sure I want to hear this story, but I have to ask, "What kind of accident?"

"I'm from one of the moons off Spectra 5, Acculmi. The mine was an old one, almost nothing left in the ground. That's why they started shipping us to the mine on Spectra 5. There hadn't been any maintenance or reinforcement on Acculmi's structure in years, except what we did ourselves. Requests for better equipment, parts, anything that could keep things running went without response. It was going dry and they knew it, so they weren't going to be bothered with putting any money into keeping it in good order. We were all non-cits anyway. Cheaper labor." She puts down the VDU and clasps her hands together tightly, almost as if she doesn't trust what they might do.

"So we had to start finding other ways to get what we needed. We didn't report all the ore we extracted, which was practically nothing anyway, and sold what we skimmed to whoever would buy it."

After a pause, she continues, "It just collapsed one night with eighty people inside. We'd had to move inside because our sun shields were badly deteriorated. I was out flying when it happened, testing some of the modifications I'd been making to our shuttle. I heard the dispatch from the mine; they were begging for help. And then . . . I picked up a communication between the Admin flight control and one of their patrol ships close to our orbit. The patrol ship asked if they should send a medical team to the mine."

My stomach cramps painfully as I wait for what she's going to say next. I already know.

"The flight ship controller just asked him why he thought that was necessary." A scary, half-crazed laugh bubbles out of her throat. "I got back to the mine as fast as I could, but there were only a few people who made it out. We couldn't dig deep enough to get to the lower chambers and we didn't have the kind of equipment we needed. I don't remember how many days we worked, trying to find anyone who was still alive. Their cries for help . . . there were less of them every hour. But eventually, we just had to give up. There was nothing we could do.

"Not long after that, a patrol ship finally landed to survey the situation, see if there was anything left to salvage. I stole it."

She looks me fully in the face for the first time since she'd started the story, a wet sheen of tears highlighting her eyes. "I was going to get revenge, you know? I was going to fly straight into the first Admin ship I found and blow them all up. I was crazy. I lost my whole family, my friends. Everything I had. You understand that, right?

"I got as far as Spectra 6 without seeing a single Admin ship. I hadn't eaten for days and had burns from a fire that broke out on the ship. There's an outpost on the other side with a smaller settlement than this one. The fire took out part of the hydraulics and I crashed. Fortunately, Captain V and Karl found me. I was delirious. I don't really remember it. When I got back to normal, they told me how sorry they were that they hadn't been able to find any other survivors. I'd been raving the whole time, so they knew most of my story. But when I told them I'd flown the ship alone, they didn't believe me for a while. They said that ship couldn't be flown without a crew." This time her laugh is genuinely amused. "They'd never met *me* before."

"What kind of ship did you steal?"

"A DC Class gun ship."

"What?" It's my turn for disbelief. DCs are interstellar cruisers with the capacity for thirty crewmembers, four of which are essential to fly it. "How could you keep it flying, much less control it?"

"Took some rigging, and like I said, no time for eating or sleeping. But I got the flight trajectories loaded and made that baby do things it was never designed for. Kept on it for three days but I lost it anyway. Without a full crew I couldn't look to the engine and once that fire started, I was done for."

It's a fascinating story, I'll give her that. Fascinating, but impossible. Or is it? I've already seen how fluidly she handles the *Sphynx*, a ship design known for having quirks in atmosphere that makes being aboard one feel as if you're riding a roller coaster through a blast zone. Something in her makeup has made her the kind of person who can read ships, understand and intuit the vagaries of flying and weather the way a master sculptor understands marble. And the modifications done to the ISPS, who better than the pilot to know what to do?

"The captain took care of me until I got back into my head again. Her and Karlie talked me out of killing myself. Even if I had managed to find an Admin ship and run into, it wouldn't have brought my family back. She asked me to take the *Sphynx* up one day, to see if I really could fly it, and that's why I'm here now, and not atomized space dust."

It's almost hard for me to match the image of a caring and concerned Strahan with the surly grunt I've dealt with, but it's easier with Vitruzzi. It's been a while since I've met people with a genuine sense of human decency. People who actually give a damn about others, not just percentages.

"Do you know why I'm telling you this?"

I honestly don't, and shake my head.

She looks at me as if I might be a little slow. "Because Cap'n V, Karlie, and Pat are not stupid, Aly. If they were, they'd have been dead a long time ago. They don't make decisions at random. They've been at this game a long time. They're smart, and they always do what's right for people who deserve it. Do you get it?"

"It seems to me as if they make a habit out of kidnapping unconscious people and making them part of the crew." I know my words are unnecessarily frosty, but I can't seem to help myself.

"Yeah, I guess you could look at it that way. But you could also look at it like they help those that need it. Even when there's a risk." She gives me a tranquil smile, her heart-shaped face and pale skin making her look like a marble angel. "The captain is a doctor, after all." And then, with a rapid change of mood to which I'm becoming accustomed, she stands up and walks toward the door. "I have to help Bodie with some maintenance on the *Sphynx*. Help yourself to anything you can find, or wander around. Whatever you want. See you later." And she leaves.

TEN

Restlessness and anxiety set my nerves on fire while my brain lists twenty different horrible things that might be happening to David while I sit uselessly on this rock. My watch has set itself to local time. It's only 1130, so I have some time to kill before meeting Vitruzzi. I've been alone for half an hour and no one has shown up to keep tabs on me, but I know they can't trust me that much. I probably have a shadow, most likely someone I haven't met, someone I wouldn't recognize if I saw them around. Probably waiting for me to leave and planning on following me. Or maybe they have video captures hidden in the maelstrom of Venus's dwelling. Could be both. If I cared, it would be enough to make me paranoid.

Fuck it. Sitting here is going to make me crazy. I'll just take a walk.

Being on foot allows me to soak up the warm air, refreshingly welcome after being aboard ship for almost a week. I walk aimlessly around the rambling settlement with no destination in mind. Basically, it's just a small collection of dirt streets that divide the spaces between buildings. It's hard to say how many people live in the area. Could be a couple hundred, could be no more than a sixty or seventy. People occasionally pass me either on foot or driving some version of a beat-up land transport. No one stops to talk, but their suspicious stares make it clear that they're aware of who I am. They all proceed as if they have something important to do. Considering the work I saw taking place inside the mine, they probably do.

Despite my wandering, my mind stays busy thinking over the things I see. Here's a group of people who have done more than fall into the deep end of space and given up. They're really trying to make a life for themselves, make it work despite the Admin restrictions that work against them. Most of the non-cit outposts I've been to in my travels have been destitute sties filled with pirates, degenerates, and criminals—hiding places for the cutthroat and brutal. I had almost forgotten that there are still people in the universe, citizen or not, who want to do more than steal and hide.

By 1200 hours on my watch, Algol A is at its zenith, setting the sky fully ablaze. A crescent of Algol B can be seen on the distant horizon shadowed by the planets between us. The brilliant backdrop only serves to punctuate how alone and unguarded I am. As if to create a safe barrier between the unknown and myself, my interior navigator leads me back to the mine entrance.

As I walk through the opening toward the main cavern, darkness quickly absorbs the dazzling outside light like an inky sponge. The tunnel is semi-illuminated by deep holes penetrating to the surface along the roof, allowing enough sunlight to provide moderate visibility. The grainy gray glow filters through suspended dust and sweeps over a metal walkway along the left side of the tunnel. As speeding vehicles pass me in both directions, it becomes immediately clear that it's the safest path for foot traffic.

The sound of a vehicle approaches, catching my attention as the hum of its engine slows. It pulls to a stop beside me. In the gloom, I recognize Desto sitting astride a large motorcycle with a gigantic faring and gun barrels pointing out of turrets on either side of the steering apparatus. I've never seen any kind of two-wheeled, terrain-limited vehicle equipped like it before. A bike made for combat?

He gives me his trademark lecherous grin.

"Nice bike."

The grin widens even further at the compliment. "You like it, huh? My own design, with some help from my man, Bodie. He's pretty decent with a wrench. But the guns were definitely my idea. Are you headed to the ship?"

"Just wandering around. Waiting for a chance to pick up communications with Vitruzzi a little later."

He revs the engine loudly, showing off its power. "So you have some time then. Why don't you come with me and I'll show you one of my favorite places on this rock." Noticing my hesitation, he continues, "Don't worry, I promise to get you back in time."

"Are you trying to pick me up?"

"You damn right I am!" He leans closer and winks. "Come on, honey. Don't be shy. We're going somewhere I know you'll love."

"Which is?"

"The shooting range. Let's see how good you are with that little carbine of yours." His very white teeth gleam at me in a challenging smile. "If you want, you can try my gun too. Hop on."

Why not? I'll do about anything to take my mind off the fact that David's been in the hands of the Admin for a week. Almost before I'm seated, Desto guns it and peels out, the sudden velocity whipping my head backward. Without time for a single breath, he slams the foot-brakes, making the back wheel skid in an improbably canted arc at the mouth of the mine. Taking a moment to let his eyes adjust and make sure no one is entering, he warns, "Hang on."

We drive fast for about fifteen klicks to a deserted stretch of land. The road we're on narrows as we enter a sprawling cluster of wreckage, chunks of twisted metal, and other scattered debris that covers a range nearly the size of the mine's main chamber. The path continues into the heart of the ruins, forming a twisted circuit.

Desto stops just outside of the perimeter and leans the bike on a reinforced kickstand the size of my arm. I nearly have to pry my clenched fists from his shirt with my teeth as we dismount. The transport is clearly as heavy as it looks, but he handles it as if it weighs no more than a bicycle. Next to us is a loudspeaker kiosk. He picks up the handset and clicks it on.

"Anyone on the range fire twice in the air. Otherwise, watch out." He lowers the handset and waits for a moment, scanning the field. There's no sound to alert us anyone else is here.

"All right, Erikson. Ever ridden one of these?" He gestures toward the bike.

"Sure."

"Good. Right here and here are your triggers, and these toggles adjust the barrels up and down about twenty degrees from center. They don't have a left or right pan mechanism. I couldn't get enough angle out of them before hitting the tank. But that's what steering is for. The bullets are caseless, so don't worry about them ejecting and burning your legs. But the thing that makes it a challenge is the kick. You'll ride forward just fine, but fire those guns and you have to compensate for the recoil." He turns to look me over, gauging my reaction to the task.

The size of the bike is daunting. It will hold itself upright once it gets going; that's not what I'm worried about. It's the fact that if I lean too far on a turn without enough momentum, this behemoth will pin me to the ground as if it were a bulldozer parked on a mouse.

Smirking bravely, I climb on. As I start to pull the bike off its kickstand, a hydraulic activator helps it extend, pushing off the ground and raising the bike to riding position. When I have control of it, I jump on the starter and the kickstand retracts. "Any thoughts on what you want me to hit?" I ask as the engine rumbles to life, growling at the same pitch as Desto's laughter.

"Anything that looks scary, babe."

I visually measure the distance and angle to a blasted old piece of mining equipment, adjust the right gun, and fire. The steering apparatus bucks furiously in my hands, vibrating as if I'd grabbed an electric fence, and jagged metal spikes bloom around the new hole that appears in the mining junk. The bike maintains perfect balance. I glance at Desto with a nervous grin. His return smile is full of both approval and pride. However overblown his libertine act, the guy knows his shit.

I'm about ready to twist the accelerator when he says, "Hold it," and opens a storage box mounted behind the seat. Keeping the bike locked tightly between my thighs, I pull on the pair of heavy plastic goggles he hands me, tighten up the strap, and move out.

Weaving throughout the range, I cover several branches of the circuitous paths, adjusting to the bike's feel. It handles smoothly, only the shocks reacting a little stiffly. But then they're calibrated for a man who easily outweighs me by forty kilos, maybe more. At first, I'm cautious, almost jittery, but nervousness quickly gives way to a sense of natural easiness. The rig almost drives itself. All I have to do is maintain control while firing. Its power is intense, and the accuracy of the guns is a lesson in perfection. I do two or three loops just for fun, carefully aiming at targets that come within range, returning to where Desto waits, with real reluctance. As I pull up and kill its inertia, the bike's heaviness seems at odds with its graceful motion.

Desto's grin is total approval this time. "Outstanding! Where have you been all my life?"

I grin back, weirdly pleased to have made a good impression. "I think I missed a couple, but as fast as it goes, no one would have time to return fire anyway. How do you reload when you're dry?"

"You can't while it's moving. She's more of an escape than an attack vehicle. Spray and pray and get the hell out of there."

We spend the next two hours practicing firing drills. Ingrained military maneuvers, part of my DNA after years of training, come as natural as breathing. Desto shows me some new ones. My shots are either dead on, or close enough to matter, but he never misses. When midafternoon shadows begin to pool between the hulking wrecks, we switch to laser sights and continue practicing. Finally, hunger and fatigue bring an end to the fun.

As we prepare to head back to the hangar, a sudden movement at the north end of the range catches my attention. There's a man there, or what used to be a man. He's deathly pale, dressed in rags, his face covered with red, scaly lesions. He leans against a rusting turbine that once belonged to a midrange transport ship, staring at us with filmy eyes that continually blink and squint. The symptoms are all too easy to recognize.

"Desto, do you know that guy?"

His head swivels on his muscular neck to follow my line of sight. "Solar stoner. Junkies from a little town east of here wander over to the range sometimes. They usually don't have enough of a brain left to figure out how to get back. I've seen a few of them

'accidentally' wander into the line of fire. It's a pain in the ass to clean up."

About what I thought. Sometime in the last couple of decades, a scientist discovered a compound that he hoped would cure the ubiquitous cases of melanoma caused by the system's binary stars. During the testing phase, he discovered that instead of blocking damaging UV light, the compound catalyzes with it and induces feelings of intense euphoria in anyone who ingests it. It has virtually no effect if you stay out of sunlight, but the addictive effects were too much of an instant hook for a lot of people. Word got out, and the process for making the compound with it, and people like the guy at the end of the range started popping up everywhere. If taken over a long enough period of time, the product and overexposure to sunlight turn these pathetic addicts into walking zombies, bodies filled with cancers and diseases, and brains fried like rotten bacon. There's no way to recover from the effects once they've gone that far. Like any junkie, they can be dangerous if they don't get their fix. That is, until they become too weak to do anything but fester and waste away. The name solar stoner is as good as any.

Desto's comment about a nearby town ignites my interest. "There's a town in the area?"

"Yeah, but you don't want to go there. Full of lowlifes and crooks. We keep the Beach free of their kind."

Does he realize the irony in what he said? *I'm* one of their kind.

"We shake down anyone from that gutter-ghetto who comes over here. More than a few have tried to take what we've got. They just don't seem to get it that you have to work for what you get in this life. No free rides. Besides, we're always ready for them, me and her." He pats the Thresher assault rifle that he'd used on the range, now resting in a scabbard along the frame of the bike. "You ready?"

I jerk my chin over to the stoner by the turbine. "What about him?"

"Can't do anything for him. He doesn't have long." He revs the bike and I barely manage to grasp his shirt in time to keep from tumbling off the back.

THE SHORT RIDE BACK to the hangar isn't fast enough to keep my worries from catching up with me. I'm sure it's too soon to have heard back from Rajcik, but every hour that passes could be one hour closer to David's death.

Desto skids to a stop next to the *Sphynx*. As I climb off the beast, Bodie walks over. He grins at Desto, very straight teeth gleaming through the tendrils of his beard and mustache. "Hey man, can you give me a hand with this toolbox?" He indicates a container sitting at the base of a ladder propped against the *Sphynx*.

"Bodie! Bring me that cylinder torque, will you?" The voice belongs to a pair of legs emerging from the rear hydraulic compartment. It's Strahan, leaning so far in that only the tips of his toes are skimming the ground. One of his feet is black-booted but the other is still encased in its brace.

Bodie and Desto both take an end of the toolbox. With his free hand, Bodie tosses me a wrench. "Here, Erikson, hand this to Karl. Thanks."

I approach the legs and hear muted cursing. "I've got your wrench."

"Great, sweetie. Just lay it on the cart there. No wait, hand it to me."

I'm confused for a second and then chuckle when I realize that he thinks I'm someone else. "Here you go."

He emerges from the hatch so quickly it's almost as if the ship spits him out. "Oh, shit. Erikson. I thought you were . . . you sounded like . . . um, I thought you were someone else."

"Yeah, I got that." It's hard not to laugh at his embarrassment as I hand him the cylinder torque. He just stands there for a moment, appearing to be at a loss at what to say. So I make it easy. "Have you seen Vitruzzi?"

A faint red blush still tinges his cheeks. Sensitive after all, it appears. "She's up in the com annex. You know how to get there, right?"

I nod and walk to the lift. When I get to the top, Vitruzzi is sitting in a chair in front of the massive satellite console, listening to something through a set of headphones. I allow myself to hope for a second that it's a message from Rajcik.

"Anything?" I ask.

She swivels around and looks at me with a mixture of disappointment and worry. My own features shift, mirroring hers.

Removing the headphones and laying them down on the desk, she says, "We'll try again at 2000. That's about twelve hours since you sent the first message."

Twelve hours, but the chances are still slim that enough time will have passed for him to respond. It would take approximately three hours for the transmission to get there, another three to get back, with a narrow six-hour window in between where he'd have to be monitoring for new messages from the uplink satellite. It's possible he's not even checking at this point, having given David and I up for dead days ago. Or the Admin could have traced him and severed his access. There are a million things that could keep him from getting that message. Thinking of it makes the balloon of anxiety in my torso swell tight, close to bursting.

"And if there's nothing, what then?"

"Then we'll have to take our chances with Vilbrandt."

I meant what would happen to me if Rajcik doesn't come through with the plans, but I don't pursue the answer. The severity of her expression makes it clear that her biggest, and only, concern is figuring out how to rescue the other crew from the Fortress. I'm here as a token of hope, one that can be chucked if there's no more reason *to* hope.

As if she hears my thoughts, Vitruzzi says, "You know, Erikson, if Rajcik doesn't respond, there isn't a hell of a lot you can offer us."

I keep my features neutral and my eyes very steady. "You can't keep me here forever."

"Nothing is stopping you from running. You've seen that. But I think it's fair to warn you that the Admin has newscast your theft. There's an at-large notice for you and Rajcik both. Everyone with a receiver from here to the moons of Spectra 4 has seen your faces. There's also a reward." She pauses, inspecting my expression.

My features feel as if they've turned to stone, rigid and cold, hiding the fear behind them. T'Kai had agreed that the operation would be anonymous. Any Corps soldier who asked the wrong questions would be charged with dereliction of duty and sentenced indefinitely to Keum Libre. If Vitruzzi is telling the truth, and I have no reason to think she wouldn't be, either T'Kai hadn't kept that part of the bargain or they'd gotten to David and made him talk. It wouldn't surprise me if T'Kai double crossed us; he's a typical self-serving Admin politician, but if it was David . . . I know my brother. If he talked, it took drugs and torture. Imagining how much he'd resist before they could break him turns my guts to antifreeze. And if he told them everything he knew, why would they keep him alive?

"They're calling it theft of Admin property, downplaying it. But they want you and Rajcik bad, that's certain."

"So you could turn me in and collect the reward. If Rajcik doesn't come through, what'll stop you?"

"Besides the fact that my crew and I are the reason they haven't caught you already? Nothing. Except that's not the way I do things. I know something about you, Erikson, that you either don't realize about yourself, or you're trying very hard to hide."

"And what's that?"

"You're not as much of a greedy cutthroat as you pretend you are."

I chuckle rudely.

"You want to know what my proof is? The way you risked your

neck to help Karl on R'Kadia. If you didn't care about anyone's ass but your own, you wouldn't have done that. You could have jumped on that elevator without a second thought. But you didn't. It's automatic for you to look out for others . . ."

"When it's in my own interest," I finish for her.

She's quiet for a moment, letting that sink in. "I don't think it's about getting rich for you. We all have our reasons for doing what we do, and I think yours are about getting even, getting revenge. I know what the Corps is like. The stories make it out this far. A soldier has to follow orders, whether she likes it or not. You deserted for the same reason you work with an arms smuggler."

"And what's that?"

"You want to get back at the Admin for trying to make you a killer. That's not you, even if it's easier for you to tell yourself it is."

Vitruzzi's words splash over me with the same harsh effect of alcohol poured over an open wound. She's right, but it's a hard truth. I hide behind my battle-hardened armor so I don't have to think about who I may really be deep inside. I buried the soldier I had been under layers and layers of carefully tended forgetfulness. What kind of person follows the inhuman orders that I had to follow? Telling myself that I had no choice doesn't make any difference. I'm no more willing to know the answer to that than I am to let my brother die without traveling to the edge of the galaxy, to hell if I have to, to save him. So I bury the guilt and I bury the hate I have for the Admin and the Corps. It doesn't matter. It's bigger than the universe. So fuck it, let me forget my feelings, and my reasons, and just get rich. "What's your point, Vitruzzi?"

"What I'm saying is this. Most of the people in Agate Beach feel the same way you do. But instead of giving up, they went the other way. We're *really* living, Erikson. We have friends, family, and a future, and we're doing it our way. We are not controlled and we make our own choices about how we lead our lives. There could be a place for you here, if you want to know what real freedom is."

"But you kept your citizenship. You still work for the Admin. Is that what you mean by freedom?"

My words are unnecessarily callous, and her face hardens. "I'm not a hypocrite. I do what I have to because I'm a doctor. Working for the Admin gives me access to the equipment and supplies I need so that the people here don't die needlessly."

"So you want to pass judgment on me because I don't pretend to be a good citizen? At least I'm honest about being a thief. Where did Brady and your crew get those weapons they carry? Found them in the desert? And what about those solar seeds? Don't try and tell me your *legally* contracted transport operation is squeaky clean. Maybe you think you have me figured out, but your business isn't exactly going to win you a 'citizen of the year' award."

Her reaction is instant and vicious. "Who the hell do you think you are?"

"Hey, am I interrupting?" Neither one of us had heard the lift that brought Bodie up.

Vitruzzi rises, her shoulders stiff and her eyes blazing with anger. "No, we're done. Be back here at 2000." Brushing by me without another look, she steps onto the lift and disappears.

Bodie watches her leave, eyebrows raised in concern and curiosity. When she's gone, he turns to me and asks, "What was that about?"

I already regret what I'd said. What good does it do to make Vitruzzi my enemy? Don't I have enough to worry about? "Nothing important."

"Yeah whatever, Erikson." He stares crossly at me, the way you stare at a child who has tried but not succeeded in lying to you. "It's all right to tell me it's none of my business. Anyway, I'm headed to an observation platform topside to take an air quality reading. Want to join me? It's a helluva climb."

I have four hours to kill, each one promising to be more frustrating than the last. Anything to take my mind off the waiting. "Yeah, sure."

"Here, put this on. It's dark in there." He hands me a light attached to a head harness and we begin to climb up a steel ladder hanging from the wall beside the lift platform. It soon disappears into a narrow tunnel drilled into the rock.

I count two hundred and fifty rungs as we climb before he stops. A giant lock tumbler grates noisily into place, and a waterfall of sunlight blazes past his frame, dazzling my upturned eyes.

"Sorry, I should have warned you. It's pretty bright after being in the tunnel."

I follow him up the last couple of rungs and over the edge of the tunnel mouth, my arms grateful for the reprieve.

We're standing on a small platform, maybe one-and-half by two meters, with a metal railing. From up here, the midafternoon sunlight scorches the planet as far as my eyes can see, turning the goose bumps on my arms from the cool cave into tiny, hot stingers. I feel the way ants must feel when wicked children level a magnifying glass over the top of them, but the sensation passes quickly as I take in the panoramic view.

Bodie unslings his backpack and now holds a small sensor wand in one hand and an analysis pack in the other. He waves it around and checks the readout from the air tester.

"Why check the air quality? Is there an atmosphere converter on this planet?"

"No, I just do it for my amusement. I used to be a geophysicist with the Ministry of Engineering before I came out here. It's habit." Aside from a catch in the back of his throat, as if he's getting over a persistent cough, his voice is almost back to normal.

"Sounds like a good job. Why did you give it up?"

He gives me a reluctant sideways glance before answering. "I lost my citizenship when I quit working for the Admin. We were researching unique life forms on the Obals and trying to convert them into incubators for specimens from the first Earth. You know, cows, horses, that kind of thing. I just couldn't stomach it. I thought we should leave them be and learn to live with the natural environment, at least what's left of it. The Admin disagreed and threatened to strip my funding. Said I was 'jeopardizing essential scientific research' or some shit like that. I decided selling out for a few bucks wasn't worth it. So I quit."

His story explains a lot to me. He's an idealist, what people had once called an "environmentalist." Mental maybe. He doesn't believe the Admin creed that everything exists purely for humanity to exploit.

So being a gunrunning pawn for the Admin is more in line with your worldview. I keep the thought to myself. I nearly killed the guy, and now he's taking me on a tour. He's too friendly to antagonize. Besides, he has his reasons for being out here, as we all do.

He puts the air tester back into his backpack and takes out a bottle of water. Motioning me over to the railing, he says, "Take a look at that view, Aly. Can I call you Aly? Calling you Erikson makes me feel like I should start with 'sir,' or 'sergeant,' or something."

"Whatever makes you happy."

"Beautiful, huh?"

"I guess. Looks dead to me though."

"You'd be surprised. We've been able to mix relatively low levels of growth hormones and fertilizers in the soil to make it viable. Even deserts are full of their own kind of life. You just have to learn what to look for." He takes a swig of the water, caps it, and hands it to me.

I glance at him. Rough exterior, untamed beard, and shaggy hair aside, he certainly seems gentle. Taking a closer look at his eyes reveals a depth and intelligence I hadn't noticed when they were still squinted in pain.

"We've been composting and fortifying soil inside the mine for years. There are some real farmers here who know more about it than I do. They started long before I got here. Most of our food still has to be grown in the typical industrial incubation fashion. You know, growing protein and carbohydrate compounds inside bean pods and banana skins, but we're getting to the point where naturally grown foods are becoming a staple. I had no idea how good a squash could taste until I grew one myself."

I take a long drink of the water and smile slightly at the idea of being excited about the taste of a vegetable. He notices and smiles in return.

Changing the subject, I ask, "So you went AWOL from civil service. Does that make you a fugitive?"

"No, I'm legal enough. Just not a citizen. That's how I can still run transport operations with Vitruzzi."

"Don't you think the Admin would be a little skeptical of your colony's success out here? I mean, there's no way you got all the materials and equipment I've seen since this morning legally. At least, not without boatloads of cash. And there are the guns."

His forehead creases and mouth pulls down in a frown. "We've been careful about keeping the existence of this colony quiet. Outsiders aren't welcome. Everyone living here is reliable and we trust each other. Nothing we do is a threat to the Admin, so why should they bother us?"

"I don't know. Because that's what they do. Bother people who aren't fitting into their grand plan." And what about me? I'm an outsider. And Vilbrandt?

He doesn't say anything, just reaches for the water and takes another drink. Blunt honesty has always been one of my attributes, or possibly flaws. "Bodie, you know that if your crew manages, by some monumental stroke of luck, to get your friends off the Fortress, the Admin will scour every single planet between the suns until they find you."

His frown deepens. "Maybe. But what should we do? Just let them rot?"

I shrug, unwilling to say it, but that may be exactly what they should do if they want to maintain the relative peace they have out here.

"Right. Well, that's out of the question." There's a bitter edge to his voice. He knows what's at stake.

We stand for another few minutes staring at the landscape in moody silence. I feel as if a load of cement has been added to my already overburdened scaffold of emotions. Am I beginning to care about what happens to these people, this colony? How did I get mixed up in this? I have my own problems, and the future of these non-cits and their hopeless wish to live in a world where the rules make sense should not become one of them.

Finally, he turns his faded blue eyes back on me and says with a stubborn cheeriness, "I have to get back down to the grow room and take care of some things. A few of us are having dinner at my place after that. You're welcome to join us."

His grin says he is not just being polite, the invite is authentic. I mutter an awkward, "Okay," and then, more loudly, "thanks."

I'm half an hour early arriving in the darkened communication room, and take a seat to wait for Vitruzzi to show up. Most of the satellite equipment is password protected or encrypted, and I can't make any of it work. My anxiety is mounting, and I'm at the point where I've decided I'm going to take my chances and try to find Rajcik myself if he hasn't come through yet. The people in the town Desto had told me about have to get to this planet somehow. I'll start there.

I spend the time waiting for Vitruzzi thinking over what I'd learned from Bodie's dinner. I don't know if I thought the squash tasted as good as he does, but almost anything is an improvement after eating nutrition bars for the better part of a month. Besides Bodie, Strahan, Desto, and Venus were present.

Their conversations had mostly revolved around the various duties the people of the colony shared to keep the place in working order. Maintenance, digging wells, growing food, the essentials. I kept quiet unless someone asked me something directly but was able to get an idea of the size of the settlement and the dynamic that's making them successful at it.

They call it Agate Beach, apparently an ironic reference to the ore once mined here and the complete lack of any large enough body of water nearby to have a beach. It has been occupied for around fifty years. The first people to make it a permanent home had originally been workers in the mine when the Admin ran it, an they'd stayed when the operation was abandoned. The town Desto mentioned is called Hell's Gate, and lies about fifty kilometers east. All of this served as useful information that my mind had automatically catalogued.

I hadn't seen Vilbrandt anywhere in the settlement since we

landed and it had been nagging at me. Seeing no need to keep my distrust of him a secret, I asked about him during the meal.

A secretive glance had passed among them and Strahan's tight-lipped response had been short. "He's around. We're keeping an eye on him." Whatever the reason for their secrecy, his comment was nonetheless revealing. If they're keeping an eye on Vilbrandt, they're undoubtedly keeping an eye on me as well.

After dinner, Bodie offered me a lift to the mine. Needing some quiet, I'd declined and walked back to wait for Vitruzzi.

When she finally arrives, we go through the process of checking incoming communications. Still nothing.

Leaning back in her chair and leveling a look that's neither embittered nor benevolent, but somehow both, she says, "We're going to have to go to plan B. If we're lucky, your team hasn't already started their assault on the Fortress. If they have, we may never be able to beat the Admin security. We'll check the uplink queue one more time tomorrow morning, but we can't afford to wait any longer. I'm sure you feel the same."

Distress and mental fatigue pull the corners of my lips into a frown, and I want to scream in frustration. Where is Rajcik? This is the outcome I'd avoided thinking about, but now I have to decide what to do next.

Again, she seems to be reading my thoughts. "Erikson, you don't have a lot of options, but you're free to do what you want." She stands up and pushes her thick hair back from her forehead, as if what she's about to say is going to be hard for her. "Truth is, we could use someone with your skills and your background to help us. I know that's a lot to hope for, considering your priorities. The only other thing you can do is head to Hell's Gate and barter a ride, if you have anywhere to go."

Disentangling her fingers, she reaches into the cargo pocket on her pants and pulls out a stack of Admin-printed cash. "We brought you here without asking you. Maybe you realize the decision saved your life, maybe not. But this money will get you at least as far as the Obals. Consider us even."

She tosses the money on my lap and walks out to the lift platform. "I'll be here early in the morning. If you're still around, we'll check the queue. Think hard about what you're going to do, Erikson. Your bunk on the *Sphynx* is open if you want to get some sleep."

She reaches out to activate the lift. "Vitruzzi," I say. Her hand stops, hovering above the controls, and she looks at me. "I am grateful. I know I wouldn't have made it."

Without a word, she presses the controls and is gone.

I don't know what I'd expected her to do if the situation came to this, but this isn't it. I sit in the darkening communication room for a couple minutes, listening to the thump of my heart, trying not to hear the whir of thoughts spinning through my head. She's right, there's no more time to wait. I'll leave first thing in the morning. I don't know what kind of town Hell's Gate is, but it's probably best not to walk in there in the middle of the night looking for a lift to the Obals. I pick up the stack of bills she gave me and its heft is a generous reassurance. Especially not with this much cash on me. I may be on the forsaken outskirts of the system, but I'm no longer stuck here.

It's still early and I'm way too wound up to sleep anyway, so I climb back up the tunnel to the overlook Bodie had shown me, some deep part of my brain hoping the tranquil view will quiet my thoughts and make it possible to sleep.

The heavy door thuds open and I reach for the handrail to pull myself the rest of the way onto the overlook. Movement in the corner of my eye alerts me that someone else is already here.

"Oh, sorry." Disappointed, I start to pull the door closed.

Strahan's voice stops me. "It's all right."

"No, that's fine. I'll leave you alone."

"Wait." He takes a step forward and I make out the look on his face. The scowl is permanently affixed but muted in the darkness. "Erikson, actually I wanted a chance to talk to you. Will you stay for a minute?"

I shrug. I've had enough one-on-one time with people trying to talk me into things I don't want to do today. Besides, what's the use? I'm gone in the morning and I'll never even see these people again.

But, if that's the case, talking to him now won't kill me, will it? I pull myself over the edge onto the landing.

The sky is blazing with a billion stars, each tiny point a dazzle in my eye. It's beautiful, peaceful in a way that is somehow different from being aboard a ship. Standing here on solid ground, watching them hanging brightly above me, they feel further away and less like a judgment, filling me with the kind of wonder the first *Homo erectus* must have felt a couple million years ago. There's a measure of relief in realizing how utterly small and unimportant our fleeting lives are.

I walk up to the railing and lightly rest my hands along it, not saying anything, just waiting.

He pulls out his cigarettes and casually leans on his elbows a few steps away from me, pulls one from the pack and sticks it between his lips. Lighting it with a match and cupping the flame in his hands so the fragile spark is hidden, he inhales deeply. Noticing me watching, he asks, with the cigarette dangling from his mouth, "Did you want one?"

Shaking my head, I respond, "You'll lose your citizenship if the Admin knows you smoke."

"Yeah, well, they can keep those forty-seven years."

He's referring to life expectancy. For a citizen it's ninety-seven years, for non-cits it's around fifty.

We both turn back and stare out over the expanse of the Spectra 6 landscape. Unbroken blackness crawls away from us, making it seem as if we are in space, not standing on solid earth.

Strahan remains quiet for some time. Finally I say, "So you wanted to talk to me about something?"

Still focused on the distant skies, he replies, "Do you like to fly, Erikson?" The question is rhetorical and he doesn't wait for an answer. "I love it. I dreamed of it when I was still a kid on Obal 10. Wanted to be on those big cruisers and see new worlds more than anything. So I joined the Corps when I was sixteen. No way was I going to be stuck in some landlocked job in the civil service. I worked hard to get assigned to a ship, and when it looked as if I wouldn't get assigned outside the infantry and maybe never go farther than the nearest moon, I worked even harder until I became a pilot. I even thought I was a pretty good one until I met Venus." He pauses, a faraway grin playing at the corners of his mouth, then resumes, serious again, "I've probably seen forty or fifty different moons and planets in this system."

He's getting at something so I just let him talk.

"And you know what I've learned?" He takes another drag on his cigarette. The burning coal reflects in his light-brown eyes, making them resonate with an inner flame. "No matter where you are, it's the people you're with that matter the most."

I bite back a sarcastic response: *Thanks for the lecture.* "Uh-huh."

"Doug Mason is the pilot of the *Sky Serpent*. We used to fly together a lot until Venus came along. He's a good man. Like a brother, really. There's nothing I wouldn't do to get him the fuck away from the Admin."

He turns to look at me full on. "And he'd do the same thing for me. What would you do to get your brother free, Erikson? Is profit that much more important?"

His words are a cleverly laid trap, but he doesn't know the real effect they have on me. I push away from the railing and turn stiffly, facing him. "Is that it?" My voice is sharp and I hope he doesn't hear the way it catches for a second in my throat.

He drops the cigarette on the landing and squashes it with a brutal stomp from his boot. "Yeah, I guess it is. Enjoy the view." Taking one long stride, he disappears down the shaft, leaving me in the wake of his disapproval and disappointment.

The view suddenly isn't quite as serene as before. Who is he to judge me? Part of me wants to follow him down the ladder and unload on him, but there's another part of me that has to admit, regardless of what difference it does or doesn't make, he isn't completely wrong. Rajcik and the rest of my crew are dangerous people. They're not the type to sacrifice profit, and certainly not the type to put themselves in harm's way for others. What good does it do me to find Rajcik? Will he bother to help me try and save David? Why do I even fly with someone I can't rely on in the first place?

The answer is surprisingly simple. There's freedom in knowing exactly how much your life is worth to others. When the answer is nothing, there are no surprises.

The chill night air begins seeping through my clothes, staunching my anger. Time to go back to the *Sphynx* and get some sleep. What are my chances of getting off this rock tomorrow? Best not to think about it yet.

ELEVEN

Standing at the rim of a canyon looking over the little town of Hell's Gate about half a klick away, it's easy to see where it gets its name. It's a densely packed, dirty little pisspot of a town with smoke stacks and mud turning the whole thing into a uniform dingy heap. One flash fire and the whole place would be smoldering toothpicks within minutes. Right now, the town is mostly quiet except for a few stray dogs that move around the outskirts looking for scraps. I idly wonder what happens to people who die here.

Still, for all its ugliness and destitution I can see three interplanetary vessels sitting outside of town. Hopefully, they're sky worthy. Now I just have to find their owners.

Turning around for one last scan of the labyrinthine canyon system I'd just come through, I feel confident that I haven't been followed and start driving down the hillside's eastern flank. I'd quickly and steadily lost elevation as I drove from Agate Beach into this maze of walls and crags this morning, and the going is now much more gradual after clearing the canyon walls. With a sliver of guilt, I check for confirmation on the navigation console of the ATV I'd stolen. I could probably have found someone to give me a ride here, but I wanted to avoid another encounter burdened with accusations and expectations. They'll know where to find the transport, and I'll be long gone.

It's nearing 0900 hours and more people can be seen up and about as I reach the town's edge. The place is gritty and claustrophobic with buildings haphazardly placed, leaning on each other for support. Trash and refuse are everywhere, tossed carelessly in the streets. The overall area is smaller than Vitruzzi's settlement, but more structures fill the space. The air is redolent of oily smoke and unusual food.

The paths running between the buildings are too small for the ATV, so I ditch it behind a large bin on the edge of town and wave goodbye. Even if I planned to come back for it, I have my doubts that much time will pass before someone steals it or strips it. Unsure of the best place to start searching for passage, I pass between the two nearest buildings onto the widest of the footpaths running through the cluster's center. Places like this always have a dive where business and drinking can occur, and people with ships seek out those who have something that needs to be shipped. I walk cautiously, but not obviously so. No need to give the impression I'm nervous. Trouble can be dealt with but doesn't need to be invited.

Instincts of self-preservation envelope me in their usual configuration: hyper-awareness, cautious movement, and hair-trigger reflexes. I'm here on business and not to be fucked with.

As I walk, I feel the heat of the morning sun bake into my neck. The bruises from Strahan's rifle butt and the watchcap I wear are the only disguises I have. If bounty hunters are canvassing the area, it won't be hard to recognize me. I just have to keep my head down and look as if I belong. Easy enough for someone with my years of practice.

"Got some spare change? Little money for a hungry man?" says a scruffy beggar, reeking of piss and the disturbing smell of cooked skin, from an alleyway as I walk by. He reaches out to grab my arm, and the red scabs covering his wrists emerge from his own tattered sleeve. His eyes are cloudy and bloodshot, rolling back and forth in his pitted and dirt-streaked face, and he leers at me in a suggestion of a smile. His teeth are all missing.

Moving backward a step before he can get hold of my arm, I answer, "Maybe. Where can I hire a transport ship?"

He coughs in a dry, wheezing crackle. "You're almost there," he answers, and points toward a building a few meters down the street. There's a glowing sign in front, hanging on a slant from its one remaining wire: Van Dieman's Land, and under that, *Roomz & Drinkz*. Perfect.

"Any ideas on who I might need to talk to?"

He shakes his head miserably. I doubt this walking shell has spoken to anyone besides rats, and maybe a dealer, in weeks. I pull out a single bill, hand it over, careful not to let his scaly fingers touch me, and walk on.

The bar has no windows and it will be dark inside. I stand next to the door for a few seconds, glancing inside whenever anyone enters or leaves, getting an impression of the interior and letting my eyes get used to the gloom. It's smoky, the shadows of men and women visible standing around a few tables, but I can't make out many details. Even this early, the place has good business. A man walks in past me without a glance and I slip in behind him, quickly moving beside the wall nearest the door.

Two more men and a woman sit at the bar near the back. The woman and one of the men don't look like much, but the second one wears clean clothes made of good material, and his boots are barely scratched. He hasn't been walking around on this rocky planet much. I'll start with him.

Crossing the room, I come to a standstill beside him—the bar has no seats—and catch the barkeep's eye.

Before I can say anything, I hear: "Erikson. I've been looking for you."

My jaw clenches involuntarily at the sound of that voice. Calmly, but not slowly, I turn around. Before he can speak again, I thrust out my hand and grip the man's crotch in a relentless squeeze. He hisses in surprise and pain, but doesn't try to move.

"MacCready." I have to wait a second for the dryness in my throat to give way before I can go on. "I didn't expect to ever see you again."

Almost two years have passed since I abandoned Marcus MacCready, a one-time member of Rajcik's smuggling crew, on a moon about to be overrun by Corps. I thought he was dead.

"That goes for both of us, Erikson. But don't worry, I've completely forgotten about that, uh, disagreement. Now would you let up a bit? You could be ruining my chances for future generations."

"You and I both know you'll never be anyone's father." I eye his sweat-sheeted face for a second. Even if he does have plans for revenge, this place is far too public for him to settle any scores. Letting go, I ask, "What the fuck do you want?"

He sucks in a full breath, reaches an exploratory hand toward his package, and pushes in next to me. The man who I'd originally intended to talk with side-steps as far toward the other end of the bar as he can, trying to conceal the wary way he glances at us from the corners of his eyes. "Our mutual friend sent me to pick you up."

It's as if his words are cold water suddenly thrown in my face. Keeping my voice low, I say, "You're here with János? Where is he?" The question I don't ask is: What do you mean, our mutual friend?

"Waiting. Let's go." Without sticking around to see if I'll follow, he heads for the door.

My nerves are on full alert. It seems impossible that Rajcik has somehow made it to Spectra 6. But then, in six years working together, I've learned not to be surprised by much of what he does. The only two ways he could be here so soon are pure luck, which I don't put much faith in, or he somehow followed me here. Either way, this situation has just become more fluid. There may be a chance of getting to David in time after all.

No longer hesitating, I go after him. We step back out into the hot sunlight and MacCready begins walking down the empty street. I want to grab him and force him to answer the thousand questions reeling in my mind, but his pace is too quick, as if time is short.

The sun scorches us and sweat glazes my neck like lukewarm jet fuel. MacCready turns into a narrow alleyway, but I stop. Part of me is eager to follow him and meet back up with Rajcik; the rest of me knows better than to let myself be led into a dead end by this man. Planting myself at the corner of a building, I ask, "Where exactly is he, MacCready? I haven't seen the *Temptation* anywhere."

There's an extensive list of men in the universe that I don't trust, and Marcus MacCready is on the top of it. For good reason. When I'd left him behind, I'd been in a hurry. Unfortunately for him, he'd been standing in the stream of deadly blowback from our escape craft's jet engine. The last thing I'd seen through the craft's image sensors before getting the fuck out of there was his twisting body engulfed in flames consuming his clothes like ravenous devils. A thing like that isn't easily forgiven, and MacCready never impressed me as the understanding type.

My abrupt questioning stops him. As he turns around, pale features fixed in exasperation and impatience, I see his face clearly for the first time. Reddened and pocked skin scours the left side of his head, peeking through in patches beneath his white-blond hair and continuing down his jaw and throat until the scarring is hidden beneath the collar of his distressed jacket. He hadn't been facing me directly inside the dark bar and I had not seen the damage. The burn scars draw the skin of his cheek together the way plastic curls up when it's melting, giving him a permanent sneer.

But it's the look in his anemic blue eyes, corneas the same yellow as a jaundice patient, that triggers the neurons in my brain to fire a high alert. Pure hate, the kind that burns a person up from inside out, threatens to ignite the air between us. He doesn't say anything for several seconds, regarding me, trying to smolder me on the spot. With slow but menacing care, I draw my Sinbad as a warning, but I keep the muzzle pointed toward the dirt. In response, he raises his hand to his jacket, where I assume he carries his own pistol. Rays of sun find their way between the building roofs and pour their spotlights on the scene, illuminating everything with perfect clarity. Before he reaches into his jacket, which would guarantee him a bullet between the eyes, his hand stops and he blinks.

Instead of doing anything stupid, he extends a finger and points up the alleyway. "Our ride is parked just outside town. We're supposed to take it to the ship. Rajcik's gone to a lot of trouble to find you."

He's not telling me something. "Then why did he send you? When did you start working for him again? Show me some proof, MacCready, or our little reunion will end right here."

His sneer deepens, but he reaches into the jacket's cargo pocket, slowly, and retrieves a handheld comsat channeler. Pressing the telecast operator, he says, "Mac for Rajcik."

Holding up the video display so that we can both see it, we wait for a response. In a few seconds, the black screen shifts and I'm looking at the face of János Rajcik in crisp detail. "Go for . . . " My boss's wide, thin lips part to reveal the edges of perfectly even teeth in what represents, for Rajcik, a smile. "Erikson. You *aren't* dead. I only half expected Mac to find you. Get back to the *Temptation* ASAP."

Uncertainty and anxiety bubble up from my guts in an acidic burp. I should be glad to have found my employer and crew again, but the presence of MacCready and unusual twist of events leaves me cold, worried. Still, I lower the Sinbad. "Rajcik, what's going on? How did you find—?"

"We'll have plenty of time for Q&A, Aly. MacCready, how quickly can you get back to the ship?"

"Shouldn't take more than an hour."

"Good. Don't use the comsat again." Without another word, Rajcik severs our connection.

MacCready looks at me and doesn't try to hide his impatience. "You ready to go, Erikson? Or do you want to discuss anything else?"

Stifling the urge to buy myself more time, I holster my pistol. My questions will be answered as soon as I get back to the *Temptation*, and right now reconnecting with Rajcik is the only option that offers me much hope. MacCready takes the cue and begins walking down the alley again. Before following, I take a final glance back toward the town to see what else could be in store. No one on the roofline, no one coming toward us. I look back toward the bar and see—

"Oh, shit." Strahan stands just outside. His back is pressed against the wall of the building and he's trying to wedge himself out of sight inside the doorway. Clever bastard. *Why are you following me?* I can't tell if he knows I've spotted him, but I'm not going to give him any more opportunities. Stepping past MacCready, I start double-timing down the alley. "Let's go."

It branches out into a T-intersection at the end and I turn to get directions. He's standing flat-footed, his jaw set and eyes stabbing me again with hatred. I realize he's about to attack, but too late. His fist smashes into my jaw with tooth-rattling force. I feel an explosion of pain, taste blood, and then my arms are yanked backward, my wrists quickly clamped tightly together with handcuffs. I try to pull free, but whoever has my arms keeps his hold, forcing me to stop before ripping my shoulders from their sockets.

"MacCready, what the fuck?!"

"Shut up!" And he slaps tape over my mouth so I'll do exactly that.

Craning my head backward in an effort to avoid the tape, I get a look at the person holding my arms. Liev Fedchenko, another of the regular crew. His dark, greasy hair covers his bushy eyebrows and he's grinning at me sinisterly, scarecrow teeth protruding from his thick lips. I may be in more trouble than I realized.

"Quit struggling, Erikson, or I'll break your jaw," MacCready warns. "We're taking you to the *Temptation*, but Rajcik didn't specify what condition you'd have to be in. I've had enough fucking trouble from you."

"Forget it, Mac. Let's just get her back. Rajcik wants to talk to her."

He snarls at Fedchenko like a dog but leans away from me. Pulling a rag from his pocket, he unfurls it and pulls it over my head as a hood. I can't see anything, but dust and rankness fill my nose, making me gag. The tape over my mouth forces me to control the reflex in order to keep from choking, and I consciously slow my breathing down, making myself ignore the stench.

"You're either going to walk on your own, or we're going to drag you. What'll it be?"

Because I can't speak, I nod and my shoulders are yanked sideways, spinning me around. Pressure that can't be anything but a gun barrel jabs into my spine, and we walk.

THE DOOR OPENS. Someone approaches, lifts the hood still covering my head partway, and presses something cold against my cheek, making me suck air sharply through my nostrils in a nasal gasp. Then the hood is pulled off.

"Welcome back." Rajcik stands in front of me, holding an icepack to my cheek.

I'm groggy and off kilter after the shot to the jaw and lack of clean air. They'd brought me back to the *Temptation*—a decommissioned assault craft, stolen and retrofitted for use as a long-range smuggling ship—and locked me up. I've been waiting for at least an hour, but, somehow, I'm not as relieved to be back as I expected to be. We'd traveled by hovercraft to get here, but even without the benefit of being able to feel solid ground beneath us, the extensive rises and dips we'd glided over tell me we're in canyon country. Rajcik has hidden the *Temptation* amid the walls of the ragged landscape, and I have no idea where I am.

I focus on him, letting my fury at being punched, handcuffed, nearly asphyxiated, and brought at gunpoint back to the ship burn from my eyes in a toxic-waste glare. He stares back with a glint of mania and rage in his own.

If people were dogs, I wouldn't be surprised to see many submissively piss themselves when meeting Rajcik. His hulking frame, grinning-skull face, and the measured threat always looming in his voice never fail to induce a lizard-brain reaction of fear and intimidation, even from the reckless and insane. His muscles fit his frame the way perfectly calibrated elements fit a war machine, both graceful and menacing. On the rare occasions that our jobs had ended up in a hand-to-hand fracas, I'd seen Rajcik move like a vengeful ghost, swift and certain, killing men before they'd even realized they were in a fight.

He examines my expression for a moment, as if trying to decide whether to eat his dinner with a knife and fork or just shove his whole face into the plate, and unceremoniously yanks the tape from my mouth.

I'm furious and confused, but I let the fury talk for me. "What THE FUCK is going on, János?" My jaw feels swollen, a hot lump that pulses with my heartbeat. I can only imagine what my face looks like now, between the damage caused by Strahan's rifle and MacCready's fist. "Let me out of these fucking handcuffs."

He swallows and a large-caliber machine gun round tattooed in black ink bobs up and down with his Adam's apple. With his flight jacket on, only the top of the vast network of tattoos that adorn his skin, winding up and down his arms, neck, and back, is visible. He is covered in savagely inked illustrations, the kind that mean something. It's not about vanity or having a jailhouse record of how many people he's killed or how many women he's fucked. A darker impulse drives his epidermal tableau. A maelstrom of guns, warships, and all the other devices for war and destruction that he buys and sells covers his body in a macabre representation of death in machine form. These are the tools he peddles in defiance of the Admin, always with the intent that they'll be used against it. It's all about money and revenge, which to him equate to the same thing.

Finally unlocking my wrists, he steps back, waiting patiently for me to either calm down or do something stupid like jump him. "I was very surprised to pick up a transmission from you, Aly. I thought you were dead. There were two squads after you on Obal 3." He scans my face, trying to read my thoughts. "Looks like I underestimated you."

He hasn't answered my question. "David and I were trapped. He held them off, while I tried to escape. I think he's been arrested and—"

He cuts me off with unmasked suspicion in his tone. "How did you end up here?"

"That's why I contacted you."

"You contacted me to tell me how you got here?" Sarcasm is frightening coming from him. "I don't think so. You're trying my patience. Now, how did you escape from Obal 3 and whose uplink did you use to transmit?"

This is his favorite dance. Not a waltz, more like the circling of a hungry wolf, the tango of a tiger. He's only interested in discovering why I'm still alive and how he can use this information to his advantage. It hasn't played into his plans that I could possibly have survived the odds we faced on Obal 3, and he probably believes that I've betrayed him in exchange for my life. He'll feint and jab until I admit it, not relenting or allowing anything from me except the answers to his questions, which he thinks he already has. My only chance is to take the lead. I have to be strategic if I'm going to convince him of anything different.

"First, why don't you tell me why you're here? You got my transmission. Why didn't you just respond? You want the story, János, you're going to have to tell me one too."

He tosses the icepack next to me on the table. "MacCready tells me you were being followed. What assurance do I have that you aren't working with someone else?"

So MacCready had seen Strahan too. "Look at my face! You think I'm working for people who did this to me? Besides, is there another gig in the galaxy with a better payday?"

My outburst has the right effect. A vicious smile curls up both edges of his mouth, making him look sharklike, all teeth. I can almost imagine flecks of meat from his last victim stuck between them. The thought makes me shudder. "Hmm." He makes a smacking sound with his lips. "You are consistently reliable when it comes to getting paid, Aly. You would think I'd know by now not to doubt that." Reaching out to lightly brush my throbbing jaw, the gesture more intimate than necessary, he says, "As for this, Mac must have taken the opportunity to recover an old debt."

It takes an effort not to brush away his fingers. "So what's going on? How did you find me and how did you get here so fast? We were supposed to rendezvous on Obal 10. That's at least a week and a half away. Why didn't you stick to the plan?"

"Plans changed."

It's clear that he's not going to give me any straight answers, but I try anyway. "Then why are you on Spectra 6?"

"No, Aly. The question is, why are you on Spectra 6"—his eyes turn feral and dangerous—"with another group of arms smugglers?"

I can almost feel the ground sinking beneath me like quicksand, and I'm suddenly not sure I'll be able to talk my way out of this. There's a shrill edge to my voice as I try. "Cut the shit. I was kidnapped! Get it? T'Kai was sloppy and someone else found out about the holodisc. Or he changed his mind about the gig and outed us. Either way, the people who grabbed me want a copy of their own." Now that I hear the story coming from my own mouth, I realize how unbelievable it is. It doesn't matter that I've spent the last six years working for Rajcik. If I don't convince him of the truth, MacCready's blow is going to seem kind. "You know I wouldn't blue falcon you."

He regards me for a long second with a sly look I can't interpret. "No, you wouldn't. You're not stupid, are you? That's something I've always found curious about you—your loyalty." Then, to my relief, he says, "Tell me what's going on."

It takes me fifteen minutes to explain everything. He listens closely, without interrupting. A grim scowl darkens his features when I tell him about Vilbrandt and Director T'Kai. T'Kai had obviously told him nothing about Vilbrandt or bothered to warn him about Vilbrandt's potential to jeopardize our mission. Rajcik's jaw clenches when I tell him about the Admin's newscast of the robbery, probably promoted by T'Kai in an attempt to cover for himself. He says nothing about Vilbrandt's interest in trading his insider knowledge of the Fortress for a cut, and stays equally mute when I share Vilbrandt's theory that David's captors would have taken him to the Fortress for questioning—and use as a lab rat. His looming silence throughout my explanation has the effect he wants; I grow more nervous and agitated by the second, struggling to keep it under wraps.

He stands in front of me like a wall, his eyes scanning my face as I conclude with Vitruzzi and Brady's proposal. "So these arms trans- porters are trying to help their friends and they're serious about negotiating with us. They want to exchange a mother load of solar seeds for the disc. It's a solid deal. I've seen the seeds and I know they have them." The expression on his face makes me decide to leave out the part about them wanting to make this a joint operation.

The room is quiet for a few seconds. Then slowly, he recites, "T'Kai, David, who's in the Admin's hands, this scientist Vilbrandt, and a group of non-cit smugglers . . . tell me, Aly, is there anyone in the *fucking universe who doesn't know about my plan*?!"

He leans over me, eyes red-rimmed, furious and wide. His mouth is inches from my face, spittle flecking his lips, his anger like a furnace on the brink of exploding, and for a moment I think he may actually try ripping my throat out with his teeth. I don't budge from the table. Drawing in a long, controlled breath and forcing myself not to move, I refuse to let him see my fear.

His nostrils flare once more, and then he straightens back up. His neck and face are flushed red, glowing the way vulnerable skin sitting too close to an open flame does, making the whites of his eyes stand out vividly. The muscles from his jaw to his neck, each almost as thick as my wrists, are flexed taut. I've seen him look this way before throwing men from the doorways of in-flight transporters. They died. I wonder if it's my turn.

Taking a deep breath, he lets it out slowly and asks casually, as if the conversation had never verged on murder, "Tell me more about Captain Vitruzzi and her crew."

Already his mind is working on an angle he can use to his benefit. The immediate threat appears to have diminished, but I well know that Rajcik can go ballistic without warning if I'm not careful. "Mostly ex-soldiers, legally released. Vitruzzi used to be an Admin doctor. There are about five regulars on her crew and they all seem reliable. From what I've seen, they're not loyal to the Admin."

"They transport arms. How did they get that kind of clearance?"

"I don't know."

His next question is so unexpected, I'm not sure I hear him right. "Do you think we can trust them?"

What's he getting at? Rajcik trusts no one, not even me. "If you mean do I think they're good for the exchange, yeah I do."

"Maybe we can use them."

He's no longer looking at me, his thoughts probing the surface of some new plan. I'm not sure I'll like what he's thinking. "What do you mean?"

"We need a way to get aboard the Fortress. Stealing an Admin ship will be too obvious and they won't let unknown transporters anywhere near their perimeter. This Vitruzzi and her team could be just the diversion we need."

"You mean use them as bait? I don't think that's—" He focuses on me sharply. "I mean . . . what about this? We could make them partners—not for the payoff, just to get in and out of the station." Suddenly no longer in control of my mouth, I barely believe what I'm saying. "They don't even want a cut of the money, just the disc so that they can break in and rescue their friends. If David's there, they're all probably being held together. Their involvement could be a tremendous asset."

He frowns, looking almost as surprised at what I said as I am. "The plan does not change. This is *my* show. Don't forget that." Leaning close again, he emphasizes, "I'm not jeopardizing this mission for *any* man. Including David."

I hear a stupefied gasp and realize it came from me. "Are you insane? We can't leave him there! They'll kill him!" I'm standing now, face to face with him, both of my hands gripping the collar of his jacket.

Grabbing my arms just above the elbows, he pulls them away with a quick jerk and shoves me back against the table. A shadow of impatient anger passes over his brow like the first ripple of a pending tsunami. "He knew the risks when he signed up for this job. So did you."

Bile begins to churn in my stomach. "You're going to regret this you sonofabitch." My voice is flat, icy, toneless. For the moment, I don't care if he kills me.

He squeezes my wrists crushingly tight, black eyes smoldering into mine. "Does this mean you want off the crew?"

Cold hatred lodges in my throat, making me choke on the threats

I want to hurl at him. Instead, I remain tense and silent, rage shaking me.

He stands motionless for a moment, scrutinizing me with insidious attention. Then he drops my hands, and a quick dip of his chin indicates that he's come to some kind of decision. "Maybe you need a little time to think it over. You know I've always liked you, Aly. Because you're smart. Don't do something that's going to change my opinion."

He turns his back to leave before I break out of my paralysis. "There's one thing you didn't tell me, János."

He looks back over his shoulder.

"Why did you bring MacCready back on the team?"

"I can rely on him to do what's necessary."

"I told you what happened last time. He put the operation at *unnecessary* risk. We could have lost the payoff. What makes you think he's reliable now?"

"Don't worry. MacCready knows what his orders are." His face is unreadable, but I can guess what those orders might be.

DAVID. DAVID'S IN TROUBLE and the only chance I had of helping him just threatened to sic his guard dog on me if I make a wrong move. David. How the fuck am I going to get to him?

Maybe Rajcik isn't my only option.

Ten minutes go by and I don't move from my seat on the table. What's the use? I'm as familiar with this ship as I am with my own weapons. I should be, it's been my home for the last six years. There's no way to break through the door to this room, an empty berth for excess gear and smuggled goods. Not even a duct from the ventilation system links into it so there are no shafts I might be able to wriggle through. I'm in a prison that's as secure as any in the system.

My mind is like a flag in a hurricane, whipping and beating itself into a shredded frenzy. Something is very wrong here. It shouldn't surprise me that Rajcik could care less about the jeopardy David is in, but something more has kindled a warning fire at the tips of my nerves. He acts as if he *expected* the two of us to be killed. As if we weren't supposed to escape Obal 3 at all. But what reason would he have for wanting us dead? We've backed this mission completely since the day he told us about it.

And there's MacCready: unpredictable, psychotic, and almost guaranteed to increase the amount of bloodshed in a mission way beyond what's necessary.

When I left him for dead, we'd been following a Corps troop transport for about a week, the kind of job we'd done a hundred times. These ships always docked at some point to rotate personnel on and off remote duty. Our intel told us that this particular crew were tasked with guarding an Admin warehouse full of munitions.

Once the squads had been switched and the troop ship dispatched, MacCready and I ambushed the new sentries. They were slow-witted and clumsy, not prepared for our little surprise, and we'd neutralized them within minutes. Unexpectedly, we also found a handful of citizens serving as supplemental staffing for the facility. Before we realized they had active DNA tags that allowed them to fire weapons, MacCready was winged by a small-caliber handgun. We were able to outmaneuver them, killing one before they surrendered, and he trussed them together while I collected the payload. Less than ten minutes had passed by the time we had everything on board our escape craft, and I'd climbed in to start the engine and check our satellite surveillance feed for company. I can still taste the metallic gush of adrenaline that filled my mouth at the sight of a short-range hovercraft full of soldiers speeding toward the warehouse.

"MacCready, move your ass! Unfriendlies are on the way and they look like they know we're here. Five minutes tops!"

His voice came back via our helmet comlink, furious. "Sonofabitch. These cits got the word out."

Something was keeping him. When I stuck my head outside the EC's cockpit to see what, he was approaching the citizens, pistol drawn. My voice felt as if it were trying to force itself through mountains of sawdust, but I tried to stop him. "MacCready! We don't have time. Come on!"

He'd ignored me and shot the first man point-blank in the face. I heard him mumbling as he turned to the next one, "Goddamn citizen fucks. Don't know when to just shut the fuck up," and raised his weapon to the victim's head.

The sickening shock at such needless carnage only held me immobile for a second, though the terror in their faces will be embedded in my mind forever. There was no time to deal with MacCready if I was going to get out of there before the Corps arrived, so I engaged the forward drive and started the EC toward the open warehouse door. Another shot echoed through the comlink and MacCready began shouting for me to stop. Instead, I overcharged the EC's engine and slammed the thruster-control to full open. A super-heated jet of fumes steamed from the exhaust port, instantly turning his running figure into a scorched scarecrow and propelling the EC through the exit like a bullet.

I made it back to the *Temptation*, certain MacCready was dead and happy to have been the cause.

Rajcik accepted the news calmly. He well knew the kind of sadistic man MacCready was, and my decision to leave him behind had kept us from losing both the EC and a pile of arms worth a sizable sum.

Yet, here he is. The thought keeps ringing through my head like a funeral bell. I don't care how he survived, and I'll leave him for dead again or shoot him myself if he gives me a reason. What I do care about is the answer to one simple question: Is he back on the crew because Rajcik intends to replace me?

There's no other explanation. I don't know exactly why Rajcik would decide to cut me loose, but I have to consider that a possibility. He's using me, just like he wants to use Vitruzzi and her crew. Right now, I'm the link between the two, and to get what he wants, he'll have to pretend he's not planning to shake me off. As unreal as it seems, I might have been better off throwing in my lot with the settlers.

But why? Why would Rajcik turn like this? Does it have something to do with David? What he'd said to me when he surrendered

*—Don't let Rajcik out of your sight—*what did he know? Is Rajcik planning to double cross us? He hates the Admin, and he loves selling weapons to people that could use them against the Admin, but he needs our help to do it. None of this makes sense.

The room is small and stifling, the lack of airflow making me sweaty and lightheaded. It's almost a relief when the door opens and he comes in. He's back to ask the only question that matters. What will it be, Aly? The answer is easy: live today, fight tomorrow.

"So are you with us?"

I let the silence hang heavily for a minute, satisfying myself with a hint of disdain before answering. "What do you think, János? Of course I'm in. I'm kidding myself if I think David's still alive. Let's make some money."

His lips curl in that frightening half grin. "Excellent. You've just made yourself mission imperative again. Your gear is in the bunkroom. Get it and meet me in operations in twenty minutes."

TWELVE

Most of the crew is assembled around a holographic 3D image of the Fortress hovering over a disc reader when I arrive on the operations deck. Looming silently in the doorway, I survey them before anyone notices me—Rajcik, Fuller Thompson, Liev Fedchenko, Valya Ortiz, and of course, Marcus MacCready. The final member, Ahsan Yadav, brushes in behind me and activates the door. As it slides closed, the noise draws their attention and they turn and look at me with suspicion and disinterest. No questions about what happened to David and me. No happiness to see me. But then, I'm not happy to see them either. This is just the way it is: we work as partners, not as friends. The only person I had cared about in this bunch was David. What's the point of all those years on the take now?

Rajcik speaks, staring fervently at the image of the Fortress. "Our only way in is through disguise and deception. The *Temptation* has to appear to be one of their regular supply ships."

Data readouts are displayed along the screens adjoining the disc reader. T'Kai, for all his treachery, definitely did his job. We have enough information here to practically rebuild the Fortress. Separate menus allow the structural design to be overlaid with the security system grid, which includes pass codes, system schematics, and personnel routines—full disclosure of every operational detail. Combing through the data makes it clear that it would be impossible to infiltrate the space station, much less pirate stolen goods from it, without these plans. Even with the disc, the operation will be anything but easy.

We pay close attention as Rajcik continues sketching out the plan. "We'll cloak our heat signature and use legitimate transport authorization codes, but the dock controller's attention has to be elsewhere. If anything ignites their suspicion or makes them look too closely, they'll lock it down and we'll never get in. Which is why we're lucky to have Erikson back on board." His sly stare rests on me, the pressure of it forcing me to acknowledge the plans he'd already made.

The words stick like napalm in my throat, but I have no other choice than to play along. "During the mission on Obal 3, while David and I were drawing off the soldiers, he was arrested and I ended up getting nabbed by a group of settlers with intel on our operation. It's a long story. The important point is, they also plan to infiltrate the Fortress and János wants to use them as . . . as bait to draw off the Admin." I glance at him, making sure I've said what he wants to hear. He looks satisfied.

Yadav, a swarthy smuggler with a thick mustache and the epicanthic eyes of a Mongol, asks grittily, "You been gone over a week, Erikson. Why should we trust you now? Maybe you're trying to set us up."

Fedchenko and Thompson nod in agreement. Together with Yadav, the three of them form the dicey edges of a lethal triad. Bottom dwellers in the smuggling cesspool, they'd worked as a team throughout the system for several years as mercs, murderers, and guns-for-hire. Alternately picking and robbing their own marks, or hiring out to the kind of scum that has the money to pay someone else to do the dirty work, they've been frequent poster boys on the Admin most-wanted list. Rajcik hired them on for a job on Ohm Lumi a couple years back, and they've been on the crew since. Neither David nor I ever cared much for their methods or morals, but the crew's successes have made it easier to ignore them. Rajcik doesn't answer Yadav's accusation, leaving it up to me to convince them, testing my commitment.

Now, I have to lie, and lie well. I may or may not have convinced Rajcik that I'm not in Vitruzzi's pocket, or that I'm willing to use her and her crew as a disposable cover for our robbery and extortion, but I better convince the rest of them. If I want to work the situation to my advantage, I can't have five suspicious cutthroats scrutinizing every move I make. I don't want to set up Vitruzzi's crew to take the fall for us any more than I want to abandon the possibility of saving David. I'm not as detached from my own moral barometer as Rajcik and most of this group are, no matter what people may think. Unlike Rajcik, I'm not willing to sacrifice others, especially others who've already proven that they're willing to help me if I ask them to. He couldn't care less about David. Or me. So fuck him. The trick is making them believe I'm on their side, but when the chance comes, I'll do whatever it takes to alter the plan to my own ends.

So I follow my usual tactic. "I don't give a shit if you trust me, Yadav. If saving your ass on Obal 3, all of your asses, doesn't prove what I'll do for this payoff, feel free to run the mission without me. And after you fuck it up and end up on some experimental slab with a probe up your ass, I'll be relaxing on Obal 10 laughing about it." It helps that I am truly furious. At Rajcik, at myself for being his pawn, at them for being too degenerate to care. At the whole fucked-up situation.

No one speaks for a second that quickly turns into several.

Ortiz breaks the silence. "Don't be fools. Erikson is here because Rajcik trusts her. That's enough."

Ortiz is a veteran on Rajcik's crew. At one time enlisted in the Corps, she'd already been with Rajcik when David and I had come into the mix. I convey my thanks with a quick glance in her direction, but it's hard to look at her too long. Ten years ago, she hadn't made it off her patrol ship when it went down after being struck by orbiting debris, and pocked and mottled burn-flesh covers her face and extremities. Her cowardly shipmates evacuated like gun-toting ants from a burning anthill, failing to follow protocol and assist the injured. After the vessel hurtled into Spectra 4, its auto-controls managing to keep the ship from going into total free fall, a non-cit doctor known to Rajcik had found her alive and helped her recover, in a way. At her insistence, he'd removed her lifemarker, making her untraceable by the Corps. Rajcik had hired her for many of the same reasons he'd hired David and me. Radically scarred inside and out, she's callous and remote, almost automaton, but still lethal and sharp. She speaks very little, but I suspect she backs me most of the time because of our shared link to the Corps, and shared hatred for it.

Rajcik finally speaks up. "This isn't up for discussion." He kills Yadav's accusation by ignoring it, letting me off the hook . . . for now. Fine with me. I've deflected enough bullshit today.

"We've got the equipment to mask our signature. We'll get the calls signs from a supply ship en route, which shouldn't be difficult. I'll have that information within a few days. For now, we sit tight. Aly and I have some arrangements to make. No one leave the ship until you hear from me."

Resentment billows through the room like caustic smoke. Nobody likes being stuck aboard a small interstellar craft for days at a time, especially when it's planet-side. But Rajcik is playing every centimeter of this gig with complete caution. As of now, the only wildcard, the only thing he hasn't precisely calculated, is the involvement of Vitruzzi and her crew. The image of the last time I saw Strahan looms to the surface of my thoughts. Why had he been following me? Can he and the rest of them even imagine what kind of danger they're in?

"Let's talk." He motions for me to follow and together we walk out of operations toward the flight deck. I can almost feel the hateful gazes of MacCready and Yadav, maybe all of them, on my back.

"HERE'S WHAT YOU'LL DO." Outside of the flight deck window screens, I see nothing but rust-colored rock walls rising from the canyon floor. It must not have been easy to land the *Temptation* between these tightly abutting cliffs. The cover, however, is excellent. It isn't the kind of place anyone would happen upon unless they were looking for something, and I know I won't get far if I try to escape. Damn you, Rajcik. His mind for strategy is probably the most nimble and ruthless I've ever seen. The Corps would benefit from having him as their Command General, but the rest of the system would be in serious trouble if that ever happened. As dangerous as he is, it's best for everyone that he'll never have that kind of power.

He hands me a disc and continues, "You're going to take this to Vitruzzi and tell her we'll be in touch with further instructions."

"Are these the complete plans?"

He raises a mocking eyebrow at me, daring me to admit that I'd made up any part of the story about Vitruzzi's crew. If I lied to him about their interest in being involved, this would be my last opportunity to come clean. Not that it would matter. If I admitted to even the smallest attempt to mislead him, he'll kill me now. Best to say as little as possible. Finally, he answers, "That disc contains everything she needs to know. Except the location."

"Which you have?" I *knew* there was something he wasn't telling me.

Without answering, he gives me a cold look, and says, "Tell Vitruzzi I want to meet. I'll let her know where and when. Make sure they have the seeds."

"We don't have a lot of time, János."

"I'm aware that there is a sense of urgency on their behalf. However, they've waited this long, and as you said, David is probably dead. Is your impatience coming from the fact that you can't wait to get paid, or is there something else I should know?"

"If you string them along, they may take matters into their own hands."

"Your job is to stay with them and ensure that doesn't happen."

It takes some effort to swallow the golf-ball-sized lump of exasperation lodged in my throat before answering. "Understood."

"Thompson will take you back to Hell's Gate. I'm sure you'll find your way from there." He flicks on the intercom and orders Thompson to meet me at the *Temptation*'s transport shuttle.

He turns to leave, but my next question stops him. "When did you have time to go back to Obal 3 and pick up the shuttle?"

His head swivels toward me slowly, the way a cobra rises from a basket. He's caught and he knows it.

The answer is that he didn't, *couldn't*, have had the time or the opportunity to retrieve the shuttle. If he'd gone back, the Corps would have blasted the *Temptation* out of the sky. Which means he never sent the shuttle to the rendezvous in the first place, explaining why I couldn't find it despite following the directions he'd given me. Had he led the Corps to that hangar, trying to set me up? But why, goddammit? It doesn't make any sense.

He doesn't say anything. He doesn't have to. If I want to leave this room alive, I'm going to have to pretend that I don't know the truth, and he's going to have to pretend to believe me.

"I guess it doesn't really matter, huh?" It's the closest I can come to playing along. "We'll be waiting for your message."

Before I exit through the cabin doors, he grips my shoulder, spinning me to face him. Strong, implacable fingers dig like stakes into my back. Every muscle in my body goes taut, prepared to fight for my life, prepared for anything. "One more thing, Aly. If they try to run, or you do, I'll find you. And end you. Then I'll wipe their little settlement off the face of the planet. If they don't agree to my terms, you make sure they *completely* understand what they have to lose."

This time I don't stop myself from shoving his hand off me. Deftly, he grabs my wrist and jerks my fist toward him, pulling me with it. I try one time to pull my arm out of his grasp, but it's like fighting the vacuum of space. His grip is relentless, demanding I submit.

Bitterly, I respond, "Whatever you say."

He releases my arm and I watch the white marks where his fingers had been slowly begin to fill with red, angry blood. Shoving the disc inside the protection of my armor, I turn my back to him and leave.

· · ·

THE DOORS SLIDE closed behind me and Thompson, a tall, gangly bullwhip of a man, is waiting in the corridor.

"You ready?" I ask.

He grunts and starts walking in the direction of the shuttle. After a couple of seconds, he says, "I'm glad Rajcik is grounding you. You don't have what it takes to be on this ship. Slags need to stay where they belong—out of our way. Ships are a man's world."

I couldn't like this cockroach any less, and in my current state of mind, there's no controlling my mouth. "Excuse me if I didn't notice where you pissed on the walls to mark your territory. I guess I should be happy that you can even remember to put your dick back in your pants."

He stops walking and turns around, his lips curled into an ugly snarl. Stepping close, trying to menace me, he fumes into my face, "I'll show you where my dick goes, bitch," and grabs at my crotch.

The dumb bastard isn't prepared for my forehead slamming into his nose. He grunts in pain and surprise, the exhalation rising into an out-of-breath screech as my knee connects full force with his groin. He doubles up, holding onto his damaged goods, blood dripping from his nose, making a pattering noise on the steel walkway that's punctuated by desperate attempts to draw air back into his locked lungs. I stand over him in disgust for a moment and warn, "Remember what that feels like next time you think about fucking with me, Thompson."

Still bent over, he turns his red, clenched face toward me and mouths "bitch" between gasps as I walk past him to the shuttle. I don't know what's going to happen next, but I realize I'll never be aboard the *Temptation* again. I'm done with Rajcik, and this crew, forever.

THIRTEEN

On the short trip back to Hell's Gate, Thompson forces me to sit in the shuttle's windowless fuselage to keep me from pinpointing the *Temptation*'s location. He barely plants the landing gear before opening the exterior hatch and telling me to get out.

Fortunately, all the money Vitruzzi gave me is still in the cargo pocket of my pants. It's late in the afternoon and more people shuffle around the area than I'd seen earlier this morning. Odds are good I'll be able to buy a land transport or a few minutes on a satcom link to contact Agate Beach and warn them. Rajcik knows where the settlement is, so there is no need for him to tail me. He's holding all the cards right now. I intend to change that.

Just outside the entrance to Van Dieman's Land, I notice that same solar stoner who had begged money off me earlier lying flat out on the dirt street. No one looks in his direction or even diverts their steps to avoid him. They just raise their feet slightly higher to clear him and keep moving. I can't tell if he's breathing. Either passed out or dead. There's a part of me that recognizes the tragedy, and the irony, in the fact that both states equal the same thing for this guy. Once you've gone too far down the road he's on, there's only one place it will end. For a second I consider helping him, at least get him out of the way of potential traffic. Except it wouldn't really be as if I'm doing him a favor. The sooner it ends for him, the better.

Bullshit. No one deserves to die like that. A man walking past gives me a dirty look as I cut in front of him, veering out into the street and grabbing the stoner's outstretched hand. Still warm. Pulling him into the shade of the nearest building—he's lighter than he looks, unhealthily light—I let go, and he slumps to the side with a deep grunt. A string of yellow drool hangs from his mouth and his eyes flutter. His sunken chest and sharp ribs burn with fever beneath my hand as I shove a few more bills into his shirt. There's nothing else I can do for him.

The bar's dark interior is refreshingly cool despite the smoke-thick air. Like all of the Spectras, being planet-side means either being rendered into an incoherent block of ice by the frost that sinks its deadly claws into your skin, lungs, and brain, or burning up from the relentless heat that fries your motivation along with your sanity. Spectra 6 is more mild than the others I've been to, but it could still be mistaken for hell. Bounty hunters on my trail are still a possibility and I keep a lookout for them or Admin personnel. But my current goal of finding a way to warn Vitruzzi makes me less careful about keeping a low profile. There are more patrons at the bar than before and catching the eye of the barkeep, I nod, beckoning her over. Her footsteps are labored as she approaches, as if she's sick or old, though she looks younger than me. Whatever this town is, it doesn't appear to be a healthy place to live. Her eyes are filmy and disinterested as she waits for my order.

"Is there anywhere around here with a satcom link?"

Her placid stare doesn't change, and she simply stands there as if I haven't said a word. So I drop some cash on the bar.

The bill disappears and she says, "There's an empty table over there. I'll find someone who can sort you out."

Uh-uh. My guess is I'll sit there all day and no one will ever show. In one quick motion, I lean over the bar and grab the arm she used to pick up the money. "I'm not fucking around here. If no one shows up within twenty minutes, that A-bill is going to be the hardest you've ever made."

My patience has already been stretched to its breaking point today and the message gets across. Her eyes widen and she dips her chin in acknowledgment.

Less than five minutes pass before Strahan pushes open the door, scans the interior, and walks up and sits in the chair opposite me. Somehow, I'm not surprised.

He looks me over, eyes resting on my freshly bruised jaw for a few seconds, and then asks, "How happy am I to see you, Erikson?"

"The truth? Not very." He waits for me to continue. "We can't talk here. This place isn't safe and we don't have the time. I need to talk to Vitruzzi right away." I'm a decent liar when I need to be, but I hope he recognizes the sincerity in my face.

He stands up. "Then let's roll."

STRAHAN DRIVES the four-wheeled Rover through the canyon at a speed I wouldn't have imagined any land craft could manage. His usual taciturn attitude gives me plenty of time to think about how to explain the situation and come up with my next move. The population of Agate Beach is as good as dead if I don't talk them into playing Rajcik's game. The hard-to-swallow fact is, Rajcik only gave up the plans to the Fortress. We still don't know where it is and have nothing left to exchange for the location. The solar seeds are worth a small fortune, but they were also Vitruzzi's only bargaining chip, and Rajcik, technically, has already struck that bargain—the holodisc for the seeds. Vitruzzi didn't realize he would take the opportunity to up the ante at her and Brady's suggestion to team up on infiltrating the Fortress. Now Rajcik will try and force Vitruzzi into carrying out a suicide mission or make her watch Agate Beach be destroyed.

He's already proved that David and I were expendable from the beginning, and now he's willing to sacrifice a town full of people he's never even met to get the Nova. He's obviously well beyond compromise, or even reason, and it's clear to me that even if I stayed on

Rajcik's crew and played everything exactly as he wants, I'd still never see a cent of the payoff.

I should be bitter. I should be livid, enraged, filled with hate. But the only feeling I'm still capable of is an overwhelming, crushing urgency to do whatever it takes to get to the Fortress and find my brother. If saving David means throwing in with Vitruzzi and her crew, then that's what I'll do. I know he'd do the same if our circumstances were reversed. If he dies, or if he's already dead, I'm not sure I can face the savage guilt, knowing that I'm the one who left him there.

In the end, that's all this is really about. My brother is the only person in this world that I can point to as evidence that I'm not just another robot, mindless and empty, trained and controlled by the Corps and its Admin puppet master. David is proof that I'm more than that. He's my brother. I'm not alone in the universe, not just another stray that no one cares about. Having a family means coming from somewhere, and knowing where to go when you need help. In a time when space flight is the norm and living planet-side with even half the luxuries of old Earth is something few can appreciate, being part of a family grounds a person. It validates the human in me and keeps me from becoming what the Admin wanted me to be—a nonentity, a tool, a unit. I don't want to be nothing.

Rajcik is prepared to let David die and make me exactly that. With calm, almost detached bitterness, I finally realize the real surprise is that Rajcik hadn't sold us out sooner.

That's all it takes for my loyalty to change sides.

We reach Agate Beach in less than three hours. Brady and Vitruzzi are waiting for us at the dwelling they share. As I take a seat, all eyes are on me, impatient for me to describe what went down with Rajcik. There's very little hope in their expressions, merely cautious examination. They're used to bad news.

Clearing my throat, I begin: "Here's the deal. Rajcik sent me back here to tell you that he would give up the disc in exchange for the seeds we took from R'Kadia." Reaching into my vest, I pull out the holodisc. "Here it is."

Their faces all register the same shocked surprise, but aggressive suspicion is also there. Brady's hazel eyes stab through the air between us, prickling the skin of my face. His dislike for me is palpable.

I toss the disc on the table and continue, "But the problem is that we, that you, don't have the Fortress's location. And he does."

Vitruzzi's voice is grim. "What does he want for it?"

"Simple. He wants to work together." I let them all see the exaggerated benevolence on my face that I'm supposed to be conveying as Rajcik's appointed representative, and all of its exaggerated falseness.

I'm not enjoying telling them this. I'm not trying to build up a dramatic sense of fragile hope in order to shatter it. I want them to understand just how dangerous János Rajcik is. I want them to comprehend that they're in over their heads and maybe they should start picking out their headstones. "Of course you already know what I'm saying is too good to be true. He wants to use you and your ship as a diversion, a set up, so the Admin targets you when we get within range of the Fortress. You get taken prisoner, or just blown to bits, and he slips in and steals the Nova."

No one says anything. I catch Strahan's expression in the corner of my eye. Unlike Brady's face, there's no dislike and distrust. It almost seems to be sympathy.

The outside door opens and Venus, Desto, and Bodie walk in. Nothing is said, but their movements become deliberate and awareness lights up their eyes, perceiving the tension in the air. Desto and Bodie look at me curiously and sit down at the table on either side of me. The corners of Venus's mouth turn downward in unhappy disappointment and she begins fidgeting around in the cupboards behind where Brady stands.

"What did we miss?" Desto asks.

"Erikson here was just telling us how her partners want to use us as decoys so they can get rich," Brady says.

Vitruzzi glances at Brady, the look in her eyes gentle but firm, and says, "Erikson, you've obviously got more to say, so get on with it."

I have to force my voice to stay even, to not give away the stress cracking through my bones like an earthquake. "Rajcik can go to hell. I'm not working for him anymore. The only way I see that we'll be able to get to the Fortress is to play along with him until he gives up the location. Then maybe we can turn his plan around and make him and his crew the diversion *we* need to get in and out undetected."

"We," Vitruzzi says flatly, but her eyebrows arch with curiosity.

"My goal and your goals are the same, at least for now. I don't give a fuck about getting rich anymore." I look directly at Brady when I say this, wanting to drive home how wrong he is, at least about me.

"Why the change of heart?" Strahan asks.

"What I want to know is why any of us are pretending to believe her," Brady cuts in, not so easily convinced. "Isn't it clear she's trying to bait us? She's a criminal, and she's working for a criminal. All of us know exactly what she's capable of." He glares darkly at me and leans forward on the table. "We know about the New Sweden Massacre." Sweeping the rest of the group with his swamp-grass stare, he continues, "Just because she's brought collateral doesn't mean those are really the plans for the Fortress, or that they haven't been rigged in some way. If she doesn't have some proof, I'm pulling the plug."

I've gone pale, my skin tingling coldly from the lack of blood. The New Sweden Massacre had been Rajcik's doing, that's true. But I hadn't been part of it.

The job happened almost a month ago, an easy-money gig appropriating a rebel cache of weapons from a non-cit settlement on Spectra 4. It should have been quick and low-risk—rush in, suppress resistance by threat and superior firepower, and be a memory within the hour. The rebels were a disorganized group, trying to plan some kind of attack on the Corps surveillance ships that sweep through the Spectras regularly. I have no idea what they hoped to get from such an attack, besides dead, and we anticipated that they would have no capacity to fight off a group with our experience. Like I said: easy.

We were on our way in, just passing near an Admin space station, when David had suggested to Rajcik that he and I divert from the operation. He convinced Rajcik that we weren't needed in New Sweden and could take the opportunity to sweep around the station in the *Temptation*'s shuttle to look for potential targets for future ops. He hadn't bothered to ask me what I thought of the plan, just assumed that I'd go along with whatever he proposed. We'd found nothing and rendezvoused with the *Temptation* six hours later. I was angry with David for pulling us off the op on a dangerous wild goose chase, but he'd been tight-lipped and unapologetic. Looking back now, I should have realized something else was going on. Maybe David knew Rajcik was going to go berserk and didn't want us involved.

Two weeks later, I caught a news bulletin detailing what happened at New Sweden. Rajcik and the crew hadn't just overpowered them; they'd killed every person there and blown the settlement off the map. The weapons cache had been paltry, barely worth the energy it took to fly out, and there didn't seem to be a reason for such dire actions. The news had upset and disgusted me, and David had been furious with Rajcik, threatening to kill him if he ever did something like that again. Murdering non-cits for no reason wasn't what we'd signed up for—we'd had enough of that back in the Corps. But it was done. Nothing would change that. By then, we had our sights set on bigger payoffs, and we hit Obal 3 eight days later.

"I didn't have anything to do with that." I'm shaken and I know it shows. For the first time since this whole mess began, I'm defending myself. "Neither did my brother. I don't know exactly what happened in New Sweden, and maybe it wouldn't have if we'd been there. But we weren't."

"Right." Brady thinks I'm lying and doesn't hide the fact. His smug expression shows that he's satisfied that he's won.

All the credibility I thought I had with this group is slipping away. If they already believed me capable of participating in that kind of ruthless slaughter, why bother trying to enlist my help at all? White-hot anger streaks through me. Have they just been toying with me all along, to get to Rajcik?

"Let me ask you something, Erikson. You know what kind of person Rajcik is. What makes you think his only interest in this Nova is profit? Hasn't it occurred to you that he plans on using it? No? Well it has occurred to me." Brady's eyes are narrow, slitted like a snake's, as he continues, "Which is why I think you're either lying and you're just as much of a low-life-scum-villain as he is, or you're being stupid."

I throw the table aside and lunge at Brady before his last word is out. I don't care that I may be committing suicide; he's gone too fucking far.

My fist flies toward his face and I register that he's pulled a pistol out and is leveling it at my torso. Then my right shoulder shrieks in sudden, sharp pain as someone grabs my arm and forces it behind my back. With a grunt, I'm pulled backward and off balance, not dropping my eyes from Brady's scarred, hate-contorted face. I jerk forward in another attempt, and a knee slams into the back of my legs, buckling them and dropping me face first into the floor. My shoulder protests alarmingly. If I don't stop, it'll be useless for weeks. A knee is planted in the middle of my back and I let myself go limp, knowing I've lost this fight.

"Fuck you, Brady! You don't know what the fuck you're talking about! If you don't believe me, then fucking kill me!"

"Everyone calm down." Vitruzzi's voice is full of collected, icy reason.

Through the water leaking from my eyes, both from pain and rage, I see Desto's coffee-black-no-cream-no-sugar hand pulling my Sinbad free from my side. Just in case.

Vitruzzi says, "Get her up." He stands, pulling me to my feet. The look on his face is more amusement than anger, which frustrates me further. "Patrick, this isn't getting us anywhere. Why don't you give it a rest?"

Brady scowls at her for a moment and slams his pistol back into its holster. Without giving me another look, he stomps out.

Venus has pushed her body tightly against the far wall, her face betraying her distress. The strain is palpable, everyone struggling to keep it under wraps. Strahan rests his hand on the butt of his pistol but doesn't draw it.

My teeth are gritted fiercely against the pain in my contorted shoulder and I have to suck air through my nostrils. After another second, Desto releases some of the pressure, giving me a chance to continue in a more reasonable tone. "I don't care what you do, Vitruzzi. Those are the plans Rajcik gave me. Take them and use Vilbrandt, if you really think he's going to help you, and storm the Fortress yourself. Good fucking luck. But bet on this. If you don't play along with Rajcik, he's going to do the same thing to your settlement that he did to New Sweden. Do you believe that?"

Well, maybe not so reasonable.

She blinks, tension spreading tightly over her already drawn features, and starts pacing across the room. "We've got our eye on Rajcik. He's not going to get a chance to threaten Agate Beach."

"How can you have your eye on him? I was on the *Temptation*, and I don't even know where it is."

The look she gives me is heavy with resolve. "We traced his location using a tracking chip we implanted on you. We have video emplacements watching his every move."

I almost missed what she said, it was so matter-of-fact. Then realization hits me. "What? What do you mean a tracking chip?"

"We bugged you."

If I'd been mad about being insulted by Brady before, I'm over-the-top, brace-for-the-storm, fucking furious now, but the sharp spike of pain in my shoulder and Desto's unbreakable grip keeps me from letting loose again. I'm forced to stand still, giving my sense of reason time to work out that she's probably bluffing. "Rajcik has the equipment to detect tracking devices," I respond. "If I had one on me, he'd have found it and I'd be dead."

"He couldn't have found it if he tried." She sounds utterly certain.

"What do you mean?"

"You don't know what I did before becoming a transporter, Erikson. Don't make the mistake of thinking you have everything figured out. You're smarter than that, and you have no idea what we're capable of."

There's no bluff in her face. "So you're saying I'm bugged. How?"

"The chip is tiny, bioengineered. It doesn't show up through magnetic resonance, x-ray, or radio frequency scanning, both because it is so small, and because it's masked by your own biochemistry. It hides from scans by cloaking itself in a genetically copied envelope of cells and integrating with the tissue around it. Its mechanical ability allows it to scramble scanners and make them see only normal biological structures. The only way to find it is by introducing viral catalysts in or near the physical instrument. It will copy viral cells, something like a cancer, but only affects the local area, thus creating a telltale lesion. It's only detectable if you know what you're looking for. I designed it peripheral to Admin research protocols, so its existence is unknown. Which makes it useful to us."

I swallow, unable to think of a response.

"I wouldn't have put you in a situation where I believed your life would be jeopardized without telling you, Erikson. I'm a doctor. My goal is to preserve life, not waste it."

"You're the one who told me I could leave if I chose to. Then you have me followed," I shoot an accusatory glance at Strahan, "and you bug me. What about all that bullshit you gave me about trusting you?"

"Did you really think that we would just give up if you decided not to help us?" She stops pacing and stands in front of me, whipping me with her words. "We knew you'd find Rajcik, or he'd find you. And since he has the information we need, we had to take the necessary steps to get to him."

"Do you have control of yourself, Erikson?" Desto asks softly in my ear.

I shrug noncommittally. Maybe I'm being touchy, but hearing my body's been used as a homing beacon makes a little retaliation feel justified. Desto releases my arm anyway and I take a slow step forward, wanting desperately to rub my aching shoulder, but refusing to give them the satisfaction.

"So where is it?"

"Your right shoulder, just under the scar. Scar tissue helps disguise the entry hole."

I pull up my sleeve to look. The scar, a remnant from the flying debris of a badly timed ammo dump eradication, is the only thing visible.

"Don't worry. It won't cause any harm. Almost everyone in the settlement has one."

Bodie and Venus begin picking up the toppled table and chairs. I remain standing, Desto's bulk near me enough of a deterrent to any half-cocked attempt at retribution I may be planning.

Vitruzzi waves her hand at the chair I'd been using before, wanting me to sit. I don't. Her eyebrows crease in anger, and she takes her own seat. After a moment, only Strahan, Desto, and I remain standing.

Bodie speaks for the first time. Leaning forward in his chair, eyes brimming with compassion, he says, "Imagine it from our perspective, Aly. We've all got friends who were on the *Sky Serpent*. We're just trying to help them. You would do the same for your brother, wouldn't you?"

What he says is 100 percent true, and everyone here knows it. I've already betrayed Rajcik, who had, despite our association with the Corps, given my brother and I an opportunity to escape that life and start a new one. You could argue that I owe him something. Or did. His decision to betray us and let David die changed that.

I take one last deep breath to rein in my temper and sit in the chair. "All right. Look. I can't prove anything I'm telling you. But the fact is, Rajcik is willing and able to do whatever it takes to get that bomb. And he won't share the profit or change the mission plan. Not even to try and rescue my brother. So fuck him. There's a chance that David is still alive, and I'm going to find him. That's the truth." And I think Rajcik plans to kill me anyway, but I'll keep that to myself.

Venus walks toward me and, surprisingly, grasps my hands between her own as if trying to reassure me. "We understand, Aly."

Vitruzzi continues to glare at me stoically for a few more seconds. Then she says, "Everyone take twenty minutes then meet back in the command room. Let's take a look at the disc and see what we have."

FOURTEEN

The room empties. Without another word to me, Vitruzzi raises her hand in a halting gesture, motioning for me to stay and wait, and catches up with Brady outside. Their voices carry through the door, modulating between loud and fast and slow and quiet, and bits of the conversation filter in to me.

" . . . trust her."

"When you're responsible for the lives of one hundred and twenty people, Eleanor, you'll think before bringing scum like them . . ."

" . . . no other chance to save Doug and Zeta! We've got Rajcik where we want him . . ."

When they return a few minutes later, Vitruzzi's face is set in hard lines, angry but determined. Brady remains surly and won't look at me. I'd overheard enough for it to be clear that he'd never agreed with Vitruzzi about bringing me to Spectra 6, and would probably prefer to have me dead and buried rather than be given any more opportunity to endanger the settlement. I didn't hear what she said to persuade him, but his opinion of me, no matter how misguided it is, could be an obstacle to a smooth mission outcome. I'll just have to keep as much distance between us as I can and hope that he listens to Vitruzzi. It complicates things, but right now he has to be considered hostile and potentially dangerous.

"Tell us what Rajcik plans to do and what he's capable of," Brady says.

There's no hesitation in my response, betrayal or not. When Rajcik had called me loyal, he'd underestimated how far that loyalty is capable of extending, and there's a subtle eagerness in my voice as I answer, "The *Temptation* isn't your biggest concern. The ship is nothing more than an escape vehicle with a few smuggling holds that allow us to hide stolen goods. Our pilot—I mean Rajcik's pilot—a man named Thompson, is good, but no match for Venus. The *Sphynx* is slower, but it's more maneuverable and takes less time to get up to speed, so she may be able to catch up to Rajcik within atmosphere if she has to. It's the *Temptation*'s shuttle that you need to be concerned about. It carries a retractable, fully auto orbital gun with nuke-tipped ammo."

"You're talking about a Nagasaki?"

"Yes. It stays on the shuttle in order to keep it hidden from Corps ship scanners. But it could tear up Agate Beach in seconds if it gets close enough."

"How close?"

"Within twenty K."

"Anything else?"

"Rajcik won't try to assault the colony by land. I'm not sure how much he knows about the area or about the mine. But if he targets Agate Beach and hits the mine, it could cave in."

The two of them share a long look and both stand. "All right, let's get to the command room."

In my mind, the issue of the tracking device is unresolved, but it's moot at this point. I may hate the fact that I have a microscopic apparatus inside my skin that's concealed by my own tissue, but I have to give Vitruzzi credit. It's difficult to believe that the Admin would let someone with her medical talents slip through their fingers. What's she doing here? Her empathy, compassion, and superlative medical skills don't add up with her choice to live in the gutters of the Algol system and risk her life in a criminal enterprise that's doomed to fail. It all contradicts what she must have come from. The only people who live on the outskirts are people with nothing to lose. The first time I saw her, wearing cross-draw holsters and an interrogator's blank expression, she seemed no different than hundreds of others I've met out here—a small-time crook. By now, I've spent enough time around her and her crew to realize that's not even close to who she really is, or was. I wonder if she has a hard time sleeping at night with the choices she's made.

The three of us take the Rover back to the mine, cold silence our uneasy companion. The tension is thick, but I'm beyond caring. I just want to see some progress. Plans have been set in motion now, and all that's left is to carry them out. To the end.

When we reach the mine's interior chamber, Brady leads the way into what Vitruzzi had called their command room, a chamber carved out of the rock walls beneath the communications annex. It must have been used as the foreman's office when the mining operations were still active. There's a heavy steel door at the entrance that can't be opened without inputting a key code. They keep it secure, and I see why once we get inside.

I don't know what I expected, hadn't even really thought about what kind of technology this rag-tag settlement might have collected, but when I get a look inside, it's almost as if I'm back in the Corps.

The walls are lined with computers and VDUs, scanners, robotic devices, and, most importantly, a holodisc reader. The far corner of the room is stocked with lab machines unlike any I've seen, but they're obviously expensive and highly specialized.

Everyone is standing around the disc reader. I walk up next to Bodie while Vitruzzi loads the disc and quietly ask, "Where does all this equipment come from?"

"This? It's . . . on loan from the local fleet." Meaning it's stolen.

"Yeah, but why is it here? And what are all of those machines for over there?" I gesture toward the bank of computers lining the north wall.

He hesitates before answering long enough to give me the sense he's hiding something. "Uh, those are for geologic analysis. Most of this stuff comes from Ministry of S&E excavation ships. That's how I find replacements when something breaks."

"And is this just a hobby, or is there a reason you're so interested in the rock on this planet?"

He smiles at me indulgently. "Solar seeds are a geologic anomaly. But that doesn't mean they're the only things in the universe that has properties we couldn't even conceive of until we found them. Maybe there's more to find." He pauses. "Besides, you can take the scientist out of the lab, but you can't take the lab out of the scientist."

Whatever that means. Is that really all this stuff is? Or are they up to something else? The more time I spend with them, the more I realize that there is much, much more than meets the eye with these people. If I weren't so concerned about my own problems, maybe I would pay more attention, but right now, I simply don't have the time or energy to investigate.

Lights beam upward from the disc reader, quickly organizing themselves into the shape of the Fortress. With each layer of the full complex illuminated, the hovering display is a chaotic jumble of lines, rooms, walls, ducts, materials, and tunnels. By selecting from different options presented on screen readouts on both sides of the table, variable views can be chosen to see exactly, and only, what interests us at the moment. It's a way to peel back the space station layer by layer and figure out what we're dealing with.

Brady makes the first choice, a schematic showing the location of all security screens, checkpoints, and sensors, and all eyes turn toward the display.

FOUR HOURS PASS like salt grains through a bullet hole, trickling thickly by, every suggestion congealing around one central barrier —we still don't know where the station is. Every possible scenario to infiltrate the space station once we're there has been discussed down to microscopic detail, and the crew's ideas have been well-informed and precise, consistent with the behavior I'm getting more and more used to. Tactical planning isn't a new vocation for them.

Once inside the station, movement should be fairly easy. Armed sentries are posted at the major sensitive areas: the weapons development labs at the station's fore, each entry into the station's command and control center, located in the belly, and the main entrances to the biochem labs at the lower-level stern and scattered around the docking bays. Collectively, the Corps units providing security on the station are a huge force, way too big for us to deal with. But if we can get in without being detected, we'll only have to neutralize the immediate on-site personnel, who will mostly be composed of doctors and scientists. With enough deception, surprise, and luck—mostly luck—we could be in and out before the main security forces know we're there.

Standing a kilometer beneath the surface in a sealed and secured room on Spectra 6, the plan sounds deceptively feasible. Except . . . it all supposes we can first *locate* and then *get inside* the station, which is where we need magic, a miracle, or an army. Rajcik's plan to gain access under the guise of a supply ship could work on two conditions: control of an Admin supply ship, or at least a similarly sized ship with replicable engine signatures, and the personnel call signs and identification numbers of a scheduled delivery run. I can only assume T'Kai packaged these details with the disc for Rajcik, but that doesn't do us any good. If he has them, he didn't include them with the copy he gave me. Besides, from what I've seen around here, there's no ship in the settlement's pool large enough to imitate a supply ship.

Once inside the Fortress we'll have to rely on wits, reflexes, and the ability to adapt. We all know that; it doesn't need to be discussed. It's not knowing the two most important elements of the plan, namely where the station is and how we're going to get in, that overstretches our nerves close to the breaking point, and the strain is beginning to show. Vitruzzi presses her palms to her temples in frustration again, yanking her thick hair, now shiny and lank from repeated handling, out of the way. The lines around Brady's massive facial scar have deepened as his irritation at our lack of resources grows, leaving a dark, severe crevasse running down his face. Desto and Strahan are the only ones who don't seem to be losing focus, their enthusiasm for cracking this problem actually increasing as the options seem to whittle down to almost nothing. Theirs is the kind of determination and intensity that you want for this kind of mission, even if it is a suicide attempt.

Finally, Vitruzzi slaps both her palms flat on the display table, causing the image over it to waver ghostlike for a second, and says, "That's it. We're not getting anywhere tonight. As much as I hate to say it," she gives me an unreadable look, "I think we have to accept that Rajcik may have given us a janky disc. We can't even tell from these where the *Sky Serpent* crew is being held. There's no indication of a prison area or anything like it."

From most people, this kind of speech would sound like an admission of defeat. But from her, it sounds like what it is: frustration, and a subtle but malicious seed of growing desperation. She's not giving up. None of them look like the thought has even crossed their minds. In a strange way, it makes me feel better. We've barely scratched the surface tonight, but being among a group that's willing to face the worst possible odds with total resolve gives me a reason to hope. Maybe I'm lying to myself about David's chances, and about their friends' chances, but if there's any way of pulling this off, we'll find it.

Brady straightens up from where he's been focusing intensely on the sub docks around the station's fore. "We need to take a break. Let's reassemble in three hours. We've got to be missing something. Maybe with a fresh outlook . . . " He trails off.

With a collective nod, everyone agrees. It's late, probably only a couple hours until sun-up. Sleep and some time to clear our heads can't hurt anything. Yet I wait at the far end of the control room as everyone else leaves, their footsteps heavy. I'm just as exhausted and my jaw continues to throb from MacCready's punch, but I can go on feeling like this indefinitely.

Everyone passes through the heavy doors except Vitruzzi. She turns to wait for me, refusing to leave me alone in the command room. "Are you coming?"

"I'd prefer to keep looking. Time is short."

She pauses, considering whether fighting with me is worth the effort, and says, "No one is giving up, Erikson. And for this to work, we all have to be operating at full capacity. You look like shit. Maybe you should try and get some sleep."

Blunt, but true. She's made her point. It has been almost twenty hours since I left Agate Beach early this morning and what I need most right now is the ability to think straight. "Yeah, all right." I follow her out and make my way to my bunk on the *Sphynx*.

It seems like only seconds have passed since I lay down when my wrist com beeps me back to awareness. Ghostly iridescent lines of the space station's schematics crisscross the darkness, permanently drawn on my mind's eye and I wearily sit up and strap on my boots. As I walk down the metal ramp to join the others in the control room, voices come to me from the front of the ship.

"He ran, just like we expected. Took one of the land crafts. Looks like he's been in the com annex, too. If he convinced Rajcik that he knows what he says he does, he may have already been picked up."

Vitruzzi and Strahan. I stop walking, listening quietly.

"All right, we planned for this. Find Desto and Venus and get the *Sphynx* up in the air. I want you all locked on Rajcik's shuttle within the hour. And check in with Bodie; he's in the control room. Tell him to find out exactly where Vilbrandt is."

That slippery bastard. Strahan said they were keeping an eye on him, but who was watching him when we'd all been at Brady's after I met with Rajcik? Vilbrandt must have gotten impatient and risked contacting Rajcik on his own. Rajcik had been angry when he heard how many people knew about the operation to steal the Nova, but what I'd told him about Vilbrandt may be enough to tempt him to consider whatever scheme Vilbrandt proposes. If Vilbrandt knows what he says he knows . . . Rajcik is no fool. He won't underestimate the value of Vilbrandt's information and may take full advantage of insider knowledge to increase his own odds. Then what'll happen to Vilbrandt? Not what he expects, I'm sure.

Vitruzzi's decision to send the *Sphynx* up, presumably to intercept the *Temptation*'s shuttle, is interesting. What good will it do? The *Sphynx* may once have been weaponized, but now it's just a decommissioned transport ship that the Nagasaki will easily turn into dust.

I emerge from the ramp, ready to jump into the middle of their plan and find out where I fit. Vitruzzi nods at me in a way that indicates she knows I overheard them. "Come with me. It's time to call Rajcik."

"Vitruzzi, there's nothing stopping him at this point from wiping out Agate Beach. What are you going to do?"

Without answering, she walks toward the lift, assuming I'll follow the way any captain assumes unquestioned authority. As if I'm just part of the crew.

On the ride up, Venus, Brady, and Strahan board the *Sphynx* below us and the lift cables begin thrumming in legato vibration as the ship's engines cycle up. Vitruzzi grips the lift's handrail hard enough to make the veins in her hands pop to the surface. It's the grasp of an overboard sailor around a life preserver, which is ironically close to the truth.

Once inside, she quickly dials-in a frequency and sends her voice into the morning: "Agate Beach hailing the *Temptation*, over."

Hardly a minute passes before the VDU lights up and the pinched, sour face of Ahsan Yadav looks out at us. "Yeah."

"This is Captain Eleanor Vitruzzi. Get me Rajcik."

He sneers. "Wait one."

The screen blanks out briefly and then comes back on. Rajcik, sitting at the familiar flight deck console of the *Temptation*, leans back in his seat, relaxed, leveling his discomfiting shark grin at us.

"Captain Eleanor Vitruzzi. Not an unexpected transmission. Did you call to ask for your scientist back?" His eyes shift to me and hold there for an uncomfortable second before he continues, "Maybe to trade one defector for another?"

Realization hits me with the force of a rocketing meteor as it strikes the planet; Vilbrandt had overheard the conversation I'd had with Vitruzzi and Brady and spilled it all to Rajcik. If I ever see that sewer rat again, he'll wish he'd died at birth.

Vitruzzi's voice is all business, almost robotic. "You still have something we need. It's not Vilbrandt."

The tiny wrinkles that deepen around his eyes indicate a hint of annoyance. "Vitruzzi, there's nothing stopping me from wiping you off the map right now. You should remember that. That's right, Aly," he focuses on me for the first time, "Vilbrandt shared your little rebellion. I knew someday you'd turn on me."

Vitruzzi cuts him off. "Rajcik, I just sent you a feed. It's in your best interest to watch it. Right now."

He gazes at her for a moment before reaching forward to his communication console and turning on a second monitor. Simultaneously, Vitruzzi switches on a display embedded below her main screen, letting us see what he's seeing.

A live feed of the *Temptation* appears, docked in a deep ravine and surrounded by steep canyon walls on three sides. A rock cornice hangs over the ship, hiding most of it, but the light glinting off the rear thrusters leaves no doubt what it is.

He looks at his display calmly for a moment, then back at Vitruzzi. "That's very clever, Captain. I don't know how you found my ship, but I feel it necessary to warn you that there's a—"

She cuts him off again, "Short-range shuttle equipped with a Nagasaki en route to Agate Beach. I know. It has been accounted for as well."

Exactly how many cards does she have up her sleeve? Rajcik has revealed something useful: he doesn't know how she found his ship. That means either Vilbrandt hadn't stuck around long enough to learn about the tracking device, or he'd hidden that information from Rajcik. Is he bugged, too? He's smart enough to realize the liability he'd instantly become if Rajcik knew they could track the *Temptation* through him, plenty of incentive to keep it a secret if he is. Even if Vitruzzi had homed in on my tracking device yesterday, how and when they had an opportunity to set up surveillance is a mystery.

She continues, "Now that I have your attention, I want you to listen very carefully. This is what's going to happen. In addition to the disc you've already handed over, you're going to give us the coordinates to the Fortress. Because we're reasonable people, we'll give you ten kilos of solar seeds for them. I'm giving *you* a chance to be reasonable and take us up on our offer."

The black bullet tattooed on Rajcik's Adam's apple ripples as he swallows, and the muscles in his jaw twitch spasmodically. "And why would I do any of this?"

"If you don't, I'll give the command to detonate seismic blasting charges loaded throughout the canyon around you and bury you under so much rock the Algols will burn out before anyone finds you. Then we'll blow your shuttle from the sky." She leans forward a little, her intensity holding his attention like a magnet. "If you don't believe me, Rajcik, I can give you a demonstration."

We're both staring at her, me in surprise, Rajcik in something like demonic hate. Finally he says, "*Captain* Vitruzzi," putting a sneering emphasis on the word 'captain,' "I have exactly zero tolerance for games." The fact that he doesn't say what he wants to say—*prove it*—makes it clear that he's close enough to believing her that he's not taking the chance.

She clicks a switch next to a microphone and, without taking her eyes from the screen, says, "Bodie."

"Yeah." Bodie's voice comes back over the speaker, loud enough for Rajcik to hear at his end.

"Give the crew in the canyon a mild shake along the north wall."

"Roger."

Vitruzzi doesn't say anything, but within a few moments small pebbles begin to jump and cascade down the side of the canyon, dust blooming like desert ghosts from the walls in all directions.

Rajcik's image vibrates just slightly as the earth around him shakes. His upper lip curls in a wicked sneer that makes my blood run cold. "All right, Vitruzzi. Now what?"

"Call off your shuttle. Meet me in two hours where your crewmember found Erikson in Hell's Gate. I'll bring your seeds. You bring us the coordinates. If your ship's engines start to cycle, I won't hesitate to bury it. Am I clear?"

Rajcik looks off to his left and gives the order: "Ortiz, tell Fedchenko and Thompson to get back here immediately." Dropping his dark gaze back on Vitruzzi, he threatens, "See you then," and closes the connection.

Vitruzzi sighs deeply and looks at me. The surprise must still be stamped on my face because she says, "You didn't really think all the equipment we have in the control room was just for analyzing dirt, did you?"

"I'm starting to not know what to think."

"We stay prepared, and we stay safe. Let's get moving."

FIFTEEN

Twenty minutes later we're in the *Sphynx*'s shuttle flying low over the canyon system headed back to Hell's Gate. We'll get there early, giving us enough time to scope the surrounding area and see if Rajcik's managed to set up an ambush. Given that up to this point he's had absolutely no idea what Vitruzzi and her crew have been capable of, it's doubtful he could have come up with anything unexpected, but with him, there's never enough margin of safety.

Two rows of crew seats are packed against opposing walls inside the narrow shuttle, filling the fuselage from the cockpit to the engine compartment. Strahan flies with Vitruzzi as copilot, and Desto sits across the aisle from me. I'm focused on the brown dirt speeding by outside the window screens when I catch Vitruzzi glance over her shoulder at Desto. Something in the look puts me on instant alert.

Desto turns to me, his left hand held out. His right rests on the butt of his pistol. "Hand over your weapons, Erikson."

"What?" I look to Vitruzzi sharply, not believing this is happening.

Desto keeps his voice pitched low, trying to keep the situation calm. "Don't make this hard, we just want to make sure everyone stays safe. Give them here, slowly."

Any ideas of resistance melt away at the implacability of his face, as if they are so much useless ice under a burning sun. "Everyone safe? What about me?" I spit the words as I pull out my Sinbad and hand it to him stock first, followed by the Mini-Derg. "I thought we were on the same side."

"We'll watch out for you, Erikson. But we can't take any chances," Vitruzzi responds, deflecting my unbelieving fury with impassivity, and turns back to the front.

I still have my body armor, that's something. But my AK-80 is hung up in the rack at the rear next to the barrel of solar seeds for Rajcik, and it looks as if that's where it will stay. Desto wedges my Sinbad under the belt of his equipment vest near his left hip and deposits the Derg in a pocket.

Sinking back into my seat, I wait for intermission to end and let this bad dream continue.

Soon, Strahan is passing the shuttle over Hell's Gate, taking a couple of low turns while he and Vitruzzi scan the streets, on the lookout for anything suspicious. I've ceased paying attention as I brace for the meeting but catch Strahan point out something to Vitruzzi on the first pass. She nods. My guess is that they've spotted the *Temptation*'s shuttle. Rajcik would have used it to get to the rendezvous.

When they're satisfied that nothing looks out of the ordinary, she turns and faces Desto and I. "This is how it will go down. Bodie is our eyes and ears from the control room back at the Beach, watching Rajcik's ship. Patrick and Venus are on the *Sphynx*, in position to deal with any other contingency." She turns to Strahan. "Once we land, get back in the air and be ready for a quick extraction. The three of us will meet with Rajcik. If you don't hear from me within the hour, tell Patrick. If Rajcik pulls any shit, make sure his ship never leaves that canyon."

As she finishes speaking, Strahan brings the shuttle to a static hover at the town's edge. Desto and Vitruzzi unsnap their harnesses and prepare to dismount.

Pulling my own harness off my shoulders, I ask, "So what exactly do you want me to do?"

She unlocks the shuttle's hatch and pushes it out to serve as our exit ramp. "Whatever comes naturally, Erikson." What the hell does that mean? "Let's move," she finishes.

The bar's atmosphere is like an ancient, primitive cave with danger crouching in every shadow. Rajcik sits with his back to the wall of the dingy room like the deity of cannibals, ready to receive prayers and pleas for mercy. No other customers are present, which I know from my previous visit is unusual. Either the patrons of this particular dive are savvy enough to know when there's too much danger to risk a drink, or Rajcik simply threatened to kill anyone who didn't leave. The only person left is the bar pilot, the same haggard woman who'd been here a couple of days ago, ready to serve.

None of this is interesting or even important to me. At the moment, my full focus is on the smuggler, looking as relaxed as an overfed snake, and the two compatriots he brought with him. It's no surprise to see MacCready's disfigured face to Rajcik's right, and Ortiz sits a short distance off to his left. I can too easily imagine a variety of possible outcomes to this situation, and few of them are good.

An electrical fizz from a broken sign hanging behind the bar suffuses the air, and the clinking of glasses being wiped off by the bar pilot with all the enthusiasm of a condemned criminal adds to the noise. The two sounds combine in a muted nerve-jangling racket, as if part of a symphony played on thousand-year-old instruments that have long since decayed into relics and dust, making my teeth want to grind.

Let's get this over with. As I cross the empty room and sit without pretense, Rajcik's relaxed posture doesn't change. Using more caution, Vitruzzi's dark eyes, their impenetrable blackness exactly the same as Rajcik's, scan the room, pausing briefly when they come to Ortiz and MacCready. She approaches nonchalantly, but her pistols are unhooked, ready for action. Desto remains standing next to the door, guarding against unwelcome intruders and keeping some distance in case of close-quarter firing.

Without waiting for an introduction, she jumps right into it. "Did you bring what we agreed on?"

Rajcik's gaze hasn't shifted from Vitruzzi since we entered the bar, but he says, "I don't like the advantage your bulldog has. Make him take a seat."

For a second, she doesn't move. Then slowly and reluctantly, as if her neck were in need of rust removal, she turns toward Desto and nods to the chair on my left. Naked hostility shadows her features when she looks back to Rajcik.

"That's the one and only demand you get to make. We've done all the negotiating we're going to. Now, do you have the Fortress's coordinates?"

His eyes flicker dangerously, anger glowing in their depths. He isn't used to being spoken to like this and it's pissing him off. Fury vibrates from him, joining the buzz of the broken sign.

After a long silence, he says, "Tell me, Captain. What makes you think you can trust her?" He tilts his chin in my direction without looking at me, and the unexpected question hits me like a sucker punch. He's trying to rattle her, put her on edge, in the process undermining the fragile bond that's begun to form between Vitruzzi's crew and I.

She says nothing, prepared to let him continue and see what he's getting at.

"I ask because I now harbor one of your former crewmembers who has already switched sides twice." He continues, "I ask because it seems you have a problem finding reliable people."

"Make your point," she says.

He leans forward, placing one palm flat on the table and glaring at Vitruzzi. "I'm not convinced your judgment is sound enough for me to trust that you'll hold up your end of our arrangement, if the people in your employ are any indication." His eyes rest on me, dead calm and filled with poison.

Vitruzzi keeps her cool. "So Vilbrandt told you he was a member of my crew?" She lets these words, heavy with the implied accusation that Rajcik is a fool for believing anything Vilbrandt has told him, settle in the vacant space between them, then continues, "This isn't about my crew, or Vilbrandt. Do you want the seeds or not?"

"Where are they? You didn't bring them with you, as we agreed, which leads me to conclude that my assessment of your trustworthiness is accurate. I have no reason to give you the coordinates."

There's an icy shift in the atmosphere, a frigid draft gusting around us that carries the realization that more than one pistol is locked, cocked, and aimed beneath the table. Almost casually concerned with self-preservation, I wonder how many are pointed at me.

Vitruzzi's lips grow tight, the tiny lines around them strained and deep. "Yes. You do. Here's how it's going to go. First, you give us the coordinates. Then we're all going to get up from this table and walk to my shuttle. We'll drop you and the seeds off at your ship and escort you off Spectra 6. When you're far enough away to make me feel comfortable, we let you out of missile range and you can go wherever you want."

Rajcik sits motionlessly, his eyes lingering in thoughtful consideration on hers for a few moments before looking back at me. "And this is your choice, Aly? You're going to give up the biggest payoff of your life on a rescue mission for your troublemaking brother, who's probably already dead, and people you don't even know?"

My words tumble out before I think about what I'm going to say. "Do you really think that matters to me anymore? That I'd sell out David for a few bucks? Fuck you. If you had any idea what loyalty really is, you wouldn't even ask me that. As far as I'm concerned, you can go to hell, and take the rest of these greedy bootlickers with you." My eyes bounce to MacCready.

MacCready half stands and seethes, "You fucking bitch! I'll . . ."

He's stopped by a casual, "Sit down," from Rajcik, and his lips wrinkle back in a hateful sneer.

Rajcik chuckles. "It's rare that I underestimate someone, Aly. You're no exception."

Before I can ask what he means, he dismisses me and returns his cold stare to Vitruzzi. After a heavy pause, he says, "It occurs to me that you could be an incredible asset in my work, Captain. Have you considered the benefits of becoming a businesswoman of the free market?"

She's hardly moved a centimeter since first sitting down, but the way her face hardens, as if made of drying concrete, and the rapidly beating pulse in her neck show that her patience is starting to dissolve. "I'm not interested."

"Why not?" He leans forward, baring more of his large teeth in that predatory grin. "From what I understand, you have no reason to remain loyal to the Admin. To be their luggage girl. For someone who's lost a husband and a daughter to their deceit—you have more reason than most to want to work for the other side. For my side."

I don't know what Rajcik is talking about, but I can see the way he's getting to her. Her body grows so rigid that her muscles strain against her skin. Desto shifts beside me, his hand coming to rest on the Thresher propped against his thigh, and my palms itch for the feel of my own carbine.

Her voice sounds as if it's being pressed in a vice as she says, "We're not here to discuss that. Now make your choice."

He appears satisfied with the effect his question has on her and leans back in his chair. "Two questions. What makes you think I have the coordinates with me? And if I give them to you, once we're escorted off this rock as you described, what makes you think I won't come back and turn your settlement into so much garbage and dust while you're en route to the Fortress, losing your personal little war against the Admin?"

He's stalling, and I want to jump across the table and carve the smug expression from his face, but Vitruzzi answers him, "Because a man like you wouldn't move an inch without keeping something as valuable as those coordinates with you. Maybe you will try to attack Agate Beach. But not if it means we get to the Fortress before you do. Erikson told us why you want the disc. And whether we're successful or not, once we hit the Fortress, the Admin will be on full alert. If you wait, you'll never get another opportunity like this. A man like you has priorities, doesn't he?" She scans his face, trying to read whether she judged correctly. Aside from a slight flaring of his nostrils, his expression doesn't change. "The truth is, Rajcik, we have no reason to fight with you. Just give us what we want, and we never have to see each other again."

He seems to consider for a moment. "You seem very sure of yourself. And I have your guarantee that you'll give us the seeds?"

My patience snaps. "Goddammit, Rajcik. Just give us the fucking coordinates."

He glances toward me with hate in his eyes. Nothing else on his face betrays the slightest hint of emotion, but that look says my death warrant has been signed and he is only waiting for the ink to dry.

Still looking at me, he reaches carefully into his cargo jacket and withdraws a small data disc. With a carefree flick of the wrist, he tosses it onto the table as if it were nothing more than a piece of trash.

Vitruzzi picks it up and plugs it into the disc slot of a portable VDU. After pulling up the information, she hands it across me to Desto. I catch a glimpse of the screen and see enough to feel confident he's given us what we want.

Desto studies the coordinates for a moment and then nods his head. "Should work."

Vitruzzi retrieves the device and speaks into her comlink. "Karl, be ready for pickup in ten minutes." Stuffing the device into the breast pocket of her jacket, she returns her focus to Rajcik.

"All right. I want you both to stand up and put your weapons on the table. Her too," she adds, glancing at Ortiz.

Rajcik smirks, appearing to be amused by something, and slowly pushes his chair back as he rises. As he raises his hands, the pistol he'd been leveling under the table comes into view. He keeps the barrel pointed toward the floor and flips the grip out to Vitruzzi as the rest of us stand. To an outsider witnessing our synchronized movements, it must look as if a bomb has exploded beneath us in slow motion. Desto reaches out with the hand not gripping his shotgun and takes the pistol. With no weapon of my own, I ball my empty fingers into tight fists, my nerves kindling in anticipation of what could happen in the next few seconds.

No one makes any unexpected movements as Rajcik reaches for the shotgun he left leaning against the table, preparing to give it over as well. Hypervigilance, a side effect of having reencountered someone I left for dead in years past, causes me to glance toward MacCready, and I don't like what I see.

Rage has contorted his features into a terrible grimace and his ice-blue eyes, dangerously lucid, are fixed on me. There's no need to think about what his expression means; instinct screams he's about to pull his weapon and start firing. "Vitruzzi! Watch him!" I yell and immediately turn to Desto, pushing him hard sideways with the full weight of my body and out of MacCready's target area.

Caught off guard by my abrupt shove, Desto loses his balance and we topple to the ground in a frantic jumble. Grabbing the pistol he'd taken from me and rolling onto my side, I fire upward through the table now blocking my view. It splinters down the center and I lunge to my feet, viciously shoving the pistol into Rajcik's chin, relishing the way he flinches from the hot barrel. My body acts on its own—thoughts, sensations, emotions, and conscience all a distant echo, far from the me that's present and handling the situation. Instinct is in control here, keeping me alive. I don't know why I'm pointing the pistol at Rajcik instead of MacCready, but I know it's the right move.

"Fuck! Christ! Fuck!" MacCready wails, leaning against the wall behind him. My shot had hit home. Blood cascades down his mutilated firing arm, which hangs askance, the fabric and flesh mixed in a shredded, smoldering waste. His weapon skitters across the floor away from him as he clutches his damaged arm.

Disjointed awareness strikes me. Everything around me except MacCready has grown completely still. My immediate focus stays on the pistol in my hand, ready to turn Rajcik's head into negative space if he even flinches. Vitruzzi stands a short distance behind me and to my right. I sense that she has one of her pistols aimed at Rajcik's chest and the other at my midsection, but this doesn't concern me. Ortiz also points her weapon at me, and Desto has a bead on MacCready with his rifle. If he fires at this proximity, its spray will cut everyone in front of him, including me, down.

Sharp smoke stings my nose and eyes as I glare at Rajcik. His head is tilted slightly back by the pressure of the gun in my hand, and his jaw is clenched so tightly that veins stand out at both of his temples. He still holds the shotgun he'd been picking up by the barrel and stares at Vitruzzi, waiting for her to pass judgment.

"Drop them." Her voice demands compliance.

"Do it," Rajcik growls through clenched teeth, thanks to the barrel wedged against his jaw.

Ortiz slowly lowers her own weapon and kicks it forward.

I remain in the same position, the frustration and anger inside me holding me frozen. I want to pull the trigger until my Sinbad is empty. I don't know what stops me.

"Erikson, we got it. Back up," Vitruzzi demands, but I can't. Rajcik has to pay.

"Erikson!" She finally gets through, the sharpness in her tone making my eyes jerk toward her. "Keep your weapon pointed. Step back."

Something—is it compassion?—in her expression carries more force than her words and my legs unlock. As the Sinbad's muzzle leaves Rajcik's throat, he lowers his gleaming black eyes to us, his lips stretched into a snarl. MacCready's face is arranged in an agonized rictus, and he drools with the pain while still holding his butchered shoulder. He's hurt too seriously to be a threat any longer.

"Move," she commands, jerking her head toward the door.

So quickly that none of us have time to stop him, Rajcik turns to MacCready. Like a battering ram, his fist hammers forward and connects with the bump in the center of MacCready's throat with enough force to slam him against the wall. MacCready gasps loudly, as if his voice is made of screeching metal being sheered from the body of a ship, and a fountain of blood erupts from his mouth.

"You won't make another mistake like that, Marcus," Rajcik says, his voice pitched low and quiet as if sympathizing with a dead man's relative. He keeps his back turned to us, unconcerned with the fact that three weapons are aimed at it. MacCready grips his throat with his usable hand, trying hard to suck air through his ruined trachea.

Blood bubbles from the corners of his mouth and joins the light, steady stream still pouring from his arm. It's hard to watch him struggling to draw breath, despite my loathing for him.

Rajcik's expression stays blank, as if he's watching nothing more than clouds shift, and without turning he says, "This must make you happy, Aly."

My throat feels tight and gummy, and my response has to be forced out. "Ecstatic."

Vitruzzi jumps in, not bothering to mask the disgust in her voice. "Time to go, Rajcik."

There's a loud croaking sound as MacCready's whole body makes one last attempt for air, then he goes completely still. His eyes continue to stare up at Rajcik, bulging like the eyes of a starved lunatic, and slowly begin to glaze over. His body remains rigidly erect.

I'm still staring at him when Desto puts a hand on my shoulder, gently nudging me forward. "I got the rear. Keep that pointed where it's most useful," he says, nodding toward my pistol.

SIXTEEN

It's been hours, maybe six, maybe more. The days are blending together as we cross the darkness of space. The crew sits in the com room and hovers around the shining image of the Fortress. We've spent another marathon session exhausting every idea, no matter how far-fetched, for cracking the enigma of how to get in. Still nothing to show for it.

Venus stops in and drops off an armload of food. Flight rations never taste good and desperation curbs our appetites further, making it hard to eat. I do it anyway, mechanically forcing down a few nutrition bars followed by some bottles of electrolyte-packed fluids. Physical and mental preparedness are paramount and I'm not allowing anything to inhibit my readiness for this mission. It's the most important thing I'll ever do. The others eat too, talking among themselves and trying to pretend things are under control, but the worry and uncertainty is taking a toll on everyone. If we don't solve the puzzle in the next thirty-six to forty hours, this will turn into a kamikaze mission. Even so, that won't stop us. That's how dedicated they are— *we* are.

"This makes me think of this thing that happened on Ammi Duc when I was still in Terrestrial and Atmospheric R&D." Bodie sits backward on his chair, head resting on his hands. "We had these burrowing creatures beneath the surface that kept getting into the food storage. Every time we'd flush them out and close another line of tunnels, it would only take them a few hours to start an entirely new system. Eventually, the thermals couldn't tell old tunnels from new ones, the critters just kept digging and re-digging so fast. We spent days analyzing their system, trying to find a way to cut them off so they'd leave the food alone. It was mind-boggling. Just like this shit." A frustrated sigh explodes from his lips, blowing the curling hair of his mustache outward.

"So how did you solve it?" Brady asks.

He shrugs. "Only way we could. Exterminated them and collapsed the tunnels on top of them. Not an option I recommend in this case," he adds hurriedly.

"No, I guess not," Desto says, pushing back from the table and starting another round of pacing. "Fuck."

Mental restlessness and fatigue is starting to push me into Crazyville, the same as the rest of them. "I'm going to take a few. Walk around and clear my head."

"Yeah, good idea. I think I'll take a shower. Want to join me, babe?" Desto asks, flashing me a leer that doesn't even scratch the surface of the crudeness of his thoughts.

"Not even if I'd just fallen into a sewer," I respond, but smile wearily, grateful for any attempt to lighten the mood.

"Hey, that's all right. I like it dirty too," he answers with his own grin, and heads toward the community washroom.

Bodie remains behind with Brady and Vitruzzi, none of them quite ready to leave the problem alone yet, and I exit behind Desto.

The silence inside the corridor, punctuated by the distant, rhythmic thrumming of the engines, closes around me like a trap. Walking through it makes me feel alone, isolated in my own anxiety. In reality, no more relaxing than slamming my head against a brick wall a few million times. I have to find something to keep my mind off the situation, give it rest before I throw myself out of the hold out of sheer frustration. I make a left toward the crew quarters, deciding to break down my weapons and clean them. Not that they need it.

When I reach the long corridor leading to the bunks, the sound of a cabin door sliding closed draws my attention. Lights come through Strahan's window, and before thinking about it, I head in that direction. Maybe a little company will be a better remedy for escaping my grim thoughts than an attempt to blank out on routine, which I know will fail.

I hit the buzzer. A second later, he opens the door and stares at me, shirtless and surprised. There's no missing the patchwork of scars, burns and a few roundly uniform bullet wounds, peppering his muscular torso. His brows are ridged in a frown and he doesn't say anything, just stands there.

I have nothing to say either. Lamely, I ask, "How's the leg?"

"Healing."

I should have thought about this before walking down here. Besides the few encounters we've had at the Beach, Strahan and I have barely spoken. We're just soldiers on a mission, thrown into the same mix by random forces. Which doesn't exactly make us friends. What am I doing here?

This was a mistake. "Glad to hear it," I remark, and spin around to walk to my own bunk.

Then I hear him step into the corridor. "Wait a sec, Erikson. I'm sorry. Hold on, will you?"

Maybe he'll drop it if I pretend not to hear him and keep walking. Instead, I turn around. I don't know why, maybe because of the understanding in his voice.

"You came by to talk and I act like an asshole. I apologize, okay? You and I started off on the wrong foot, and things are getting more fucked up lately. I'm just edgy." He gives me a lopsided grin. "I tell you what—I've got a bottle of peacemaker under my bunk. Have a drink with me. We can chat, you know, try to be civil for once. Wait right there." He ducks back into his cabin, re-emerging moments later holding a clear plastic bottle. "What do you say?"

I'm not sure what to make of this. I'm still the outsider here. But four days from now we'll all probably be dead, so what is there to lose?

"Thanks," I say, and step in.

A bunk juts from the left wall, blankets meticulously tucked, a door to the bathroom opens to the rear, and a cargo box that looks as if it may be used for a table sits on the floor against the right wall. It's exactly the same as my cabin. Feeling cramped, I sit down on the box and he follows me in, leaving the door open. Wrestling on a shirt that's the same dull uniform gray that everything washed time and again in a ship's water-recycling system becomes, he says, "Shit. I don't think I have any cups. Hold on a second and I'll go get some."

"It's all right. I don't need one."

With a grin, a look as unfamiliar on his face as it has lately been on mine, he sits down. The top of the bottle comes off with a quick twist. "To comrades," he says, swallowing deeply. His eyes fill with water and he passes it to me.

"Right." I take the bottle, tilt the neck toward him in a salute, and take a swallow of my own. Instantly, my tongue curls up and I have to force my throat to open wide enough for the burning liquid to pass. "Oh my god, what is that?" It streams into my stomach with the same caustic flow as molten lava.

"Like it? I got it as part of a trade for some mining tools we lifted a while ago. We had about sixty bottles, but we're down to just a few. Good stuff." He takes another drink.

You're insane could be written on my face. The stuff tasted as if it were radioactive pond scum filtered through gasoline. He extends the bottle to me, but I shake my head "no." So he puts it on the floor between us. The closeness of the cabin makes it seem like a good idea to have something solid between us.

"How long—?" I start.

"I know—" he starts.

We both stop. This time he waits for me to go first.

"So how long have you and Vitruzzi been flying together?" I'm fidgety and find it hard to sit still, so I grab the bottle for another drink. My throat rebels with slightly less outrage this time.

"Since just after the Soldier's Rebellion. I was in the hospital when it happened, just three months shy of my time being up. I'd been part of a suppression squad, dealing with a manufacturing riot on Obal 4 and lost my real leg. Vitruzzi was my doctor." He takes another long gulp. "She's brilliant. The technology that saved my leg from amputation, bioregeneration, she developed it. I was the first patient to have the procedure done. Took eight months to get everything working right, but Eleanor was persistent. Stubborn, in fact. She wasn't going to fail. Anyway, we had a lot of time to get to know each other."

"So what's she doing flying cargo now?" I still haven't puzzled this out.

"I'd already been planning on buying my own cargo ship when my time was up. Had a few bucks saved, and planned on working as a pilot until I could get the rest together. Flying interstellar cruise ships or corporate jobs. You know, where the real money is."

Strahan's personality isn't exactly a model of the conventionally affable, easy-going cruiser pilot, and I smirk at the idea of him giving deck tours to sliced and molded women in overpriced evening gowns. Catching my expression, he smiles back.

"Yeah, it was just an idea. Anyway, V decided it was time to change careers after the shit hit the fan during the Rebellion. She had the capital and she was able to get the weapons contract because of her standing in the medical branch and high-profile achievements, and we went into business together."

He's avoiding telling me the full story, but I know it's no good to press. There's a reason, probably a damn good one, that Vitruzzi decided to "change careers," as he puts it. "And what about Desto?"

"Bomani? Another deserter. He was into small-time black-marketing on Chum Miro. That's where the *Sphynx* came from. He needed a job and we needed someone who wasn't afraid to break the rules. Desto and Bodie are the best two guys I've ever had at my back."

"Best two guys, huh?"

"Except recently. I mean . . . well, you took care of business out there on R'Kadia. So, now I've got three . . ."

I hadn't intended to fluster him, but his surprising embarrassment is amusing. I take another drink, beginning to enjoy the signature fireball spreading through my guts. If not for the nutrition bars helping absorb the asbestoslike liquid, I would probably have a hard time walking. The room is beginning to feel hot and smaller by the second. We both look at the bottle so we don't have to look at each other. Neither of us are much for small talk, apparently, so I decide to make my exit. Maybe the booze will help me catch a few minutes of sleep. But he asks another question.

"So what will you do once we get your brother off the Fortress?"

It's the first hint of optimism I've heard in regard to David, and it's strangely comforting. "You mean if we don't all get blown into tiny molecules of space-born carbon?" My optimism, on the other hand, is tempered by my realism. "Business as usual, I guess. The black market is fairly competitive, and we've got a lot of experience. We're done with Rajcik, though, if that's what you're getting at."

He gives me a considering look. "Sounds a little pointless to me," he says and hands me the bottle.

He isn't trying to pick a fight or pass judgment; the comment comes across as a detached observation, so I let it slide. Taking the bottle, I bring the subject back to him and Vitruzzi. "If you and Vitruzzi are partners, why is she captain?"

"She's smart, she's capable, and she had the money. I've never been anything but a soldier. It just makes sense. I don't want to be in charge of a ship. This crew is . . . they're more than friends, you know? Eleanor just has what it takes to lead, and it's easier for me to follow. She knows how to keep things from coming unraveled. It's hard to explain."

He doesn't need to. I know exactly what he's saying. It's not hard to take command, but people like Strahan, and like me, reject leadership. Independence is easier; inviting people to rely on you is asking for trouble. It's asking to be let down, or to let them down. And that's hard to live with, that kind of pressure. It just means you have more to lose. People like Strahan and I have seen how ugly the universe can be. We have that joyless ability to look ahead and see all the bad things that can happen, and who wants to be responsible for leading others into them? It's not cowardice—in a twisted way, it's hope. If you're not close to people, you can't hurt them. We're quite a pair.

Swigging another drink from the bottle, I'm astonished to find it more than half empty. We'd killed a lot of it while talking. It's strange how easy it is to be with him, now that we've both relaxed and forgotten to be enemies for a second. Or maybe it's just the rotgut, melting away my instinctive caution and numbing my live-wire nerves. Whatever, it's time to go. "Look, thanks for the drink. I should get going. We don't have much time left before we reach the Fortress."

He gets up too. "We should take another look at the disc in a couple of hours. I know there's something we're not seeing, but it's there. We just have to keep at it."

Is he stalling me?

"Sounds good."

He nods but looks distracted. Nothing left to say, I start to step through the door. Strahan stops me with a hand on my elbow. I turn, and his face is inches from mine. I can feel the heat that radiates from his body. Or is it just me?

No.

Yes.

No.

As delicately as I can, I pull my arm out of his grip.

"Strahan, this can't happen."

"Why?" His eyes are gentle, and the same color as fall leaves right before the icy winter wind takes them. The emotion in them is intense, confining. It's hard for me to speak.

"It's just not possible. I can't let anything complicate this mission."

On a hair-trigger, his face grows hard and his brows knit together. "Dammit, Erikson, are you so focused on killing that you don't know how to live?"

The strike-first-or-strike-back instinct in me makes me want to hit him, but I bottle it. Yanking my elbow from his grip and careening into the corridor, nearly falling down the stairs in his doorway, I lurch toward my bunk. There's a thump against the wall behind me, like a fist striking it in anger, but I don't turn around to look. Maybe it's impossible to get along with someone so like yourself. Maybe it's just impossible for us.

<h1 style="text-align:center">SEVENTEEN</h1>

"We should've killed him."

I'm sitting in the navigator's seat in the *Sphynx*'s flight control deck, both hands clasped tightly around the seat mounts, staring across a few hundred meters of space at the *Temptation*'s stern. It isn't that the seat isn't stable; the reason my knuckles are white is because we're about to let Rajcik go.

Venus sits at the helm, swiftly punching through systems checks. Whether she's ignoring me or just can't hear my under-the-breath comment through the din of her own clamorous thoughts isn't important. Vitruzzi made it clear that we're holding up our end of the deal, believing, recklessly in my opinion, that Rajcik might still be useful.

The speed in which new schematics pop on and off the pilot display creates a chaotic strobe effect, fracturing my focus. But Venus seems to be absorbing the split-second information with casual ease, speaking in her customary rapid clip as she does.

"There's a slight tension that we can't work out of the ejector coils, but it's easily offset if we just run the core rotor at .05 amps higher . . ." Her voice becomes part of the background as she explains each observation, quickly oversaturating my interest.

"Whoa, hold it, Venus. Can you go through that a little more slowly?" A curious image catches my eye. "That can't be what it looked like."

Shrugging, she reverses the system feed, stopping when I point. "There."

A starboard missile launch tube glows from the display in as much stark detail as the real thing.

Scanning the image closely anyway for a few seconds, I just want to make sure I'm not mistaken. "I'd really like to know how you've managed to hide functioning weapons systems from Admin inspections."

"Oh yeah, it's not that hard actually." She smiles. "You see, the missile tubes are here, beneath the cargo bay floor, instead of on the outer flanks of the ship like it was originally designed. Bodie, Desto, and Pat built the new launch tubes after the captain brought the *Sphynx* to Spectra 6. The Admin had just yanked off the launch activators and pulled all the tube plating off. Bodie and the guys rerouted the afterburn jets into the old tubes, covered them with heavier graphite plating, and added a little extra piece. Lead inner walls. Pat took some radioisotope aluminum freezers and lined the tubes with their parts to keep the lead from getting too hot. So, the jets help keep the inside of the ship warm, but the heat can't get to the lead walls, which makes it impossible for scanners to see what's inside. Namely, the missile tubes."

Vitruzzi hadn't been bluffing when she'd told Rajcik we'd be keeping him in missile range. This bird is still hot. I look closely at the schematic and have her zoom out so I can see the outline of the whole cargo bay. As I suspect, the armory doubles as the loading room, and the missile tubes can be fed directly from inside. They're well camouflaged; I hadn't suspected a thing when I'd been there to get ammunition from Desto. The vault being reinforced by blast walls and located midship isn't just a convenient accident. If the ship were attacked or damaged, anyone inside would be safe and able to feed and probably even launch the missiles until they ran out or the threat was eradicated. And from the outside, there's no way to tell what secrets lay hidden in the heart of the *Sphynx*.

"So where are the ejection portals?"

"The hydraulic doors, disguised as off-gassing vents beneath the main engine. If anyone even notices them, they know not to open them without depressurizing first. We've got the real off-gassing chambers linked into the tubes, so if we need to shunt into them, I can either do it from my console, or from the backup console in the armory."

"There's a system controller in the armory?"

"Yep. It's all there, in another room. You get to it using a code in the door keypad."

"Who knows the code and how to operate it?"

She looks up from the display and raises an amused eyebrow. "You have to be in the secret club, Aly." Satisfied with my nonplussed expression, she continues, "Kidding. It's all of us, the regular crew. And Pat."

I almost have to laugh. They've been in total control of this situation from the minute Rajcik landed on Spectra 6. Vitruzzi could say the word anytime and blow him out of the sky inside of seconds. With the *Temptation*'s onboard weapon detection system, Rajcik knows it, which explains why he hasn't tried even once to shake us in the six days that have passed since we left Spectra 6.

Why hadn't they told me any of this? Rationally, it makes no sense for me to resent being kept in the dark, about everything, starting with the tracking device and going all the way to the *Sphynx*'s battle capabilities. Why would they have trusted me with information that could have benefited Rajcik? They couldn't have taken any chances; if I'd been lying about my loyalty to him, I might have given him everything he needed to sweep into Agate Beach and take anything he wanted any time that was convenient for him, even if Vitruzzi's crew didn't go for the joint-effort assault on the Fortress.

Still, a spasm of, I don't know, disappointment, regret . . . some emotion I'd rather not examine twists through me. Almost two weeks we've been together, working side by side, fighting, planning, hell,

I've even risked my life for them. What does it take to make them trust me? Accept me as part of the crew?

Venus stares at me quizzically, reading the thoughts play across my face, and I turn away. Forget it. This is how it is. We're partners. Not friends, not comrades. Business associates locked into an arrangement, a contract of defiance against the odds threatening to tear our lives apart. I better get used to it and stop letting things that don't matter distract me.

We've flown more than three-quarters of the distance to where Rajcik's coordinates put the Fortress. Three hours ago, Vitruzzi and Brady informed the crew that the time has come to cut him loose. We're so close now we can almost feel the Fortress's malignancy like a black hole in our flight path. It's a gamble to believe Rajcik will keep his promise and continue his intended mission instead of doubling back to attack the Beach, maybe the biggest gamble any of us have ever been forced to make. Vitruzzi says the settlement has an evacuation procedure in the case of such an event, and the equipment to know if he, or anyone, is coming. While I have my doubts about the settlement's preparedness, each passing day reveals something new and astonishing about these people, pushing those doubts further into the dust.

Vitruzzi hails Rajcik from the com room and I shove my concerns aside, all my focus on what's about to happen. From our seats on the flight control deck, Venus and I watch the linked pilot's VDU.

"This is it, Rajcik. We're done here. Remember, we did everything we said we would. You have your seeds and you have Vilbrandt. I suggest you take both of them and disappear."

Standing up before his video uplink and crossing his arms over his wide chest, his response is woodenly sincere. "Captain Vitruzzi, make no mistake. This won't be the last time we see each other." He lets his gaze linger on her for few seconds and motions to Thompson, standing behind him. "I want you to tell Aly something for me. Tell her I'm sorry to be losing such a competent crewmember, but it was inevitable. I knew that long before she did." He pauses, and a cold feeling begins creeping through my guts. Outside the flight control deck screen, the *Temptation*'s main engines start cycling rapidly in preparation for hyperspeed.

"Tell her she should have trusted her instincts when she realized I hadn't left the escape shuttle on Obal 3." Another pause, and a shadow comes across his features as if he's uncertain whether or not to continue. "She accused me of having no loyalty, and she's right. But loyalty is one of *her* flaws, not mine."

Black eyes shining like crystals, he continues, "Just let her know: I *gave* her and David to the Admin before his misguided ideas of moral superiority convinced him to turn on me. Vitruzzi, are you listening?"

She doesn't respond, and he keeps talking. "Make sure she knows that her brother is at the Fortress. I made that a special part of my arrangement with T'Kai. I'll be there too, waiting for her. And I'll be looking forward to our reunion." His teeth flash in a savage grin. "And one last thing. Give her this; it's *her* payback for the mission. Tell her to enjoy." And he reaches for his console.

"What the hell . . .?" There doesn't seem to be enough air in my lungs to finish the question. Stunned, I rise from the seat and stare into the empty void where the *Temptation* had been before it suddenly disappeared deeper into space, too fast for the eye to see. Rajcik has made his break, out of weapons range already.

The flight control VDU abruptly goes black, then lights up with a new image: a video feed. I instantly realize that I'm staring into a prison cell. Dingy green-painted walls seem to absorb all the high intensity light coming from fixtures on the ceiling, but it's the man sitting next to the wall, his head resting on his knees and his arms around his legs, that catches my attention. It's David.

The cell is completely empty besides him. He's wearing the same clothes as the day I lost him in the Obal 3 sub docks, but now the gray material is spotted here and there with tarnished maroon streaks that can only be dried blood. The fact that I'm looking at my brother in a cell on the Fortress isn't something my mind has to grasp; every cell in my body already knows it. My legs seem to disappear, collapsing from beneath me like so much rushing water. Falling forward, both of my hands come to rest alongside the display, but my eyes don't budge from the console. I feel as if I've been hit in the stomach with a sledgehammer.

There's a tinny clang in the background of the video feed. Alarmed, David quickly raises his head from his knees and my mouth goes dry as I glimpse his hardly recognizable face, thoroughly misshapen and swollen. Bruises cover everything and a deep laceration splits the skin above one eyebrow. His lips are torn in at least two places. But his eyes are the worst. The lids have puffed up to the size of tennis balls, stuck fast to his cheeks by a dried puslike fluid seeping from behind them. There's no doubt that he's reacting to the sound, but he can't possibly see what it is.

As quickly as the image appears, it's gone. I remain leaning over the display, my body devoid of sensation for the moment, just waiting . . . for Rajcik, for the image to continue, for my screams to split the ship open and spill me into space. The room around me begins to recede, shrinking into blackness, and my focus dims down into two tiny points before my eyes. Finally my legs give out completely and I land on my hands and knees, torso clenching in dry heaves.

"Erikson, hey, Erikson. Just take a deep breath."

Strahan's words seep through a disconnected part of my brain. When had he come in? His hands gently grip my shoulders, senselessly trying to help me hold it together. And then everything in me suddenly breaks free from reality, from rational thought, from control.

"NO!" I'm on my feet, flailing madly at his hands. If I get by him, I'll knock Venus from the pilot's seat and take control of the *Sphynx*, chase Rajcik down and kill him, the way I should have back on Spectra 6. The scorching desire propels me into a frenzy, wildly punching Strahan and lunging to get free of his grip, but it's useless. He's too strong, too prepared. My frantic onslaught is no more effective against his restraint than fire against water.

"Take it easy, take it easy, Erikson." He keeps talking, his voice too calm to punch through my anguish. But his grip is relentless and he presses my body firmly against the rear wall, not letting me free. "Calm down. We'll get him. We'll get your brother. Just take it easy."

My body isn't listening to me anymore; it has come undone. This must be what if feels like to plummet so far into hopeless, agonizing despair that you become embedded in the bottom, glued and trapped, drowning in poison. I'm powerless to do anything but collapse against the wall, held up by Strahan. My eyes close, and I hope I never have to open them again.

His warm breath puffs against my cheeks. "Look, Aly, we're going to find your brother, okay? He may still be alive. Are you listening? Don't give up, because we're going to find him. We need your help. *He needs your help.*"

I open my eyes and see his face centimeters away, rearranged into an expression I hardly recognize. His sepia eyes are filled with concern, staring into mine. Hot tears burn my cheeks. Patiently, he holds onto me, providing a solid foundation, letting me process the image of my wounded brother, but keeping me from harming anyone, or myself. Finally, my breathing steadies. Time begins ticking again and awareness creeps back. In another few seconds, I take a deep breath, and let it out slowly.

He relaxes some of the pressure on my shoulders and I straighten up. "Are you all right?"

Nodding is an effort, but I don't trust myself to speak yet. The cockpit door opens and Vitruzzi steps hurriedly through, worry stamped on her face. Taking in the situation quickly, she doesn't need to ask how I'd reacted. She looks at me and asks, "That was your brother?"

Swallowing and swiping an arm across my hot face, I answer in a choked voice, "Yeah."

To Strahan: "Do you think that was a live feed or recorded?"

With a final examination to make sure I'm in control, he lets his hands drop from my shoulders. "It had to be recorded. How could he get a live broadcast from the Fortress?"

"Unless her brother's not really at the Fortress. Do you think he could be using him as bait, Erikson? Trying to set a trap for us?"

Vitruzzi's questions pierce the shock-fog enveloping my brain. What would Rajcik have to gain by sending me footage of David, suffering and beaten, other than a sick sense of retribution for our betrayal? No, Rajcik isn't trying to lead us anywhere that we're not already going. He does know me well. He knows we'll be coming to the Fortress and that he's given me all the incentive I need. He knows I won't stop until I find David, or we're both dead.

I shake my head. "No. He's trying to keep us close. He wants revenge." There's no longer any need to emphasize how cruel he can be. They've finally seen it for themselves.

From the corner of my eye I see Bodie and Desto join the group, standing just outside the flight deck hatchway. They must have heard me scream. Venus has turned around to look at me, for once entirely still, a sympathetic frown etched across her pale face. The depth and sincerity of their concern is real, making me uncomfortable. At what point did they start caring about my brother?

Vitruzzi glances around the room, taking in everyone's condition. No one says anything, as if we're all waiting for the next thing to happen. Finally, she says, "Okay, this is it. Karl, you and Bodie take the controls for a couple of hours and give Venus a break. Stay alert. Rajcik is unpredictable. Everyone else, take a break too. We're not going to get many chances from here. We'll all get back together in the com room in four hours. According to the coordinates, we're within three days of the Fortress. That's all the time we have. We need to make some decisions. Any questions?"

No.

"Erikson, can I talk to you in private?"

My legs are stiff as I follow her off the flight deck. Before we're out of range, I hear Desto say in a low voice, "Man, that was some of the most fucked-up shit I've ever seen. For Rajcik's sake, I hope her brother's alive."

Rajcik's a dead man. Whether I find David or not.

WE STEP UP a short stairway into the com room, situated astern and above the flight deck. After closing the door, she turns and says, "Look, Erikson, I know you're only with us because you're hoping your brother still has a chance. But there's something I have to know." Her focus is intense, uncompromising. "We don't know how old that video is. He may already be dead. You realize that."

She pauses, and the words seep like acid into my brain. "Yeah. I know that."

There's deep concern in her eyes, but her voice doesn't waver as she asks her next question. "What if he is? Are you going to stick with us if we get in there and don't find anything, or maybe just his body? I have to know how far we can count on you to go."

It's a fair question, but one I don't have to think about. "I'm in this until the end, Vitruzzi."

She stares at me for another second and nods. There is zero equivocation in my plans, and she knows it. Maybe she can see that if David is dead, the only thing I'm going to care about is revenge. Which means, no matter what, I'm in to the bitter end.

It takes me a few minutes to get myself together after talking with Vitruzzi. Standing in the washroom of my bunk and splashing cold water on my face gives me a chance to think deeply for the first time about how I'm going to cope with it if we don't find David alive. The thought has always crouched in the recesses of my brain where dark and hateful things live, things I rarely allow myself to think about. Now as I stare into the mirror, cold water dripping in rivulets down my nose and cheeks, the same resolve that helped me escape a loveless home, then desert the tyranny of the Corps, and has now freed me from Rajcik's control, is still there. If there's a chance David's alive, I'll search every centimeter of that station until I find him. And if he's dead, nothing in the universe will keep me from finding Rajcik and ending him.

EIGHTEEN

The sound of Brady's voice over the intercom yanks me harshly from a restless sleep.

"Everyone to the com room! An Admin patroller is boarding us. Get your asses up here now!"

Panic and adrenaline send sparks of electric saliva shooting into my mouth. Within seconds, I'm fully dressed, jamming the Mini-Derg into my boot and racing to the com room.

The crew piles inside, everyone strapping on or zipping up the bits of equipment they'd grabbed on the way, and Brady lays out the situation. "They pinged us two minutes ago. Routine sweep ship. They said they're looking for a fugee. I'm sure they mean you."

There's no way to interpret the look he gives me. "How could they know where I am?"

"Not the issue. We have to get you hidden. Go to the ammo vault with Desto." He turns to him. "Hide in the fire control room. We've got legal manifests that put us in the area, so, as long as they don't find you, we shouldn't have any trouble. Stay put until I give the all clear. They'll be here in five."

I'm already on the way to the vault by the time he's done talking, with Desto following closely. Once we get inside the ammo vault, he uses the interior keypad to open a hidden hatch in the floor.

Climbing in behind me, he slides the door closed overhead. "Keep quiet. We'll shake these guys fast. Nothing to worry about."

It takes a few seconds for my eyes to adjust to the dimness, helped by the glow from a console anchored against one of the steel walls. The background hum of the *Sphynx*'s engines begins to grow quieter and a couple minutes pass before they stop altogether. The ship's slowing motion creates the disconcerting feeling of reaching the vertex of an arc, hovering for a moment, and then plunging back downward in an unchecked dive. There's a sharp jerk as the Admin ship's boarding shuttle connects with the external airlock, reinstating the sense of gravity. Standing totally still, I listen with my entire body, trying to hear what may be happening on the cargo deck. Of course, it's futile; the overhead bay floor is engineered with thick steel plating designed to sustain the ship's integrity in the case of a ballistic attack, muting all sound and cutting us off from everything happening above. We're locked in the dark with no way to control the situation.

But not helpless. One benefit of being on ship for nearly ten years in the Corps: I know my way around a flight control deck and weapons systems. A quick investigation of the fire control console and I easily locate and enable the target acquisition sensor. Desto doesn't notice, standing at the top of the stairs with his pistol drawn, waiting for a reason to jump out like a bogeyman jack-in-the-box. The image display lights up sharply with a schematic of the *Sphynx* floating inside a dull green circle, overlaid by a grid pattern. I'm seeing a 360-degree view from the perspective of the ship's current position relative to everything outside. Triangulated guidance points hover in the display's upper corner, waiting to be trained on their objective. The diagram only shows a one-kilometer circumference, which is nothing but emptiness. Placing my fingers on the zoom controls, I'm able to enlarge the visual area. As I do, the image of the ship shrinks on the screen, but now I can make out the Admin sweep ship about three klicks from our stern. Zooming closer, I get a bead on her main generator and bring both missile guidance points to lock on. If anyone at the *Sphynx*'s helm is also attempting to operate the system, apparently this console has override power. Good for me. A single, nonrepulsed missile from the *Sphynx* could blast the Admin ship into dust if I hit it right. And if anyone comes through the hatch besides one of the *Sphynx*'s crew, that's exactly what I'll do. One strike and you're out, two and you're annihilated, you bastards.

Desto turns and sees what I'm up to. "Erikson, what the hell—?"

Both of us suddenly freeze in place as the door to the weapons vault above opens and footsteps belonging to two or three people enter the room. The cargo bay floor may be soundproof, but noise travels more easily from the vault through the hidden hatch. Desto's eyes move in a plane from the hatch, to me, to the console, and he gives me a short nod. He knows what I'm doing.

"Your manifests look legitimate, Captain Vitruzzi. We just have to check every room in case you have a stowaway. Someone you don't know is here, of course." A male voice. Unfamiliar. Probably the Admin ship's commander.

"I understand, Major." Vitruzzi's composure is unearthly; even through the floor she sounds as cool as ever. Knowing she can lie so convincingly marginally increases my sense of security.

"I have to admit," the man continues, "it's rare for a citizen to have such a generous contract. An unarmed ship carrying this caliber and volume of weaponry could create problems if it were to get into the wrong hands."

What is he implying? Is he playing with us? My head is tilted, my ear toward the ceiling trying to hear his voice more clearly, looking for a cue that it's time to render the Admin ship into fragments of unidentifiable space trash. Vitruzzi says nothing, but I can imagine the way her jaw clenches at his barely concealed accusation. More footsteps overhead.

"Sir, everyone on the ship is accounted for. One thing seems out of place. We found an extra bunk that has recently been occupied. It's empty now, but there are no passengers listed on the manifest."

Shit. They found my bunk. There's a grating sound and I picture the insufferable officer rotating on his boot heels to face Vitruzzi. "Captain?"

"We took a non-cit passenger from Letum Uti to Dro'an. Dropped him off yesterday. You can verify that with my nav-planner." That same casualness. There's no hidden challenge in her voice, but if they look and the nav-planner hasn't been fixed to show landings on the two Obal moons—landings we didn't make—we may get a trip to the Fortress after all. Of the one-way variety. My fingers dance jerkily on the targeting console, ready to launch the eagles.

"That's all right, Captain. I know there are numerous difficulties involved in living on the unsettled planets. Anything to make a little extra cash, right?" I can't speak for her, but I'd like to bust the smug bastard in the mouth.

"Thank you, Major."

His portable manifest reader emits a beep as he shuts it off, saying, "Your cooperation has been excellent. I'll make a note of it. We're done here."

Their footsteps retreat and the vault door slides shut again. That was too fucking close, but it doesn't mean they'll be leaving. I'll just keep my eyes on them for a while, see what happens. Fifteen minutes later their shuttle flies into view and docks, their engines spin up, and they're gone. Sitting in the semidarkness waiting for Vitruzzi to give the all clear, I'm thinking now would be a good time for another slug of that paint thinner Strahan and I had been drinking a few short hours ago.

"We've swept the ship for surveillance devices. Come on out."

Vitruzzi stands at the top of the hatch and beckons. She doesn't have to ask twice; two hours of killing time in this dungeon, time that should be spent working on the Fortress op, is plenty.

"What did you find?" Desto asks, coming up behind me. Despite the sober inquiry, I can practically feel his eyes crawling over my ass.

"Usual. Bugs, a couple of imagers. We fried them. Venus says the ship's out of range, so they're not coming back to ask why."

That's all I need to know.

After grabbing a box of compressed fruit blocks and a jug of water from the galley, I head directly to the com room, prepared to spend every remaining minute locked inside with the disc. Three days left. Three days until I know whether David is alive or dead. Thirty-six hours until I spill every drop of the toxic sludge that stands in for Rajcik's blood. Everyone lives for a reason, and I have two.

Strahan and Bodie walk in. Barely glancing up, I nod and quickly return my attention to the plans.

"Anything new?" Bodie asks.

"Not a goddamn thing." My voice is strained in frustration.

I feel Strahan's gaze, like a hot ray of light, resting on my face. When I look up, he's passing me the jug of water. "Let's see what we can see."

Bodie takes a seat and Strahan leans against the reader, their scrutiny equaling mine. For a while, no one talks, the time seeming to pass instantly, and far too slowly. Even after manipulating the schematic's angle, shifting perspective in new ways, and changing structural overlays, it still feels as if I'm staring into a blacked-out window and seeing nothing but my own reflection mocking me. The plans are impenetrable, like a fucking Gordian knot.

Leaning against the back of a chair, I recite the same litany of questions we've all gone over a hundred times. How are we going to get in there? Where are the prisoner cells? How much more time do they have? What the hell are we missing? Our last chance to figure out how to achieve the impossible is being shot away like so many wasted bullets.

According to the plans, a bank of surveillance satellites encircles the station, picking up everything within a ten thousand kilometer perimeter. It's completely impossible to get close to the thing undetected.

That's *if* we're right about where it is.

Brady, proving the word "optimism" isn't in his vocabulary, had earlier voiced the practical reality that the coordinates we have are only good as long as the Fortress doesn't move. At this point, a week after Rajcik gave them to us and two weeks since they were originally stolen, it's entirely possible that the station is no longer where we expect it to be. On Spectra 6, Rajcik had said something to the crew about picking up the call signs for a supply ship en route. Was that all he was picking up? It would have been easy for Rajcik to give us bogus coordinates, and why wouldn't he have? He had told Vitruzzi that he would see us at the Fortress, so it seems that the coordinates are correct, but . . . what if? He could easily have been bluffing.

The unknowns are piling up too high. The only way to maintain my focus, and my sanity, is to assume the station is where we expect it to be and concentrate on the central problem.

With no feasible chance of docking by surprise, the only way to get in is if we're supposed to be there. The security reports T'Kai included with the disc indicate that incoming and outgoing flights have been preplotted for over a month, but the precise schedule is missing. We can reasonably assume that there will be intermittent resupply ships, and we're far enough from any of the Obals or Admin outposts that ship traffic is irregular at best. It wouldn't be impossible to scan all crafts that come within range of the *Sphynx*'s radar and hope we're lucky enough to pick up a supply ship. But the chances that we find one on its way to the Fortress are slim to the point of being almost nonexistent. That's not good enough.

Bodie asks a question about entry and exit points, launching a discussion over the station's traffic patterns, which we guess at based on the number and size of its docks. I pull shipping access points into view, their boundaries highlighted in sharp red within the floating blue lines of the holograph. Looking through the margins of the after-deck diagram into the laboratories, it's hard not to imagine what could be happening to David and their friends in there. And then—

"Look at this," I say, pointing to a docking bay near the base of the station. "You see this bay? It's labeled 'Supply Docking Bay 5.'"

They both look from me to the schematic, then back at me, not sure what I'm getting at. "Look at the dimensions. See how small it is? It can't dock a ship much bigger than the *Sphynx*. And look where it's located, right next to the water storage and reclamation system, on this side, and an incinerator on this side." I point at the image, my finger almost shaking in excitement.

"Then over here, beyond the bay control rooms, are the two main labs. Bio and chemical. The weapons development center is on the other side of the station. If they wanted to bring supplies in from this bay, they'd have to take them through the labs. Think about it. A complex this size is going to need a hell of a lot more room than this little dock for bringing in all the essentials—food, more water, equipment, whatever."

My eyes lock on Strahan's, demanding he understand. "I think this is where they're bringing in prisoners. Human subjects."

Bodie looks at me surprised, but Strahan is nodding his head, excited now too. Standing, he points to a series of small rooms running between the two labs. "Look right here at these rooms, Storage A–J. If you're right, they bring the prisoners in, and take them right to these rooms. These have to be holding cells."

He's right. With the exception of the areas labeled "Living Quarters," no other compartments on the station are configured the same way. Perfect jail-cell size, and located right next to where we know they're testing their inhuman shit on living people.

A fragile tendril of an idea starts growing in my mind. "Yeah, makes sense. The docking bays near the front of the station are much bigger. *That's* where they're bringing in supplies and everything else. But they don't need a big dock for this. And they don't need to advertise it by labeling it what it is, in case some honcho with a weak stomach or sense of puritan morality ever gets a look at these plans."

Bodie still looks slightly perplexed. "So what? They'll be guarding that dock just as closely as everything else."

"Yeah, but if we can land there, we'll be right next to where they're holding David and the others. And the only way they'll be able to come at us is through the labs or from the outside. They'll have to be careful too, or they'll destroy their own water system, which will force them to shut down the whole place. They're not going to want to do that."

"Okay, yeah, I see. That still leaves the problem of docking, Aly.

They're not going to let a civilian ship anywhere near it. If we even look as if we might be getting too close, regardless of what our manifests say, they'll send someone to intercept us and probably arrest us."

I have a plan for that too. Walking to the intercom console, I buzz Vitruzzi. "Captain, I think I have an idea. Can we get everyone to the com room?"

NINETEEN

Everyone assembles and I quickly explain our theory. I'm grateful when Strahan jumps in at critical points, giving my ideas some credibility. Brady's face is a mask of cynicism, but he doesn't call bullshit. It's a relief to not have to defend the idea against his automatic suspicion; time is far too short for divisiveness.

After everyone looks over the schematic and sees what we're talking about, I take over. "So Bodie, your question, *the* question, is how are we going to get permission to dock? Easy. We're going to give them a prisoner." They're all looking at me with focused concentration, wondering what I'm talking about. No jury ever handed down a sentence with more conviction than mine as I answer their unspoken question, "Me."

Strahan begins shaking his head. "Uh-uh, Aly. You're not going in there alone, and we're not a registered prison transport anyway."

"You're right. But we know where to get one."

Vitruzzi knows what I'm talking about. "The ship that boarded us today."

"Exactly. I got a good look at them while I was hiding in the fire control room. It's an MCACS—Multi-Containment Armored Carrier Ship. Commonly used by the Admin for prisoner transport. They're probably taking a load to the Fortress right now and got tasked with checking us out because we were in the same region and getting close to the station. Their commander wasn't very interested in doing a thorough inspection of the *Sphynx*; he didn't even want to look at the nav-logs. Why? Because that's not his job. He just wanted to follow orders and wrap up his primary duty—dropping his cargo, the prisoners, at the Fortress."

"What's your point, Erikson? That ship is faster than us, armed, and loaded with security personnel." Brady's playing Captain Obvious, not trying hard enough to understand.

Opting to ignore him, I continue, "Look, they've got twenty personnel max. An MCACS isn't much bigger than we are and all the prisoners are locked up, contained, whatever the hell they do. They're basically an armored transport ship. And they aren't going to be too far away yet. Hell, they may even be following us."

Venus chimes in, "Nuh-uh, I've been keeping my eye on the radars. There's no one out here but us."

I don't want to be a jerk, she's just a kid after all, but the point has to be made. "The minute we underestimate them, we lose our advantage. They can cloak themselves if they want to."

She frowns, slightly stung, but my bluntness stoppers their doubts long enough for me to continue, "It's easy. Just call them back and say you found me on board after all. I'd been hiding or something. They may not believe you, and they don't have to." I stare intently at Vitruzzi, wanting to impress on her the importance of giving the plan all due diligence before rejecting it. The final decision will be hers, and everything rides on what she chooses. "Let them think that being boarded spooked you and made you realize how much shit you were in, so you decided to give me up and pretend like you didn't know anything. It doesn't matter. They'll come back for me because they've been told to. And when they do, we take their ship. The coordinates to the Fortress will be in their nav-system. Brady, if you're right and the Fortress has moved or Rajcik gave us the wrong coordinates, it won't matter. We've *got* to do this."

Their expressions testify to the fact that they think I've gone completely off my nut, but it's the best plan anyone's thought of so far. The *only* plan.

"Venus, do you think you can fly an MCACS?" Vitruzzi asks after a moment of consideration.

Without hesitation, her lips spread into a wide grin. "Shouldn't be a problem. Their engines are modeled after these, but with a higher output. The stabilizers have to compensate for that by creating more drag, but that's offset by a larger bore combuster and higher torque on the turbines."

Does she study ship designs for fun, or is it just wired into her mutant brain? Either way, good news for us. "Then we just have to make the call. People, there's no other choice. We do this or they die."

"She's right." Desto stands, no smile on his face this time. "It may be crazy, and probably impossible, but I've always wanted to hijack an Admin ship. I'm in."

It only takes another second before everyone is nodding. "Okay." I'm also nodding, relief and excitement flooding through me. We may be grasping at the shortest straw ever made, but we finally have a plan. From this point, there will be no more doubt, no more confusion, no more uncertainty or fear. Right or wrong, we are finally, inevitably, in motion.

"The best way to take control is to capture their commander. With a little persuasion, he'll order the crew to stand down. There may be a couple of heroes, but we can deal with them. Once we own the ship, we'll bring Venus on board. Until then, she and someone else can stay here and cover us."

Worry dances circles in Venus's wide eyes, threatening her nerve. I smile confidently, trying to reassure her. As long as we can keep her out of harm's way, no doubt she'll be able to manage the hijacked ship.

Talking fast, I lay out the strategy my mind has already processed. "Whoever stays on the *Sphynx* will provide us with a distraction. Once they're convinced I'm the fugee they've been tasked to find, we'll be forced to make the delivery. Take me to them. They're vulnerable if they split up and their shuttle is launched." I shift my eyes back to Venus. "You keep their ship in firing range. After we're on board—and I don't mean after we dock, but after we're on board and *off* the shuttle—you line up and blow out one of their auxiliary engines. The MCACS can still fly without it, but the strike will confuse them and give us enough of a distraction to take the ship."

"You're saying that four or five of us are going to take out twenty of them?" Desto asks.

"We don't have to kill them. Just take away their initiative and make them *our* prisoners. Once we blow their auxiliary and they realize they're under fire, if they follow SOPs, they'll try to make a run for it. But not if we have their commander hostage." I stop talking for a minute, considering the biggest obstacle to this plan. "But what we really need is a way to jam their coms, make them unable to transmit a SITREP or SOS. The plan hinges on us being able to surprise them, and then use the ship as cover to get inside the Fortress."

"We've got a pulse emitter in the fire control room. If we splice it to our transmitter and draw from the *Sphynx*'s engine, we may be able to scramble their transmissions by overloading all frequencies," Bodie says. "It's old, and it'll take a lot of power from the *Sphynx* to create a big enough electrostatic wave. I'm not a hundred percent it'll even work at all." He looks around the table, one eyebrow raised as if to ask, *I know it's a long shot, but what else do we have?*

Vitruzzi asks, "How much power? Will the *Sphynx* be able to make a break for it if things go wrong?"

"*If* it works, it'll draw . . . maybe eighty percent of the engine's energy. All at once. The only thing on board that will work is the grav-stabilizer and life support. That's for one static pulse, which should disrupt their communications for three, maybe even five, minutes. If they send a transmission, it'll be garbled and anyone hearing it won't know who it came from." He draws a long, slow breath. "I think."

"How long will the *Sphynx* be down?"

"I'd guess about ten minutes."

"Is that enough time?" Strahan asks.

"The MCACS is a small ship, and they don't have much more firepower than the *Sphynx* does. But they're a lot faster than we are, even with a burnt-out auxiliary. Their orders will be to send an SOS and make a break for it. But it will take them a minute to diagnose the damage. If we take their commander hostage before they can respond, we can make him order the ship to stand to. They'll know what we're capable of and do as commanded."

"And if any single thing goes wrong . . ." Brady doesn't finish the sentence.

No one else says anything for a few seconds, thinking over what I've outlined. Strahan's brown eyes are on mine, and this time I meet his gaze. He stares right through my resolute, no-compromises exterior, recognizing the deep fears now pushing me into risks that seem beyond reckless, and he nods. He understands. I, *we,* have no more options.

"Okay. This is how we'll run it." Vitruzzi takes over and we spend the next forty-five minutes ramping up for the mission that decides whether David and the *Sky Serpent* crew live or die.

TWENTY

The *Sphynx* is about two kilometers behind us and the shuttle-docking doors opening on the top of the MCACS are just ahead. Vitruzzi made the call and they'd responded exactly as we'd hoped. It's small and close inside the shuttle. Sweat runs down my back and I see it beading up on Desto and Strahan's temples. Vitruzzi is as impassive as ever, piloting us to the shuttle dock with the same even determination as when she's sewing up one of her crew or lying to an officer of the Administration.

Turning to Strahan, I tell him, "Put me in restraints."

"What?"

"Put some wrist restraints on me. They won't believe us unless I'm cuffed."

"You'll be helpless . . ."

"If you think that, you don't know me very well. Just do it. Fill the lock core with a fingernail's worth of E-10 right before we get off. It'll melt through in about two minutes and my hands will be free. But take this," I hand him my Sinbad pistol, "and keep it in the back of your pants. Stay in front of me. I can fire with restraints on."

We all have guns, all well hidden. We need the Admin crew to let us inside the dock with the doors shut and the airlocks activated if this is going to work. For them to do that, Vitruzzi and the others have to appear to be innocent citizens giving up a known fugitive. Possessing guns is illegal, and if ours are seen, our cover is blown.

"Shit," he mutters under his breath but puts the cuffs on. I try to smile at him while he's balling up the E-10 wax, but it feels forced. He grins back anyway and pushes the Sinbad inside his belt in the small of his back. "Don't pull that trigger until it's clear, got it?"

Vitruzzi eases us down through the open doors and we hit the bay floor with a screech of metal. I hear the hydraulics engage, and the doors above us begin to close. Here we go.

Green lights flash inside the bay indicating the airlock is engaged and pressurized, and Vitruzzi activates the shuttle ramp. It lowers slowly, giving us time to note the positions of the commander and half a dozen other uniformed personnel in the bay. Every one of them has a weapon pointed at us. Vitruzzi takes the lead and begins walking down the ramp, followed by Strahan, me, then Desto. I raise my hands waist high, hovering just behind Strahan's back.

"Be very careful, Captain. I want to see empty hands in the air."

I take my first look at the officer, and to my complete lack of surprise, he is almost exactly as I'd pictured. Regulation cropped hair, barely long enough to be seen beneath his commander's cap, sharp blue eyes attentive beneath the cap's brim, and a rigid stature that makes his starched uniform look nailed on. Distinct lines drape from the edges of his mouth toward his chin, reinforcing the frown that he now levels on us. He's not much older than I am, but life transporting prisoners to the fringes of space has not been gentle on him.

All of us keep our hands in plain view except for me. Once we're all on deck I step only slightly beside Strahan so I can draw the 'Bad without having to shift my body. The others line up horizontally as the crewmen approach to search us. The air tastes electric with tension and I can read in the major's face that he knows something is up.

Just as the first man reaches to pat down Vitruzzi, a voice stoked by urgency booms through the ship's com system, "Major Donnelly, we're getting an unexpected reading on our weapon sensors."

Bodie is locked! *Fire now!* I scream in my head, reaching for the Sinbad. The major's sharp eyes dart toward us, and then the ship bucks crazily, throwing everyone through the air.

The auxiliary engine's explosion reverberates throughout the chamber like water breaking through a dam, forcing my eyes to squeeze tightly shut. A yell followed by a meaty thud comes from nearby and I open them in time to glimpse Desto kneeling over the nearest crewman, trying to disarm him. Vitruzzi lines up a shot at another, and Strahan has Donnelly by the collar, forcing the officer in front of him to use as a shield. Another crewman lines up to fire at me, and I roll aside just in time, then back, aiming for his face with the 'Bad. My shot is off by a few centimeters and only grazes him, but the pain and surprise are enough to make him forget to fire back. His weapon clatters against the floor as he reaches for his wounded neck, allowing me the time I need to take aim at his head. He knows the deal and reaches high.

"Everyone drop them or your commander is dead." Strahan's voice slices through the chamber like a scythe.

As if they were a single unit, the security team freezes. Strahan scans the bay, one arm gripped around the major's neck, the other pointing the pistol he had strapped to his calf at the man's temple.

"Do as he says," Donnelly gasps through his half-closed throat.

"Sir! We've been fired on! Sir, what are your orders?" The same frantic voice as before shouts through the com system.

The men remain still, but it's a fifty-fifty chance they'll disregard their commander's order. It only takes one overhyped gunman jerking his trigger, and like dominoes, the rest will open fire. The docking chamber is small, the walls deflective—it would be suicide to continue shooting standard-issue metal rounds in here, but the human mind doesn't always believe in its own mortality. Rising slowly, I draw the Mini-Derg with my free hand and point it at another crewman, already regretting that I'll be useless to my brother and he'll die alone inside an Admin torture chamber if we lose our momentary advantage. But then Donnelly finds the motivation he needs to force an unquestionable command through his constricted throat. "Drop your weapons, now!"

This time, the remaining crewmen comply, and the room echoes with the sound of rifle butts banging on steel. Desto and I quickly kick them out of reach and wave the men against the far wall with the non-negotiating ends of our weapons. Strahan continues to hold the major in a throat-crushing grip, and the man's face begins turning an alarming purplish color as Vitruzzi approaches them.

Despite being choked, he manages to whisper, "You're making a huge mistake, Captain."

She nods at Strahan, who eases up on the pressure, and Donnelly draws a whooping, pained breath.

Vitruzzi ignores him. "Call your flight deck and get a SITREP. Tell them not to report to any other ship until you get back up there. Am I clear, Major?"

He nods, eyes squinting in fury, keenly aware of the gravity of his situation. Strahan pushes him toward a com console near the airlock.

Pressing the link, he clears his throat and says, "Captain Roby, SITREP."

"Sir, the ISPS fired on us! The auxiliary engine is completely gone. And there's something wrong with the transmitter. We're trying to get a lock on the craft, but it's moving erratically. What are your orders?"

The major shifts his eyes to Vitruzzi, waiting for his orders.

"Tell him to hold fast, you're coming up. Have all crew not dealing with the engine meet you in here."

He gives his subordinates the command. Within seconds, six more men rush into the bay from the forward cabin, completely unaware of the situation, and are quickly subdued. Desto ties their hands and feet to each other, immobilizing them, and covers their mouths with tape. It takes less than two minutes. While he's busy with the crew, Strahan and I provide security, and Vitruzzi interrogates Donnelly for information regarding the location and duty of any remaining crewmembers. Ten minutes later we're standing on the bridge, in control of the ship. I'm having a hard time swallowing the rising sense of dread our unlikely streak of luck brings—there's no way things will go this smoothly again. No way.

TWENTY-ONE

Twenty-four hours have passed. Venus has been at the helm for the last eighteen, but seems as fresh and lively as if she'd slept eight perfect hours a night, each and every night of her life. The good news: no shots were fired when we took the bridge. The bad news: the bridge commander, Captain Roby, immediately changed the ship's course and locked the nav-system when he realized they were compromised. Donnelly and Roby are the only crewmen with the encryption pass codes to get back into the nav-system, and without them we're flying blind. Not part of the plan.

Donnelly consistently denies the ship's destination is the Fortress, but he's lying. He doesn't even try that hard to hide it. So what if we reach the Fortress? He knows it's crazy and our odds of being blown out of the sky, or worse, picked off to be used as more test subjects, are much greater than our odds of achieving whatever idiotic plan we've cooked up, so why bother to try and be convincing?

When the MCACS doesn't make its rendezvous with the station, they'll begin a search and our plan, along with all of us, will be dead in the water. Vitruzzi has been explicitly clear that none of the Admin crew should be needlessly harmed, instantly rejecting my suggestion that we shoot one every ten minutes until Donnelly gives up the codes. I'm not bloodthirsty, but it's as Rajcik once told me: they knew the risks when they signed on.

Brady has been piloting the *Sphynx*, keeping her within firing distance in case we lose control of the situation, while Bodie and Venus keep the MCACS flying. We locked the crew in the galley, rather than with the thirty-eight prisoners aboard, for their own protection, and Desto and I switch guard duty every six hours. I'm standing on my third watch, staring through the galley door at the imprisoned crew, shifting my weight from foot to foot to stay conscious. None of us has slept since intercepting the MCACS and I'm starting to lose the battle against the fatigue threatening to take my eyelids prisoner.

There's a noise in the corridor and I look up to see Desto approaching. "Your relief is here, honey. You ready to catch a nap?"

"No. I couldn't sleep even if I wanted to."

He chuckles. "That's not what it looks like. Go ahead, rack out for a few. I just did and I feel a million times better. Captain started us on a sleep rotation for three hours each, and you're up. Take it while you can get it."

"Is that an order?" I try to keep my tone light, but it doesn't work. My voice sounds gruff and resentful, even to me.

"Does it matter? You need it, trust me."

Even if I don't, my body wants to accept the invitation. My arms drop heavily to my sides and my knees waver, forcing me to lean back against the wall.

"Yeah, that's what I thought. Head up to the top level. It's the bunk nearest the flight deck. Any troubles here?"

"They're as calm as kittens. Keeping the temp at thirty-seven C doesn't inspire rebellion."

A DENSE CURTAIN of fog moves around me like a shroud. It's cold and damp, a heavy mist, and there's a strange grating sound—metal against metal—coming from somewhere not very distant. I'm on full alert, feeling danger in the mist with me, but none of my senses can locate it. I want to call out to

David, to see if he is here too, but I can't risk drawing unwanted attention to myself. Any noise could give away my location, and I won't be able to see it, whatever it is, coming.

I don't know what to do, so I begin stalking quietly toward the sound. If I find it first, I may be able to identify it without being detected.

As I take a few tentative steps, curdles of thick fog blow back from my shape like smoke, quickly replaced by more of the same. Continuing forward, I look down to get a sense of what kind of ground I'm walking on, trying not to make any noise. One more step and the mist shifts for an instant, long enough for me to see that there is nothing. Nothing but black, empty space below me.

The moment this realization hits me, the sense of having solid ground beneath my feet dissolves, and I'm suddenly falling—hurtling—through space, gaining speed though there is no gravity. I feel cold wind and needles of ice burrowing into my skin, as if being stabbed by a million tiny knives. I begin to kick and claw at the emptiness around me, trying to slow myself, to break my fall, anything. I hitch in a deep breath, preparing to scream—

—and wake up gasping. Wild-eyed and panicked, I look around the room and pick out Vitruzzi leaning through the doorway.

"You all right?" she asks.

I can't speak for a second, still partly paralyzed in the free fall of my dream. The haggardness in her face, eyes deep-set in dark pockets, almost mournful, helps bring me back to the present. "Yeah, I'm fine."

Time to get back to work. Leaning down and pulling my boots on, still trying to get a grip, I hear her footsteps as she comes in. She watches me quietly for a moment and says, "We can't wait for Donnelly anymore. We need the pass codes, and we're going to have to make him tell us." She doesn't say it, but I know what she's thinking: *I wish like hell it didn't have to come to this.*

"Are we going to use his crew?"

"No," she answers immediately. "We're not going to make them pay for his mistakes."

"Vitruzzi, you know we can't let any of them go. They know who you are. They know your ship. Even if we pull this off, if anyone lives to report what happened, you and the others in Agate Beach will be targets. The Admin will come eventually."

Anger flashes across her features, but it's not about me. She's angry with them for putting her in this situation, and no one can blame her for it. I still don't know why she gave up her comfortable life on Obal 10 before all this, but the more I see, the more I'm convinced the Admin had something to do with it.

"Let's just get this done." She heads for the flight deck and I follow her.

Strahan stands over Donnelly, who's been taped to the copilot's seat. He doesn't appear to be frightened, but dark smudges beneath his eyes reveal a wary concern and lack of sleep. When we enter, Strahan glances up and the major cranes his head back to look at us.

Vitruzzi positions herself rigidly beside the seat, looming over him. She's relaxed, nothing in her stance overtly threatening, yet no one would mistake her mood for anything but serious. Deadly serious.

"Major Donnelly, give us the pass codes to the nav-system. Now."

"You have control of the ship. What difference does it make?" He's trying to remain curt, but there's an unmistakable strain in his voice.

Strahan pulls a vicious-looking knife from his load-bearing vest and presses the blade against the man's jugular. "Major, you're going to tell us those codes, or you're going to watch yourself bleed to death. I suggest you think very carefully about what you say next. You've got five seconds."

Donnelly's face grows pale, the depressed circles around his eyes becoming more like bruises. Or like the sunken eyes of a corpse. "You'll never get away with this. You'll kill me anyway, even if I give you the pass codes."

Strahan remains stolid, staring the man down with the intensity of a predator locked on its prey. Finally, Vitruzzi says, "Karl, take him to the galley and put a bullet in his head in front of his crew. Then bring the captain to the deck." Her eyes never leave Donnelly's. "Erikson, go with him."

I look from her, to Strahan, to Donnelly. The same resolute calmness is in all of their faces. Venus remains seated in the pilot's station, keeping her head turned stiffly to the front, refusing to acknowledge the scene playing out around her. *If only we could all wish it away.*

Donnelly stands up after Strahan cuts through the tape holding him to the seat, and without a word turns toward the flight deck door. Vitruzzi, still staring at the seat he'd been sitting in, says quietly, "Last chance, Major."

He steps through the doorway without looking back.

KILLING HIM WORKS. The ship's new OIC, Captain Roby, complies without hesitation, inputting the pass codes himself. Once the nav-system is unlocked, Venus and I locate the Fortress's coordinates. We're all a little surprised when they match those Rajcik originally gave us. He'd kept his word after all, confirmation that he's been baiting us, even as we'd held him captive. It leaves me feeling sick.

We're within eighteen hours of the prisoner ship's scheduled rendezvous. They'd been ahead of schedule before we intercepted them and Roby informs us that Donnelly's plan had been to remain in a holding pattern until their expected window. By reinstating their previous course, we'll be arriving at the Fortress just in time.

I'm sitting in the navigator's station poring through the flight logs when Vitruzzi walks onto the flight deck. Without a word, she takes the pilot's seat. Venus put the ship on auto about two hours ago and left to catch a few minutes of sleep, finally. Or maybe she just needed to put some distance between herself and the horrible shit happening around her.

Glancing up at Vitruzzi, I see the same look in her eyes that I've seen too often in my own. The haunted way the eyes trip around a room, not seeing anything, covered by a dull sheen that says they've seen too much violence and senseless death. A look stained with the knowledge that our own end is coming, and fast. That look is the reason most soldiers don't own a mirror.

"You had to do it, Vitruzzi. It was the only way."

She looks at me gravely. "Have you ever been a parent, Erikson?"

It's a strange question. "You know I haven't." Corps troops are sterilized at in-processing to keep the ranks and population in order and ensure perpetual combat readiness—a Malthusian reaction by the Admin to guard civilization from ever reaching critical mass again.

"I know you've never had children, but that doesn't necessarily mean you've never had to help raise a child. Then, I imagine you've never had that kind of opportunity, the life you've led."

I shake my head. I'm not sure what she's talking about, but her grim tone extinguishes any impulse to interrupt.

"That's just another freedom the Admin takes from people." She stops. Part of me hopes she's done, but after a minute, she continues, "Karl says you're curious about how I became an Admin contractor."

"Yeah. You've got some good people around you, but let's be honest, it isn't much of a life."

She studies me blankly for a second, then begins speaking rapidly, as if the words have been dammed up too long and can no longer be held back. "I was Head Surgeon of the Cyber Prosthetics Unit at Mercy Hope Hospital in Tunis City before I went into business with Karl. My husband was a molecular chemist, working on biological pacification projects. We met at the hospital. A year after we were married, we had a little girl. Evie." She stops again. There's something she wants to say, something painful, and in another second, I'm going to hear it. Only I'm not sure I want to.

"Six years ago, an Admin-engineered virus was brought to the hospital. John couldn't tell me where it came from, but it wasn't hard to figure out it was developed at the Fortress. Everyone had heard the rumors about the place. He was so excited about being part of such a highly sensitive operation. I still don't know why the Admin exported it. There was no reason to bring it to a civilian population center.

"Somehow, the virus got out, and before they could contain it, twenty-five thousand citizens from Tunis City and the surrounding area died. My husband and daughter included." She continues staring through the flight deck screens, her lips the only part of her body still animated. "I went to work early on a Saturday morning, and that afternoon they locked down the hospital. No one was allowed in or out. By the time the epidemic was contained a week later, my family was dead. I never saw either of them again. All the bodies were incinerated."

I remember the news. It happened right before the Soldier's Rebellion. Rumors claimed the outbreak, dubbed the "Crowers Croup" by the Corps ranks because of how bad it made people cough, so bad it shredded their lungs and throat, was the reason for the rebellion in the first place. Or at least the catalyst. The units sent to quarantine the infected and clean up the mess weren't properly outfitted for the bug, no one was even sure what it was and the Admin spun the news reports to keep people pacified and in the dark. Word was that it was transmitted through body fluids, mucus and saliva, but soldiers were dropping like flies before anyone realized it was airborne. Estimates say fifty thousand citizens died in the Obals—no one bothered to count the non-cits in the Spectras—but over seventy-five thousand soldiers were sent to the cremation chambers.

"I wasn't a very good mother. I worked too much and spent more time with my patients than my own family. My husband was just like me. By the end, we were just familiar strangers to each other. I like to think Evie died knowing that her parents loved her. But most of the time, I doubt she did."

An involuntary shiver traces up my spinal cord. I don't know what to say; not that anything I come up with would matter anyway. I knew people who died from the Croup, but no story I've heard is as horrible as hers.

She stops talking, battling with herself over whether she wants to relive this nightmare by telling it to me, but eventually, she goes on. "The Admin never acknowledged that the virus had come from their experimentation at the Fortress, and everyone who knew the truth was dead, like John.

"I couldn't stay at the hospital after that, working for a government that killed my little girl and then lied to me about it. I dropped off my resignation two days after the quarantine was lifted, and I think the only reason they let me go was because they suspected I knew the truth. They gambled I'd keep my mouth shut if they let me leave without restrictions."

"Why did you?"

A bitter chuckle escapes her. "How could I have proved it? Besides, it isn't hard to guess what would have happened to me if I had tried."

I don't know how she chokes off the rage she must feel over what the Admin did to her and her family without going crazy, but even as she tells me the story, she seems calm. Bitter and hateful, but calm.

She swings the pilot's seat around and looks at me for the first time. "Erikson, I'm telling you this so you'll understand something important: I have no regrets about what happened to Donnelly. That was simple justice. Those scientists on the Fortress, scientists like Vilbrandt, kill people, *people,* in ways that no one deserves, and Donnelly was helping them do it. He got what was coming to him."

There's no trace of guilt in her words. She's not trying to make me see things her way; she wants me to know how far things have gone and the consequences for anything or anyone that gets in our way. If I had not just heard these words, I could have lived fifty lifetimes before seeing this deeply into Vitruzzi. She hadn't brought Vilbrandt on board just because he presented an opportunity. Her motives were never that straightforward. Her plans for him, once he served his purpose, were almost certainly every bit as grisly as what Rajcik will probably end up doing to him. This isn't just a simple mission to save her friends from bad luck. It's personal. It's a vendetta, and it's driving every decision she makes, good or bad. So far, those decisions have been exact, calculated, and flawless, but there's no telling what tiny little nudge might be all that's needed to send her over the edge and out of control. She could be close and no one would know it. If Vitruzzi loses it, it's hard to know how the rest of this crew will react. They're smart, strong, and capable, but like any tower, when the foundation crumbles, it all comes down.

"In a way, I've had more of a relationship with the prosthetic in Karl's leg and the *Sphynx* than I ever had with my own daughter. She was only seven years, two months, and nine days old when she died."

. . .

"Fortress, this is MCACS F-205, prisoner transport from Keum Libre, requesting clearance to land. Over."

"Roger, Major Donnelly. This is Lieutenant Stevenson. Redirect to the lower docking bays and provide your authentication code."

We've arrived. The monstrosity looms at our bow, gleaming against the blackness like a hellish, mutant asteroid. According to the disc, there are fifteen levels in the bow of the station: two that are strictly traffic corridors spanning the entire length through the center, and ten levels in the stern. The main generators encircle its core, generating the energy needed for both operations and mobility, completely enclosed in an impenetrable structural shell. No way to take those out, even if we had ten ships with ten times more firepower.

We approach facing the two main flight deck levels where the transit ship launch tracks run into the interior, terminating at the station's primary loading bays. The tracks, being the station's most vulnerable design component, are buttressed on each side with jutting missile tubes that ensure nothing gets near without clearance. Prismatic lenses, which capture and relay all visuals from outside, are located directly above the launch tracks' gaping airlocks. Coupled with the segmented design of the station's hull, the overall effect creates the impression that we're flying toward the snatching jaws of a giant carnivorous insect.

Vitruzzi, Venus, Brady, Strahan, and I occupy the prisoner ship's flight deck. We'd left the *Sphynx* crewless and in stasis when we entered into communication range of the Fortress, and everyone now wears the MCACS's security personnel uniforms. I hate it; my own body armor is light and flexible and this stuff is like wearing a lead suit, but we have to look the part. Even so, I removed the lower plates from the torso section to give me marginally better maneuverability and speed. Security guards are hired for size and strength, and their heavy vests are not designed for my short, compact frame. All of us are now ready and waiting for the action to begin, with Bodie and

Desto docked in the *Sphynx*'s short-range shuttle inside the MCACS's bay in case there is need, and opportunity, to bug out.

"Fortress, this is Captain Roby, OIC. We've encountered hostile activity and Major Donnelly is in the infirmary. I've taken command. Over," Strahan answers, assuming the role of the ship's second in command.

"Why didn't you send a report?"

"Our coms sustained damage, Lieutenant. We haven't had the chance."

"Describe your situation, F-205. Over."

"We were tasked to pick up a fugitive by the name of Erikson, located aboard a contracted vessel. Their crew resisted us and Major Donnelly was injured during the fugee's extraction. His situation is critical. We need immediate clearance and a medical team ready when we dock. We also have a faulty auxiliary engine that needs maintenance. Over."

"Roger, Captain Roby. What's your authentication code? Over."

He flips off the com. "Shit." The rest of us hold our breath, frantically trying to think of a way to get this asshole to open up the Fortress and let us in. We'd left the real Roby with his crew to keep him from blowing the whistle once we made contact. It's too late to run back to the galley and retrieve him; the hesitation might serve as a warning to the Fortress's boarding command. Before anyone says anything, Strahan switches the com back on. "Lieutenant Stevenson, stand by for authent code. STY-0038-9762-98. Over."

Where did that come from? After a moment the LT's voice comes back. "Captain Roby, that authent code is inactive. It actually belongs to a former Tech 3 Sergeant, Chief Pilot, Strahan, Karl S. Over."

I look over at him, genuinely surprised. It's a dangerous gamble for Strahan to give them his prior active-duty flight officer code. If we manage to get away with this, there's no doubt that he'll be investigated, which will lead back to Vitruzzi and the *Sphynx*, and eventually, Agate Beach. It doesn't matter now. The option of turning back is obsolete.

"So?" He's playing a pissed-off commander flawlessly.

"Sir, we can't let you board without a valid authentication code. What is your authentication code? Over."

"Lieutenant Stevenson, I've got my ship commander leaking brains and blood, a hull full of pain-in-the-ass prisoners and one fugee, and a busted engine. I've got enough problems to deal with today. Don't become one of them. Some goon database tech who can't read his fucking alphabet entering my authent code into the system wrong, is *not* my problem. Do you read me? Now, are you going to clear that fucking dock? Over."

There's a pause after his transmission that feels too long to be anything but a death sentence. Then: "Captain Roby. Please proceed to Alpha Dock, Bay 5. They are clear and waiting for your arrival. Over."

Everyone in the cabin starts breathing again. Strahan looks genuinely pissed off and finishes the transmission. "Good job, Lieutenant. And make sure they have a goddamn mechanic crew on standby when we get there too. Out."

He switches off and the deck falls into total silence. Once we're inside the station, approximately ten minutes from now, all of the planning, running, hiding, and fighting that got us this far will stop, and the real battle will finally begin. I don't know what thoughts are spinning through their minds, but the face of my brother, bleeding, hurt, and afraid, fills mine like a cancer. But instead of enervating me, the image replenishes my determination to get the bastards that did it to him. Whatever the cost.

Finally, Venus breaks the silence. "Captain, what are we going to do with the prisoners?"

Vitruzzi and Brady look at each other and he says, "We let them go."

"We what?"

"If we leave them on the ship, they're sitting ducks. And we don't really want to cart them back to the *Sphynx* if, *when,* we get away. Besides, they'll make a good distraction."

"Do you really think that's a good idea, Brady?" I ask. "We've got enough to worry about without giving them a chance to turn on us too."

"Do you have a better idea?"

I don't. This time I keep my mouth shut.

Vitruzzi takes a deep breath. "I'll go tell them."

The four of us walk through the guard annex to the holding bay. Vitruzzi activates the hatch and the din of voices inside quiets down as we enter.

"Listen up." All heads turn to her. The walkway we stand on is about two meters above two metal-barred cages that separate thirty men and a handful of women. The room is brightly lit, casting garish light over their upturned faces. They look mean, pissed off, and violent, but there's no fear in their faces.

"By now you've probably realized that this ship has been hijacked. We're not here because of you, and now we have to figure out what to do with you. So we're going to let you go." No cheers. No applause. No smiles.

"It's fair to tell you where we're going, if you don't already know. The Fortress." For the first time, murmurs of anger and disquiet wash through the air, quickly whipping into a wrathful gale.

Someone shouts, "You can't cut us loose in there! They'll kill us!" More yelling, interspersed with gems like, "Fly us outta here or you're dead," "I'll fucking hunt you down, bitch," and more similarly empty, useless threats. No doubt about it, these are not the type we'd be interested in recruiting as partners, and I'm not surprised they've been earmarked as future human lab rats. Still, I can't help but feel some sympathy for them. Like Vitruzzi said: no one deserves to die the way they certainly would if we hadn't hijacked the ship and changed their fates. Whether or not their new futures will be an improvement, however, is not so certain.

"Quiet!" Her voice rings throughout the confined space like doom, and they fall silent. "We're not taking you anywhere you weren't going already, so quit complaining. This is the only chance you're going to get. We're not here to save you. But like I said, we're giving you a chance."

Thirty-eight pairs of eyes are now fixed on her, some with murder in them, but some are starting to show interest.

"How many here are deserters?" A little over half of them raise their hands, listening closely now. "There are a lot of guns on this ship. Most of you should still be able to activate them if your records were destroyed in the Rebellion. You're going to have full access. For the rest of you, there are some grenades, maybe some incendiary units. Once we dock, which will be in about three minutes, my crew and I are going to disappear. These doors will open five minutes later and you can all do whatever the hell you want. Claim your freedom. If you're smart, you'll team up and get systematic about dealing with the security shit show that I guarantee will be coming."

She turns and we walk back into the guardroom, an angry furor flooding the bay behind us. Hitting the code, she lets the door close them out. "Karl, get some E-10 in those locks as soon as we land then hustle back to the exit ramp. Let's get these gun cages open."

The entire scenario is a lunatic's nightmare, but the fact is the Admin is going to have a, as Vitruzzi put it, a shit show on their hands very soon. We're dead if they catch us. But if we're lucky, this swarm of gun-toting degenerates with nothing to lose will thin out the Fortress's security force, and we'll just slip silently through their fingers.

TWENTY-TWO

Venus maneuvers into the launch track and hovers at the end until the dock controllers activate the airlock. The vibration of the ship's floor slackens underfoot as she lowers it onto the dock and disengages the engines. The rest of us stand at the exit ramp. Three out of the six of us came from the Corps, but being back in uniform makes cold sweat seep from my pores. Or maybe it's this place.

Staring through the window hatch into the bay, things seem too quiet. "I don't see any mechanics."

The communication console lights up, and a second later the dock controller starts speaking. "Captain Roby, we're experiencing a security situation and need you and your crew to move directly to the debrief room. Just leave your cargo and injured on board. We'll send medics and a maintenance crew soon. Over."

The six of us turn to look at each other. "Rajcik?" Vitruzzi speculates.

I shake my head, not knowing what else it could be. "Unreal."

"Answer him, Karl."

Strahan clicks on the transmitter. "That's affirmative. Out."

Bodie releases the ramp and we walk onto the Fortress, where the coldness of space wraps its burial shroud around us.

The dock is relatively small with only three bays for ships no bigger than the one we're flying. We cross as a group to the debriefing room. No one needs to be told where it is; we've all scrutinized the holodisc long enough to know exactly where to go. As we pass by the prisoner ship's bow, I look up and see Venus staring out at us with worried eyes. She's locked inside the flight deck, ready to get us the hell out of here the instant our mission is complete. I nod and give her a small smile of encouragement. She acknowledges the gesture with a smile in return, and raises her hand to her temple in a mock salute.

There is no one waiting in the bay to meet us. Unusual. Their security protocols are tight enough that we'd anticipated an armed escort but something else must be keeping the soldiers busy. The dock controller didn't sound overly alarmed, but I can almost taste the panic and disorder that's happening somewhere on the station. Whatever the cause for the alert, it's well timed.

As we cross the bay, Brady snaps his fingers. Once he has all of our attention, he points to his throat mic, indicating that it's time to switch them on. By pressing the throat radio sensors against the trachea, we're able to speak much more quietly than normal and still transmit clearly to each other. If there are listening devices around, they won't be able to pick up what we're saying.

Brady's voice carries through my earpiece: "Once we're in the debrief room, we'll split into our teams. Strahan, Bodie, and Erikson, you sweep holding cells alpha through echo, we'll take the rest. If we don't find the crew, we start sweeping the labs."

He's not saying anything we don't already know. This is the plan we decided on days ago, but hearing it spoken now that we're inside the Fortress gives it a heavy finality.

Our group steps into the debrief room, everyone working hard to appear relaxed. As the door sweeps closed behind us, the high reverberating octaves of an alarm erupt throughout the complex. Beside me, Vitruzzi inhales sharply. Adrenaline surges through my body, flooding my motor and sensory neurons in a building storm that will soon settle into a slow drip until this thing is done. The sound of the team breathing around me is loud, rhythmic and heavy, but aside from Vitruzzi's first breath, no one sounds panicked. Looking to my left, Strahan's pupils dilate with the same intent focus as my own. We are ready. I reach forward and input the code that unlocks the debrief room, opening out into the bowels of the Fortress.

Instantly swinging my carbine barrel out and down the left side of the corridor, I glance quickly in both directions. The hallway is clear. Looking back over my shoulder, I give the rest of them a quick nod, and we begin advancing in bounds up the corridor. A set of stairs at the end will take us to level two and the first set of holding cells. Vitruzzi, Brady, and Desto will check these and the rest of us will continue up one more flight to the last five cells. Level three is also where the biological and chemical laboratories are located. Part of me hopes we don't have to search them. Christ knows what we might find inside.

We reach the end of the hallway without seeing anyone and race up the stairwells. Entering the third floor corridor, Bodie trains his rifle down its length. The alarms continue to bounce back and forth against the walls, but there's no sign of other people. According to the disc, SOP in a code five or higher security breach is for non-security personnel to evacuate to a safety chamber on an upper level. If that's where this section's personnel are, the security breach must be severe. Good.

A rumbling boom thuds from behind us, sounding in or near the debrief room. The prisoners must be loose. We don't slow, continuing up the flight to the first level of cells.

The first door is a quick jog down the corridor. Strahan inputs the pass code and it slides open on its track. Simultaneously, we realize we're not looking into a holding cell but into some kind of anteroom, like a guard station. This wasn't in the holograph. What other surprises will we find?

Two chairs are parked in front of a control console. A one-way window looking into an empty cell beyond dominates the far wall. Strahan gets on his mic. "Vitruzzi, Brady, be careful. There's a security antechamber for the holding cells. Over."

Vitruzzi's voice comes back. "Roger. We just discovered that. Let's just hope there aren't any more surprises. Find anyone? Over."

"Negative."

"All right, keep moving."

We exit and race to the next door, ten meters down the corridor. Strahan reaches for the keypad just as the door starts sliding open on its own. With reflexes as taut as overstretched wires, Bodie swings his rifle around and shoots the exiting soldier point-blank in the face, then drops to a knee and fires at another soldier inside as he jumps off his chair. As a bullet tears through his chest wall, a sadly comical expression of surprise affixes itself permanently to the dying man's features. Ensuring no one else is inside, the three of us leap into the room and pull the body of the first soldier through the door with us.

The window to the holding cell is grayed out, not allowing us to see what's behind it. Bodie leans over the control console, searching for the function that will clear it or open the door to let us inside. In a few seconds, he finds it and the glaze begins to dissipate.

A row of stacked bunks line one wall. A lean woman with a galaxy of black curls spread around her lies on the closest, her head turned away from us. A short man who looks as if he could single-handedly trounce a squad of wrestlers stands with his eyes fixed on the one-way window. His jaw is bruised and his lip swollen, and his fists are balled into bludgeons with knuckles that look as if they've been through a shredder. He can't see us, but his rigid stance indicates that he heard Bodie's shots. On another bunk, a small woman with dark brown hair sits upright, also staring at the window.

But no David.

"Karl!" Bodie cries.

Strahan presses the speaker on the guards' console. "Doug, Zeta, Jade—it's Karl and Bodie. We're going to get you out of here."

Instantly, the woman on the bunk jumps to her feet and looks toward the window. Both of her eyes are surrounded by dark bruises shot through with shades of green as if she's been in a hell of a fight. She squints through the remaining swelling and half whispers, "Oh my god, how did you . . .?"

Still on the mic, Bodie says, "Did you think we'd leave you here?"

The smile that spreads across her face is huge. The man, also smiling, responds, "Took you long enough."

Strahan busily cycles through the security codes for the door while I take position by the entrance, ready for anyone who tries to come in.

Bodie stays on the mic. "Are you hurt, any of you? Can everyone walk?"

"We're all okay," Zeta answers. "Just get us out of here."

What's taking Strahan so long? I glance back and see a laser reader buzz to life on the console. "Dammit!" Strahan growls. "Biosensor. We need a hand. Bodie, help me lift this guy. Quick."

They grab the man who was shot in the face by both arms and drag him back to the console. Strahan holds his limp hand inside the wavering red field but nothing happens. He curses and cycles through the operations appearing on the console as precious seconds slip away. I can almost hear a clock ticking.

"What's the problem?"

"I don't—wait! It won't open unless it reads a pulse." He reaches out and grabs the other soldier, laying his fingers against the inside of the man's wrist.

"Anything?" Bodie asks.

Karl's strained grin is almost a sneer as he nods. Yanking the guard's arm violently, he brings his hand up to the sensor. The red light wavers for a moment then turns green. Steel bolts on the security door retract and it slides open.

The three prisoners rush into the guardroom, their expressions a mixture of disbelief and joy.

"Where are C.M. and Kazaki?" Strahan asks.

"Dead," the older woman says.

Bitter sadness tightens their features momentarily, then melts into acceptance. Gratitude that we've found anyone at all will come later, if there is a later.

Facing the woman who'd spoken, I ask, "We're also looking for another prisoner. A man named Erikson. David Erikson. Have you seen him?"

She looks at me curiously. "I haven't seen any others. It's just us."

It feels as if a giant vacuum sucks my heart straight from my chest, collapsing my chest wall in the process and making me breathless.

Then the man says, "No, I saw a guy when they brought us in here. Couple hours ago. They were taking him somewhere on a gurney."

My voice is almost a whisper. "What did he look like?"

"I didn't see much. He had reddish hair like yours, and he looked like he was beat to hell. His eyes were all jacked up."

"Was he alive?"

"I don't know."

I don't know . . . the words chip through my composure as if they were daggers of ice. "Do you know where they took him?"

"No. No idea. I'm sorry."

"V, we've found them. Over." Strahan presses on with the mission.

"Everyone?"

"Just Zeta, Jade, and Doug. The rest didn't make it."

"What about Erikson's brother?"

"We don't know where he is. You haven't seen him?"

"No."

I break into the transmission. "Vitruzzi, I'm going to sweep the labs. I'm not leaving until I know something."

There's a pause. No doubt Vitruzzi is questioning whether she's willing to add more to the risks we're already taking by spending time we don't have searching for David. Then: "We're on our way up to your level. Is everyone mobile?"

"Roger."

"We'll start aft and meet you in the center. Out."

Bodie and Strahan hand extra weapons to Zeta and Mason. Strahan takes point and risks a quick glance outside the guardroom door. He gives us a nod and begins moving down the hall. Bodie immediately follows, then Zeta. Mason goes next. Before I bring up the rear, I turn to see why the short woman hasn't moved out. She is visibly shaking and pale, scared shitless. I don't have time to babysit, so I strip the Mini-Derg from my shin holster and push it into her hands. My face is inches away from hers. "Do you want to get out of here?"

Her eyes, already wide, bulge. *Goddammit, where's your survival instinct?* "Do you want to live?!" I have to be harsh, make her mad, make her realize she doesn't have time to be afraid.

She nods.

"All right." Remembering her name, I add, "That's good, Jade. 'Cause if you're ever going to see the light of day, you better move your ass and keep that gun up. Do you understand?"

She nods again with more energy. Checking again to see if the corridor is still empty, I squeeze the girl's arm—she can't be more than seventeen—and nudge her out the door.

Moving in a ragged formation, we cover the last three holding cells, all empty. The corridor opens up into a semicircle at the end, like a stadium. The schematics show the labs branching off from this central area, but there's little cover inside that nexus. For now, it's clear and we rush to the first lab.

The room is easily as large the *Sphynx*'s cargo bay with a door at the far end leading into a smaller storage room. Nothing moves inside and the lab is dark except for the illumination of several workstation VDUs in rows along the room's center.

I grab Strahan's elbow. "There are four labs on this level just as big. We need to split up if we're going to cover them quickly."

"All right. Bodie, you four check out the next lab." Pressing his throat mic, he says, "V, what's your position?"

It's Brady who answers, "We're taking fire! Stuck in the elevator at the far end of level two. They can't get in, but it's disabled. It's going to take us a few minutes to get to you. Desto is trying to rig it to move."

"Dammit," he mutters.

"Strahan, you and the others watch your asses. It's not the soldiers, it's the prisoners. They're rampaging."

"Fuck." This time he curses loudly. "We need to get down to level two and help them."

I'm *not* giving up the search for David, even if I'm doing it on my own. Strahan shoots me a look, reading my face. With a tiny shake of the head, he turns to the rest. "You four, take the stairs and flank the shooters, but watch your backs. Security could be on us in any minute. Try to get the rest of the crew up here to help cover these labs. Aly, I'll stick with you." He turns back to Bodie. "Let V know you're coming. Let's move."

I'm not expecting the wave of relief that washes over me. Having someone with me is good; having Strahan is ten times better. David's still got a chance, if he's alive.

They take off at a run down the corridor to the stairwell we'd come up. Strahan gives me a nod, and we duck into the lab and scrub the room, finding no one. It's abandoned and it looks as if they left in a hurry. The consoles and lab equipment are still running and several tubes with who knows what kind of biospecimens rest in containers on a few counters. As we approach the door to exit, a noise from outside alerts us that we're no longer alone. Quickly, we crouch behind a nearby cabinet, securing clean fields of fire to the doorway.

"I just need to grab a few things. Won't take a minute."

The sound of that voice throws me, and it takes me a second to realize why. It's Vilbrandt. I'd almost forgotten about him, but the fact he's here now confirms that Rajcik is too. I glance toward Strahan, and the look of contempt on his face makes it clear that he recognizes the voice too. Two sets of footsteps enter the room.

"What's in here that's so important?"

My eyes widen at the sound of the other voice. Ortiz!

"Things! Things that your boss wants! Now please be quiet and let me find what I need."

We stay kneeling silently behind our cover as objects are shoved quickly and haphazardly out of the way while he searches. The Nova is in the station's fore, stored in one of the weapons labs. What could be so important to Rajcik that he would send the scientist to this end? The answer is only too obvious and I stifle a shudder of revulsion.

Rajcik wants Vilbrandt to bring back whatever feculent biowarf specimens he's been developing. That kind of shit brings limited interest on the black market. There are still buyers, but maybe Rajcik's not planning to sell it. If I know him, he'll put it to more personal use. Maybe dose the drinking water of an Admin office complex, or just wipe out a military base. With the right resources, Rajcik's brutality has no limits.

I look back toward Strahan, wondering what he's thinking. I have no problem shooting Vilbrandt, in my book he's the lowest form of life, but Ortiz is another matter. She's committed her share of crimes, the same as I have, but she's never displayed the lack of human feeling, or conscience, that some of the others in my old crew have. Inside, she's not a monster, and maybe she would rather help me find David than continue to work with Rajcik. If I can talk to her, maybe I can turn her.

Strahan readies his pistol, preparing to stand and fire. Before he can, Ortiz says, "Drop that shit, Vilbrandt. You're not taking it."

A quick look around the edge of the cabinet shows Ortiz standing in a marksman's pose with her carbine aimed at Vilbrandt's head. He's facing her with several sealed tubes held up and his lips pulled back from his teeth in rabid hate.

"Don't be stupid. Drop it? Do you have any idea what would happen to both of us?" His question is followed by silence, and he continues, "Your boss wants it. You're going to help me get it."

"No, you're wrong about that. I'm—"

Before she can finish the sentence, gunfire erupts in the hallway outside. Instantly, I crouch lower, bracing against the cabinet, and lose visibility of the lab. A pistol fires inside the room, and there's a heaving *gghhhhht!* sound, as if someone got the wind knocked out of them. Before either Strahan or I can move, running footsteps enter and another shot is fired. This time there's the unmistakable sound of someone's head opening up and spilling its contents at peak velocity against the floor and walls. People are yelling, their voices moving down the corridor outside, but the room is quiet. Whoever entered is still here.

"Strahan?"

"Vitruzzi!"

She's standing inside the open door, guns up and ready to fire, looking out into the hallway. At the sound of her name, she jerks her head back toward where Strahan has leapt out of hiding.

"Where's Erikson?" she asks, and I step into the open.

Ortiz lays to my right, blood burbling from her chest. Vilbrandt's body has been blown backward and flops awkwardly over a desk. One fist is clenched around a pistol grip and blood flows in a growing pool beneath him. I didn't need to see what happened, experience explains everything. The scientist had been crafty enough to hide a pistol and shot Ortiz when the gunfire from the corridor distracted her and Vitruzzi fired on him when she came in. The vials he had been holding lay scattered around his body, unbroken.

"We have to move. Venus has been picking up transmissions from security and they're on their way toward us. They could lock down the docks any second and we won't be able to launch."

Strahan bounds around the equipment, ready to get the hell out of here. Despite the urgency, I squat down next to Ortiz. She'd been the closest thing to a friend I had on Rajcik's crew and something about her going out this way triggers compassion for her I didn't know I had.

Her eyes open when I put a hand on her arm and she recognizes me. "Aly." Blood speckles her lips as she whispers, "You've . . . got to stop him. Rajcik. You've got to . . ." She coughs and more blood erupts from her chest.

"I'm sorry, Ortiz."

"Listen." Somehow, she finds the strength to grab my hand. "He's going to drop the Nova on Tu-Tu-Tunis. Kill everyone."

My eyes widen. That sick bastard. "Why?"

"Crazy." A fog begins to dull her eyes and the blood seeping from the side of her mouth has become a dark, thick red. Her chest stops its desperate hitch to draw in air and I think she's gone, then her fingers tighten on mine again for a moment and she whispers, "He has . . . David."

"What? What?" But it's useless, she's dead.

Dropping the Nova on Tunis City? It's . . . exactly the kind of thing he would do. And he has David, just the way he'd promised. Rajcik's duplicity and craftiness and his ability to play multiple hands of poker at once are traits I've always recognized in him, admired even. How could I not have seen that he was playing T'Kai and maybe his own crew in the Nova job? He had certainly played David and I from the start. Do the rest of him know his plan? Do they care?

I look up and see both Vitruzzi and Strahan staring at me, their faces mirroring my own turmoil. Vitruzzi presses her mic. "Patrick, what's the situation?"

"Elevator is operational. Three squads are on the stairs headed for your level. Get down here now!"

As Brady finishes his sentence, a pistol report erupts inside the room. Strahan and Vitruzzi drop instantly, but I'm still crouched by Ortiz's body. Vitruzzi fires through the open doorway and the body of a prisoner falls inward, face down on the floor.

"Get to the elevator."

She covers the entrance, peering down the corridor. In a smooth motion, she brings one of her pistols to shoulder level and fires down the hallway, five, six, seven times. Then she turns back to the room and says something. Oddly, I can see her mouth moving, her eyes wide and emphatic, but I can't hear what she's saying. I feel as if I'm inside a thick plastic bag and nothing from the outside can penetrate. Hearing that David may still be alive has stunned me, making me realize how certain I'd been that he was already dead.

Vitruzzi's eyes shift from me to Strahan and she begins yelling more urgently, pointing at me, but it's as if her voice has been whipped away in a strong wind. Strahan's head snaps back and his eyes widen. I start to rise, but my leg refuses to hold me and I tumble forward, hitting the wall in front of me with my palm. He runs up beside me and kneels, his face inches from mine. "Aly, you're hit!"

Sound returns, bringing a searing shock of pain along with it that suddenly bursts from my left thigh. I look down and see a rip in my pants with blood oozing through, about six inches below my hip. "Fuck." My voice sounds much too calm.

"What's it look like, Karl?" Vitruzzi yells.

He leans forward and pulls the tatters of the rip apart, saying to me, "Shallow. Looks like it went through. Can you walk?"

"Yeah." Through numb lips. With gritted teeth and a timid nausea beginning to take hold of my stomach, I push myself up. No way is this going to stop me.

"Good." He yanks open a pocket in his vest, pulls out a field bandage, and deftly wraps it around my thigh, tying it off with a tight yank. "V, got anything to numb this with?"

She pulls a syringe from a med bag she carries and tosses it to us. Strahan rips through the packaging with his teeth and not bothering with delicacy, presses the needle into my thigh. "Dammit! Careful!" Searing pain rips through my wounded flesh and quickly begins receding to a suggestion.

He gives me a half grin that's calm and cool, not a normal expression for someone outnumbered by both Corps and criminals, all ready and willing to cut him down. "Let's get out of here."

Back in motion, we leapfrog up the corridor to the elevator, passing the bodies of the prisoners Vitruzzi shot. Brady holds the elevator doors open and the rest of the crew is lodged inside. Just as we reach it, we hear the stairwell door at the other end of the hallway slam against the wall.

Vitruzzi steps inside first, crowding against the others when a sudden, explosive *WHOOMPFFF!* echoes throughout the complex. The floor bucks beneath us and the elevator jumps slightly on its rails. Immediately, thick black smoke begins pouring into the corridor from every direction.

"Get in!" Brady yells.

Strahan and Vitruzzi cram into the elevator. I don't.

"What are you doing, come on!" Bodie cries.

"I'm not leaving."

Strahan pushes to the front of the elevator. "You're going to find your brother?"

Nodding, I respond simply, "I can't leave. He's all I've got."

"I'll help," he says, and steps off the elevator, followed by Desto. "We're with you, Aly. We've come this far."

I can't speak, my disbelief more paralyzing than shock. But I know I probably won't get much further alone. My voice shakes as I finally respond, "Rajcik will be in the docks at the front of the station. Nearest the weapons labs." Even while studying how to infiltrate the Fortress, I'd also been calculating what his plans might be. I knew he would never give up, just as I knew instinctively that our paths would cross again.

Vitruzzi scowls, considering the situation. She knows I won't change my course, but she won't abandon Desto or Strahan either. Not when there is any chance, no matter how small. "You've got twenty minutes to get back to the prisoner transport. We'll be waiting." The elevator door closes.

The smoke filled corridor gives us enough cover to duck into the nearest lab before the advancing soldiers see us, and we hunker together for a minute to sketch out a plan.

"The ninth floor is the most direct line to the bow. The connecting corridor, if it's still accessible, is going to have the least amount of cover. If we move toward the docks near the weapons labs and don't run into any security, it should take us five minutes." Strahan looks me directly in the eye, the message *we'll never make it in time* stamped on his face. He's probably right, but that's not going to stop me.

The squad securing our level runs by, not bothering to clear the rooms, apparently just trying to reach the elevator and get away from the smoke-filled hallway, a perfect cloak for an ambush.

"I'll take point. Karl, you get our six," Desto says. He glances outside and breaks for the stairs with us on his heels.

We scramble up the stairwell and reach level nine without encountering anyone. Running fast now, taking chances we wouldn't ordinarily take, we speed directly down the corridor as a unit. There's no time to check if each feeder hallway is clear, and the corridor itself is wide, designed for high traffic. We may as well be running down the middle of a bull's-eye. Desto skates past the opening of an adjoining hallway and a bullet glances from his armor, blowing puffs of fiber into my face. I'm right beside him, running as hard as I can to keep up, and have to duck across the opening, firing blindly as I go by. Strahan doesn't even slow down, skidding across the opening on his knees, firing into the squad racing to catch us. I reach back to grab his hand and pull him back to his feet. We keep running, blowing our lungs out to make it to the next hatch before they can get behind us and fire up the corridor.

We make it.

Strahan stops long enough to disable the entry mechanism with a ball of E-10 wax and catches up as Desto and I reach an intersection. Desto peers around the corner, then jumps backward. With his back pressed against the wall, he signals to us by sliding one hand under the other. *Find some cover!* Then waves a hand in front of his eyes. *Get out of sight!*

There's a doorway right beside me and I slip inside, expecting them both to follow but they don't. The door clicks quietly closed, cutting off sounds from the hallway. Where are they? For a moment the only thing I hear is my breathing, then an unfamiliar voice cries out, "Contact!" and shots begin echoing down the hallway. I hear someone running, more shooting coming from right outside the door, and a stampede of boots rolling down the corridor like thunder. Shadows pass under the gap at the bottom of the doorway. I tense up and press myself harder into the wall, forcing my hand to stay away from the doorknob. It would be suicide to jump into the middle of them.

As soon as the footsteps begin to fade, I try to raise the other two in my throat-mic: "Strahan, Desto, what's your position? Do you copy? Over."

There's no response for a long second, then Desto says, "I sweet talked them into following me, but they couldn't keep up. I'm a floor above you now. I'll meet you at the hangar. Over."

"Copy. Strahan?"

"Right outside." He presses the door open with the barrel of his rifle. "Let's go."

I don't know how he gave them the slip, but the soldiers took Desto's bait and have all double-timed out of the area. Moving quickly, we cover the last hundred meters to the connecting corridor. Luck is with us—it's clear. We take the speedwalking belt running along one side and make it to the far end in just a few breaths. The weapons labs are a floor below us, immediately adjacent to the docking hangars.

An empty guard booth at the end of the corridor provides enough cover for us to stop for a few seconds to catch our breath. The bandage Strahan wrapped around my thigh is holding tight and the wound is barely bleeding. I can't feel a thing. Strahan crouches inside the booth and activates his mic. "Desto, where are you?"

"Coming up on the first hangar, level seven. Looks like there has been some activity. I'm looking at one, maybe two squads of wasted soldiers. Over."

We exchange a knowing look. *Rajcik's work.*

"Hang tight. We're still on nine. We'll meet you at hangar zero-one. Out."

With a nod, we move out, running left toward the end of the corridor where another stairwell will take us down. I bang through the door and train my carbine down the shaft. No one. Strahan's right behind me and we begin descending.

Passing by level eight, my feet barely touch the steps. The sound of the door swinging open above me causes me to jerk to a sudden stop on the next landing and nearly topple over the side. Gripping the rail, I spin around and see a squad pouring through the door between Strahan and I. He manages to come to a stop a few stairs above them and trains his rifle at the three who have crammed onto the landing, but who knows how many are on the other side of the door? I begin reversing direction back up the stairs to get a clean line of fire, but Strahan suddenly turns and starts running back up. The sound of his boots on the metal stairs draws their attention, inciting them to follow. Strahan's voice comes through my earpiece: "Keep going, Aly. I'll shake them and meet you in the hangar. Over."

They don't have a firing solution on him and he has a solid lead. I press my back against the wall to stay out of sight and continue to slip down the stairs. Strahan wouldn't tell me to keep going if he isn't certain he has an out, but that doesn't stop my pulse from going into overdrive. I have the advantage with every soldier in this section probably chasing Strahan and Desto, but now I'm on my own. There are no guarantees in this, no matter how good at the game we are. It's possible that I'll be able to slip into the hangar unnoticed. But then what? Will Rajcik still be there?

Quietly cracking the door onto level seven, I study the corridor and go through. Motorized transports line up along niches in the wall along the wide corridor, ready to transport newly off-loaded supplies to their destinations throughout the station. Dead soldiers crowd the hall a few meters away, their blood streaking the walls. Yet another advantage, but there's no pleasure in seeing the carnage. Judging by the burned and mangled condition of their corpses, whoever did this used an explosive.

"Desto? Strahan? Anyone copy? Over." No answer. Maybe they're already in the hangar.

The wall separating the corridor from the docking hangars is a meter thick and built from high-strength, low-alloy steel with a melting point of over 3,000 degrees, more than capable of protecting the complex from the engine blowback of incoming and outgoing ships. A service tunnel into hangar zero-alpha opens up just beyond the pile of corpses. It has been nine minutes since we left the bio labs, leaving eleven minutes until the crew dusts off and disappears for good. It doesn't matter. I'm not leaving without my brother. He wouldn't leave me.

My VDU displays the saved pass code and I step to the side while the door slides open. Thick blue smoke pours from the gap, enveloping me and creating a fuming cloud in the corridor. Pushing away from the doorway, I fall flat against the floor waiting for a fire to rush out but none does.

What the hell is going on? A fire inside one of the hangars should trigger the Fortress's hull security response, completely disabling all of the doors leading in and out. If the integrity of a hangar is compromised, the entire complex could by destroyed, ripped to pieces by the vacuum of space. Somehow, the internal security defenses have been disabled. The station has taken a lot of damage from the prisoners, but not that much. It has to be Rajcik.

Blaring fire alarms inside the hangar slice through the air, mixing with the ever-present dull *whump* of the general alarm and setting my teeth on edge. Tendrils of the smoke caught in the service tunnel trail out and a quick look through the doorway reveals that it's empty. Still, I can't see much of the hangar beyond. A rotating red strobe light fixed on the entryway roof flashes in circles, giving the tunnel a crazed funhouse kind of effect. I'll be target practice if anyone is guarding the entrance from hangar-side, but I don't have time to look for another way in. Keeping the AK-80 stock pressed firmly to my shoulder and crouching low, I run for everything I'm worth to the other side.

Caustic vestiges of smoke line my lungs, but nothing stops me from reaching the bay. Two parked track tugs sit beyond the entryway, one partially obscuring it, the other about thirty paces forward and to my right. Random crates and barrels are pushed into groups and a catwalk with a control pod for maneuvering a ceiling-mounted crane traces the wall on the bay's left side. Clouds of smoke rise toward the ceiling but no fire. The tracker offers good coverage and I lunge toward it.

The best vantage of the bay floor is the catwalk, but the tracker's left runner conceals me while my eyes adjust to the auxiliary lights flashing in yellow strobes on the ceiling. Climbing up the ladder to the cab lets me peer over the side to see what lies beyond. The *Temptation* sits near the launch track airlock.

How did he get clearance to land? It's hard to believe a ship with the *Temptation*'s notoriety could, but it hardly matters at this point. The ship sits in the middle of the dock, loading door still open and engines cycling in preparation for launch. There is no movement around the ship visible from where I hide and the flight deck screens face the airlock. Whoever's inside the cockpit, probably Thompson, won't be able to spot me. The dock control room is about sixty paces to my right. Either Rajcik or Yadav must be in there prepping the interior airlock to open so the *Temptation* can enter the launch track. Is the Nova already on board?

Carefully climbing back down to ground level, I prepare to move in closer to the ship. The only other crewmember is Fedchenko; Rajcik wouldn't have had time to enlist more cohorts, but he could be anywhere. It's just me against four. Even if I try to raise Strahan and Desto, the mic is useless in this kind of noise.

As if reading my mind, the shrieking alarms cut out abruptly. The good news is short-lived, however, as the dock control room door opens and Rajcik comes through, staring in my direction.

And he's not alone.

He pushes my brother in front of him to use as a bullet-stopper, one of his muscular arms locked around David's neck and the other jamming a Sinbad into his temple. Before thinking of the consequences, I shout, "David!"

Rajcik's arm tightens around David's throat, almost jerking him off his feet and making him unable to respond. Deadly calm, he says, "Aly, you never fail to impress me."

I can't risk the shot. If I expose myself, Rajcik will drop David before I can pull the trigger and I'll either hit my brother or miss altogether. Dammit, Strahan, Desto, get your asses up here now!

Pressing my back into the tug's track, I shout, "You don't have to do this, János! I don't give a fuck about the bomb or the money, just let him go!"

An icy chuckle wafts across the bay to me. The only other sound comes from the *Temptation*'s engines as they slowly gain momentum, building energy for flight. "Negotiations don't work with me, Aly. When will you learn? You and your brother have caused me far too much trouble, and I want retribution."

I risk a glance around the track. He's dragging David toward the ship, his eyes fixed in my direction. David's eyes are blackened and still swollen, but they're open. But he's moving strangely, swiveling his head left and right, squinting as if he's trying to locate the sound of my voice. His eyes never seem to focus.

Rajcik shakes him. "Go on, David. Tell her what I plan to do with the Nova. I want Aly to know before you both die."

My line of sight is cut off as they move behind the track vehicle and continue to close the gap to the ship. If they get on board, there's no way I'll be able to reach them. Sweat drips from my forehead, running down my cheeks and neck into my shirt. Not a muscle in my body relaxes and my carbine stays steady at shoulder level. I have a window of about eight meters from when they become visible on the other side of the tug to when they'll be walking up the ship's loading ramp. Those eight meters are my only chance of stopping Rajcik.

"Tell her!" Rajcik yells.

David's voice, strained by the pressure of Rajcik's tight grip, cuts through the smoke. "He's going to wipe out Tunis City. There was never going to be any extortion. He's just a sick fuck and—" He's cut off.

Christ, he knew? Goddammit, David, you should have told me! If you had, we wouldn't be here right now! This is no time to get angry; I need to get in position for the shot. I hear Ortiz's dying words again, *"He's going to drop the Nova . . . kill everyone."* But how had David known? The reason Rajcik wanted us dead is finally clear. We never would have helped him get the holodisc and steal the Nova if we'd known what he intended to do with it. We would have done anything to stop him, and he knows it. I don't know how David found out or how Rajcik knew he had, but he's seconds away from paying the price for not shooting Rajcik when he had the chance. Unless I can do it first.

I'm going to kill you, Rajcik. If it's the last thing I do.

"There you have it, Aly! Now you can see what a monumental pain in the ass you two have been to me! But I think we're done now. Get out here and say goodbye to your brother." It almost sounds as if

Rajcik is laughing, but as they move around the other side of the vehicle, there is no grin on his face. His black eyes are fierce and his lips are pulled back from his gleaming incisors in a snarl. Dragging David along, he shuffles backward toward the open hatch of the *Temptation*. I catch a glimpse of someone's rifle barrel from inside the hatch, providing Rajcik with more cover.

There's a noise above me, a sharp gonging sound like metal on metal. Everyone looks toward it simultaneously. Strahan!

David drives his head back into Rajcik's face and a wet, smacking sound reports across the bay. Then he lunges forward toward me, staying low, and I open fire. A fine, red mist of blood erupts from Rajcik's shoulder as he takes a bullet, but the sonofabitch is so fucking fast. He starts running before David gets more than a few steps away and quickly takes cover inside the *Temptation*. Strahan fires a screen of bullets from above me, keeping the shooter inside the ship from getting a clear shot while David runs for his life across the bay.

"RIGHT HERE! I'M HERE!" The sound of my voice helps him make it to the tug in a blind shambling run that proves his vision is jacked up, and I grab him by the shirt, pulling him to safety. Strahan continues to keep Rajcik and the shooter inside the ship busy. Holding David by the arm, I start to run, pulling him toward the tunnel to the other side. Almost the instant we break from cover, automatic rifle reports issue from the dock control room. I leap backward, still holding David and he lands nearly on top of me, just as bullets bounce off the steel floor in front of our feet. We're covered from every angle.

Leaning back against the tracks again, I crane my head up to see Strahan on the catwalk. He has good coverage of the entire dock and is well hidden behind a stack of cargo bins. Whoever's inside the dock control room is completely concealed and has a perfect line of fire between where we're hidden and the tunnel I came in through. Rajcik, firing from the *Temptation*'s loading ramp, also has a direct line of fire at us if we leave the concealment of the tug. Strahan can't hold off both of them and David can't see to either fire or run to the tunnel. Basically, we're fucked.

Tapping my mic, I whisper, "Desto, do you read me? What's your position? Over."

Silence.

The sickening realization that Desto is probably dead washes over me, but I squash it. I have to. Brushing the sweat soaked hair from my face, I call Strahan, "I'm going to try and drive this tracker to the exit. When I stop, see if you can make it to the other side and help us get out of here."

"Roger."

Cutting through the ties on David's wrists, I realize how thin he's become. His clothes hang from his skeletal frame and I'm surprised he even had the strength to run for cover. "Can you see at all?"

"Not a goddamn thing," he says, and then adds, "How the hell did you get here?"

"I'll tell you later. Look, we're hiding behind a track tug. There's a handhold about a meter above you, by your right hand. You're leaning against the step. I'm going to go up first and get it started. When I yell, try to get up. I'll help. You ready?"

"Yeah."

I scramble up the tracker's side and into the open interior. It's too high up for anyone on the ground to get a shot at me, but as soon as they hear the engine crank up, rifle fire begins clacking off the sides. The doors are reinforced and nothing but a direct, level shot is going to get through them. Leaning out from the open left-side door, I call down to David. He reaches up, hand scrambling along the side and I direct it to the handhold. Grimacing, he pulls himself onto the cab's floor, keeping his body low and compact.

Reversing fast, I force the tug into the wall and we come to a shuddering stop. Bullets continue to bounce off its thick tracks, having no effect, but our angle is good; we're between the dock control room and the exit tunnel. The *Temptation* now has the only line of fire and Strahan won't ease up to let them get a shot.

I launch over the side and direct David's feet to the ladder rungs, helping him down. "We've got to run like hell. Just hold onto my shirt."

He nods and we take off at a sprint through the tunnel entrance. The safety door at the other end is still open and I push him against the wall while I check the corridor. Clear.

The sound of rifle fire from the hangar stops. We pause at the end of the tunnel for a few seconds, hoping to hear Strahan. Seconds later, his voice echoes down the corridor from my right. "Hold your fire!"

Appearing through the smoke about twelve meters down the hall, he races to us and engages his mic: "Vitruzzi, Brady, do you copy?"

"Where the hell are you, Karl?"

"Look, we found Erikson's brother, but we're still at the loading docks. We need ten more minutes."

"Dammit, Strahan! You've got eight! Out."

He takes one of David's arms, ready to run.

"Wait," I say. Strahan stops and turns, his expression tense and expectant. "You take David back to the ship. I'll meet you there."

The disbelief on his face might be funny in other circumstances. No, probably not.

David says, "Aly, what are you talking about?"

Strahan looks as if he wants to shoot me himself. "No fucking way. We've got to *go*."

"No! If Rajcik gets out of here with the Nova, a lot of people are going to die!"

"No way, Aly, there's no time!" Strahan argues. "Don't be so fucking stubborn. For once—"

I grab him, both of my hands gripping the straps of his equipment vest, and shout, "He's going to detonate it, Karl! He'll kill millions! I can't let that happen. Take David back to the MCACS, okay? If I'm not there in time, just leave. Don't risk it. I'll find another way out."

David starts to argue, "Aly, no . . ."

"Just go!"

He reaches blindly toward me, his eyes somehow able to find mine and lock onto them. I grab his searching hand. Strahan studies me for a bitter second, grabs David's shoulder, and turns to run. With a final squeeze, David turns away and they double-time down the corridor.

TWENTY-THREE

Gulping a lungful of acrid air, I make my way back down the service tunnel into the hangar. Even Rajcik won't suspect I'm crazy enough to come after him. He's probably dead certain that we're headed toward the escape we should be making—that Strahan and David *are* making. Right now, that's my only advantage. Creeping deftly along the wall, I can't make out any movement in the bay. The smoke that had hung like a thin fog has diminished to a minute tendril, more an oily taste in the back of my throat than something visible. There had been no indication of chemical fire retardant self-ejecting in any of the sectors we've been through, so the fire, wherever it is, must be burning itself out.

Crouched low, nearly squatting, I reach the end of the tunnel and run for the cover of the tracker. The voice telling me I'll never see my brother, or any of them, again makes my hands feel shaky as I train the carbine around the tracker's side, looking for my next move. The auxiliary lights still spin in sinister yellow flashes, but the bay is clear of my old crew. At least from what I can see. Climbing into the tracker's cab, the sound of machinery suddenly catches my attention and I duck low behind the control apparatus. The only thing I can see is the ceiling, and finally the thing I'd missed all along becomes obvious.

The Nova hovers fifteen meters above the bay floor, suspended by a network of steel chains from the ceiling crane. Parked directly beneath it, a four-wheeled electric cart is prepped to carry it on board the *Temptation*. As I watch the weapon's slow descent, my eyes track to the catwalk and the man standing at the controls. It's Fedchenko, and he's completely focused on the bomb. He doesn't know I'm here.

The Nova is surprisingly small, only about two meters in length, cylindrical in shape and narrow enough that two grown men could reach around it by linking their arms. The housing is a dark, burnished steel divided into two segments. I know from the schematics that Rajcik had obtained before the operation that the bigger segment contains the triggering mechanisms. The missile seems so small and nonthreatening that it's hard to imagine it could ever cause the devastation we'd been warned of. Taking careful aim from inside the cab, I wait for the crane to descend farther. When I pick off Fedchenko, I don't want the thing falling.

Tock, tock! I double tap him in the head and as predicted, his body hurls forward, shorting out the crane's circuit board and sending the Nova into a fast descent. It lands squarely on the cart. With Fedchenko, MacCready, and Ortiz down, that leaves Yadav and Thompson, along with Rajcik.

The sound of someone running and then—*holyshit!*—a grenade lands nearly in my lap. I fling myself back through the cab door, landing next to the tug and tucking myself into a tight ball. *KURRUMPPFFF!* The blast goes right over the top of me, bursting outward and upward. With my position compromised, I geronimo out from behind the ruined vehicle straight for the cover of the four-wheeled cart sitting between me and the *Temptation*.

Reaching relative safety, I squeeze myself against one of the rear wheels, keeping my carbine at shoulder level. On the other side of the cart, the *Temptation* sits on the bay floor like a menacing predator, loading ramp still open and engines still cycling up. Approximately six meters of open bay lie between it and me. If my guess is correct, my three ex-shipmates are now all aboard, waiting for me to expose myself.

I just start to catch my breath when the cart begins to roll slowly toward the ship. Shit! Must be controlled by remote. All Rajcik has to do is direct it onto the *Temptation,* launch, and he's free.

Not if I stop him.

I fire into the vehicle's tires, first the rear, then the front. Its engine continues to strain against the drag, so I grab a metal rod lying in a tool bin mounted on its side and thrust it into the cart's local control box. Sparks erupt in my face, momentarily blinding me and dotting my skin with burning pinpricks. One side of its wheels makes another half revolution, forcing it into a lopsided turn, and with a whining buzz, it dies. With smug self-satisfaction, I imagine Rajcik inside the ship, wondering how he's going to get the Nova on board. He can't get a shot at me from the ship, and wouldn't want to fire at the Nova anyway. With the bomb as my cover, I'm at the perfect position to ghost anyone who shows so much as an arm outside the loading ramp. David and Karl should be at the MCACS by now. I have maybe five minutes left before they launch and then I'll be stranded on the Fortress with Corps fighters guaranteed to be on their way. My momentary smugness disappears like an empty promise. I need to get the hell of out here.

As I gauge my chances of making it back to the service tunnel, the hydraulic hum of the *Temptation*'s ramp catches my attention. In an eternity that lasts maybe ten seconds, it climbs back up into the ship's belly and seals shut. He's leaving! Relief pours over me like a shower of hot sand, instantly filling me with a crazy excitement, as if maybe this will all be over soon. Rajcik might get away, but at least he's not taking his lethal payload with him.

It's time for me to go. Standing and setting my sights on nothing but the service tunnel entrance, I'm preparing to run like hell when my guts explode in a white-hot nebula of pain. It's as if a phosphorous grenade has just detonated inside my torso. It isn't until I clutch my stomach, my carbine falling from my hands, that I hear the pistol report.

I didn't know it was possible to feel this much pain, and I suddenly understand what it's like to wish to be dead. Then it gets worse. Every thought, every instinct for survival, every driving force that's ever gotten me from one second to the next is suddenly wiped away by pure, visceral agony. All I'm capable of is standing, motionless, my hands gripped to my torso while blood backs up behind them and then starts to stream over the top in a crimson waterfall. A hand clamps onto my shoulder, twirls me around, and Rajcik leers down at me. The look on his face is a demented mixture of serenity and rage.

"Aly, you just never quit, do you?"

I'm stunned, my guts bubbling, unable to speak.

He looks at the disabled cart carrying the dormant Nova, then back at me. "Still," he begins, his tone strangely magnanimous, "a lot of useless people will have you to thank for not being blown into oblivion. Too bad they'll never know, huh?"

Desperately, I look to where my carbine landed, but I'll never reach it before he shoots me again. My hands are plastered to my burning belly, the hot blood continuing to seep between my fingers like grisly lava. With tremendous effort, I reach up and jerk his hand violently from my shoulder, not wanting him to touch me. The movement takes the last of my strength. I would crumple to the floor except for his fist that flies out and squeezes painfully around my throat, cutting off the air I can't draw anyway because of the pain in my guts. Blood drips from his nose from where David had head-butted him, forming a gory mustache, which streaks down his jaw line. Holding me up and staring coldly into my eyes, he casually licks it from his lips as if savoring the taste. Before I can struggle, he jerks me forward and throws me into the floor like an empty sack.

I land on my back and draw air through my clenched teeth. It hurts. He stands above me, glaring. I try to tell him to rot in hell, but a spark of pain shoots from my belly up into my chest and I writhe on the floor, feeling my face contort from the agony. Drawing up into a fetal position, I'm helpless to do anything but watch as he opens a compartment on the Nova's sleek black housing and reaches inside.

Squinting my eyelids against the hot tears welling up, I hear him chuckle. His face grows deadly serious as he leans down over me. "I want you to know something, Aly. You're going to die right here on this floor. When this detonates, your body is going to be the first thing it destroys. You'll disintegrate and be blasted into space like so much human waste."

An uncontrollable shudder, not of fear but of pain, wracks me and makes him pause. He squats down and leans forward, pressing the barrel of his pistol against the floor as a prop. My eyes pick out the fact that he has blood caked under his thumbnail.

"In another nine minutes and thirty seconds, you won't feel a thing," he continues. "But when I find your brother, if he and your new friends manage to get away, he's going to feel *a lot*. His suffering is going to make what you're going through right now seem pleasant. That's my parting promise to you." He gives me a last look of almost fraternal pity, then stands up and walks across the bay to his ship. As he climbs back into the *Temptation*'s cockpit hatch, which he'd used to exit the ship and sneak up on me, the station's inner airlock doors engage and begin to part, allowing the ship to enter the launch tracks. Rajcik is going to escape, and I can do nothing to stop him now.

I need to warn the others. "Vitruzzi, if you're listening, get out of here. The Nova . . ." My throat convulses and I start to cough, another eruption of blood spurting from my ruined stomach. Getting it under control, I finish, "Get out of here. It's counting down."

There's no response, but I'm not going to die here on this floor. I won't give Rajcik the satisfaction. I might, just might, be able to make it to the MCACS. It's an impossible lie, but the thought gives me the motivation I need. I know it doesn't matter, but I don't want to be next to that thing when it blows. Trying to direct my attention away from the molten pain in my guts, I grab the sidewall of the cart's tire, reach for my carbine, and drag my body up into a standing position. Once on my feet and forced to hold my own weight up, pain and nausea twist through me in a secondary explosion. I double over, vomiting bright red blood, and see more blood pattering out of the hole in my torso and onto my boots. I'm not sure if the amount coming from my throat or out of my stomach is more disturbing. The red is so bright, glowing as if it really is composed of phosphorous.

The *Temptation* starts rolling down the launch tunnel. In seconds, the doors close behind it. It's just me and the bomb now, and I can feel my strength evaporating like so much smoke. Have to push hard, get away.

Staggering, I make it across the bay to the service entrance and lean against the smooth metal walls, already needing to rest. The corridor seems to be an endless tunnel blurring in and out of clarity. Slumping against the wall, feeling my insides leaking out, I search for the strength to start walking, or crawling, to the other end. The hatch is down there, and if I can get to the hatch, I can get away from the Nova.

The lights on the ceiling waver and pulse, getting darker with each beat. I've been standing here for less than five seconds, but it might as well be five years. I don't think I can make it.

My arms feel heavy and begin to go numb. Ordering myself to move forward, I push one leg out. As I rest my weight on it, it feels odd, as if my knees aren't bending the right way. I lean onto the leg anyway, grateful that it holds my weight, and will the next one forward. Something clanks beside me, but it sounds tinny and far away. Distractedly, my brain records that I've dropped the carbine. I can't pick it up—too weak. If I bend over I'll fall and that will be it.

Another step, then another. I stumble and brace against the wall with both hands. They leave a wide swath of blood behind. Not good. Warmth is spreading down my hip and thigh. I'm not going to look, just keep walking.

The pulsing lights are getting much darker. A couple more beats and I won't be able to see at all. Is this what dying feels like? Just blacking out and not waking up?

I trip over my own feet once more. But this time, my hands just slide along the metal corridor wall, the blood making them slick. I hit like a dropped corpse, my face banging into the grated floor. Its cold-ness presses into my cheek. It's not refreshing. It hurts.

Come on, Aly, come on. You got to keep moving.

Reaching out and digging my fingers into the grated floor, I grab and pull with all the strength I have left. I make about five centime-ters. Just need a break. A short break.

I rest my cheek on the floor again. Air rushes up through the small squares made by the grate. There's an oily, faintly burned odor to it. My eyes fall closed.

Something wakes me up, or pulls me out of unconsciousness, I can't tell which. Noise. Clattering . . . no, tromping. Boots. They're moving fast. I just hope whoever it is kills me quickly. I don't care, just let me sleep.

"Aly? ALY! Oh shit!"

The runner's speed increases, and then I see Strahan's face above me. "Get . . . out. Nova . . . run," I whisper, feeling blood that had started to dry cracking on my lips.

"Jesus, Aly. I'm going to get you out of here! You're not dead yet!"

Yes, I am, I try to whisper, but then he's picking me up, and the radiation from a thousand suns bursts through me. And it all goes black.

SHRIEKING ALARMS AND LIGHTS. My eyes flutter open, everything around me in chaos. The only pain I feel is my splitting eardrums, as if the nerves in them are being ripped from my cranium. A voice, "ohmygod, it's going to hit us," filled with terror, "HOLD ONTO SOMETHING!" A giant *CRAAAASH!* and the sense of being hurled through space, as if gravity suddenly changed direction, everything around me flying through the air. As the world drains into darkness again, all I feel is relief.

PEOPLE SPEAKING, murmurs that I can't understand. Then, something warm against my cheek, like breath. "Hang on, Aly. You're going to make it. You're strong. Strongest person I've ever met." David? No. Strahan.

Later.

There's a sound, a low-key beep going off in a constant rhythm. Kinda soothing. I listen for a while before realizing I'm awake. How long have I been unconscious? It's too much effort to open my eyes. Just lay here. *Beep . . . beep . . . beep.* Eventually, the sound becomes annoying.

"Can someone turn that off?"

Air exchangers whispering. Pain everywhere. My nose, my throat, my chin, my guts. My eyes flicker open inside a dim room. In my peripheral vision, I see stands loaded with hanging bags of blood, saline, and other liquids, tubes dangling everywhere, connected to my body in different places. Thankfully, I sense drugs doing their work, dulling out everything, making the pain just an unwelcome visitor, not part of me.

A silhouette looms next to me. "I told you you weren't dead."

"Where's David?" I don't recognize my own voice. I sound like a breathless crow.

"He's okay. He's in the other med-station."

" . . . see him."

"Not yet. You've got to stay still for now. V says you've just started to recover. You need to rest, recuperate."

I have no strength to argue, even if I want to. "Thirsty."

"Aly, you've been shot in the stomach, so I can't give you anything to drink. But here." He rubs blessedly cool ice over my lips. The room seems as if it isn't there, just a gray backdrop. The only thing that comes into focus is Strahan.

" . . . crazy to come back for me."

"Yeah. You're rubbing off on me."

My eyelids start to rebel and slide closed. I sense him still standing next to me and I force them back open. His hands rest on the gurney, his features arranged intently, concerned, maybe even a little afraid.

"Karl."

"Yeah?"

"I . . . owe you."

A tragic grin spreads across his lips and his moist eyes gleam. "Not this time. We're even."

TWENTY-FOUR

D ays, maybe a week, go by; I'm too in and out of it to be completely sure. I start waking up more and more, longer each time, my body healing while its monuments to pain shrink in achingly slow decrements. Almost every time I open my eyes, Strahan is there, asking me how I am, if he can get me anything. Vitruzzi monitors every pump, tube, and screen attached to me with clockwork diligence. Everyone visits. By the time we arrive at Agate Beach, most of my many questions are answered.

Why had Strahan come back for me? And how had we made it back to the MCACS before either Vitruzzi launched or the Fortress blew?

On our way back toward Agate Beach, I'm itching for another shot of morphine, sweating like a leaky faucet from the recurrent spasms of pain in my insides, when Desto comes by and fills in that part of the story for me.

About the same time I had persuaded Strahan and David to make a run for it back to the *Sphynx*, Desto finally managed to get back down to the seventh-floor hangar but was cornered by a security squad in one of the weapons labs.

"I had to duck behind the door too fast and it tore my mic right off. Couldn't transmit and tell you what happened. The security squad had me covered. There was no way I was leaving that lab the way I came in, so I headed toward the back door and damned if they didn't throw a grenade. I probably would have bought it, but an explosives testing shield hit me in the back and knocked my ass about five meters through the air. And here's the funny part—those dumbshits threw a grenade into a weapons lab. Something else in there blew up when it went off and burned up half the squad. Incinerated them in a flash so fast they never even had time to scream. That shield was thick and heavy as hell, but it kept me from getting turned into a human torch too. The rest of them must have been worried something else was going to go off because they double-timed out of there like Corps Comp master runners." There's a burn along one of his cheeks, a raw pink furrow that looks painful. Other than that, his glowing smile is as reckless as ever.

"They headed for the next level and I took off the other way, toward the hangar. When Karl and your brother came around the corner, it was nearly the end of it for everyone. I almost shot them, and Karl had me dead to rights. Once we regrouped, Karl heard your transmission about the Nova. He could tell from your voice that you'd bought at least one bullet, but if you could still talk, you were still breathing. So, we gave David a pistol and told him to keep it aimed forward, and we all doubled back to the hangar. We carried you as far as the midstation tunnels before you died. But Captain V and your boyfriend weren't having it."

I blushed when he said that, no doubt in my mind he was talking about Strahan. "What do you mean 'before I died'? And since when is Strahan my boy—?"

He cut me off with a patronizing laugh and left, telling me I needed to get some rest.

The havoc that the prisoners had wreaked upon the Fortress's security grid had not only overridden fire-control protocols and left the entrances to the docking bays operational, but none of the airlocks or launch tubes could be locked down. Despite needing to get the hell out of the area before Corps detachments came to the

Fortress's defense, Vitruzzi still had the option of staying put as long as needed. The crew weren't about to leave friends behind if there was even a slim possibility of rescue, and against monumental odds, Strahan and Desto had gotten David and I back to the MCACS, the ship launching at the last possible nanosecond before the Nova blew.

But it was Vitruzzi who explained this part to me. A few hours later, she came into the med-station looking more tired than I've ever seen her, but no less composed. I noticed that the tenseness that had dug itself into deeper and deeper grooves around her mouth and eyes every day since I first met her seemed shallower. She no longer looked like a forty-year-old woman pushing eighty, and I was surprised by how relieved it made me feel.

While she scanned my medical readouts, I repeated the question, "What was Desto talking about? He said I died."

"Yes, you were dead. You had a stomach that was more hole than tissue from the bullet wound, but that was the least of your worries. By the time Karl and Desto found you, you'd lost a critical amount of blood and went into heart failure, flatlined. The MCACS's med-station had the equipment necessary to revive you, but we needed to get you back on the *Sphynx* if there was going to be any chance you'd make it. We launched just as I got your heartbeat back. Then the station blew."

The brief fragment of consciousness I'd experienced was caused by the blast concussion from the Nova exploding. But it had been too close; the blast crippled the MCACS and caused more injuries among the unprepared crew. Most escaped with minor bruises and abrasions, but David had been unable to brace himself because of his sight limitations. He had several broken ribs caused by a heavy gear locker slamming into him, and Venus's right arm was fractured from the blast's force shoving her against the flight control console. Because of having been strapped to a stationary gurney as soon as Strahan carried me on, I was the only one aboard that wasn't hurt. At least, not more hurt. Despite her injury, Venus was able to coax the MCACS back under control and Vitruzzi, escaping with only a few minor contusions, had immediately gone to work helping the injured. With luck and sheer strength of will, the crew patched the ruined ship together enough to fly it within shuttle range of the *Sphynx*. They got me to its onboard infirmary and an emergency surgery kept me alive. Vitruzzi had been accumulating specialized medical equipment for some time through both legal and black-market transactions. Thanks to her criminal initiative, she had what she needed to save me. After the surgery, I'd been interred in a pressure suit and given several blood transfusions, but despite all of it, another four days had passed before I came out of the coma. Vitruzzi hadn't believed I'd make it until I started breathing on my own again, a week ago. Since then, a constant IV diet of tissue regeneration- and hemo-stims has brought me a few steps closer to a full recovery everyday. This is the second time I've woken up from unconsciousness aboard the *Sphynx*. I'd really like it to be the last time.

There are other questions: Like how did we escape being tracked down by Corps ships detached to the Fortress's aid? And what happened to Rajcik? No one has the answer to these. And that worries us all.

WE'VE BEEN BACK at Agate Beach for two days and I'm at the point where I can stand and even walk a few feet before pain and exhaustion force me prone again. I've asked to be helped into David's room a few times, but so far he hasn't been awake. In his weakened condition —he'd barely been able to stay on his feet while fleeing the alpha-zero hangar—he needs to retain all the energy his body can summon to help him heal and Vitruzzi has kept him sedated. His ribs are knitting gamely, and she's been running tests to determine what the Admin did to his eyes, trying to figure out whether or not he'll ever see again.

The settlement's makeshift hospital occupies three of the smaller rooms inside the mine. Brady had warned the people living here while we were still en route about the possibility of Rajcik attacking them. Since then, everything necessary to keep the settlement safe, fed, and protected has been brought inside the network of underground shafts and caves, leaving the outdoor settlement virtually abandoned. Everyone now lives in a constant state of alert. We can't take any chances that Rajcik won't try and get his revenge. He may not have cleared the station before it flared into a billion blazing fragments. But what if he did? Neither Vitruzzi nor I have forgotten his promise to destroy Agate Beach. Not for a second. The *Sphynx* and her short-range shuttle sweep the skies night and day, and a rotating schedule of locals continuously monitor the radar systems from the subterranean control room.

I hadn't been able to walk off the *Sphynx* on my own two feet and the inability to help out has been frustrating. I'm tired of being an invalid, relying on others. It's time to get back to the Aly who never asks for help and gets it done on her own. Leaning over to pull on my boots is a textbook lesson in misery, but once they're on, I carefully push myself upright and begin a slow, methodical shuffle next door to David's recovery room.

He's stretched out flat on the bed, looking pale, worn, and haggard. If I didn't see the beat of his pulse in his neck, I might think he was dead. Then, to my surprise, his eyes peel open in slow motion as if he's falling asleep in reverse.

"Hey, little sis." Fatigue and injuries make his voice soft.

Lurching to his bedside as fast as I can, I wrap one of his white hands in both of mine. It's not as cold as it looks. "Hey. How did you know it was me?"

"Easy. You're the only one who doesn't walk in and start prodding me or pulling on these tubes sticking out of me."

I grin. "How are you feeling?"

He considers the question for a minute, taking inventory. "I think it will be a couple of days before I'm ready for a rugby match, but nothing really hurts. Captain Vitruzzi is ninety-nine percent sure that the shit that screwed up my eyes—she says they're retinal ganglion-inhibitors—will wear off. That's a relief."

Patches of fading blue bruises still mark his arms and the top part of his chest not covered by his gown. His face is the only thing that looks really bad, even though it's probably the least of his injuries.

"When did you wake up?" I ask.

"Just a couple hours ago. I told Vitruzzi not to bother you if you were sleeping. How are you doing?"

"I'd say fantastic by comparison."

This makes him grin crookedly, only using one side of his mouth so he doesn't reopen the split in his lower lip. Watching him lie there, something inside me, some wall of emotion that I'd defiantly controlled, finally lets go.

"I shouldn't have left you on Obal 3." Guilt withers my words into skeletal leaves that crackle to the floor, and my eyes fill with water.

"Don't be crazy, sis. If you hadn't, we'd both be dead." His eyebrows are furrowed with concern, that older brother expression that always makes me feel as if I'm still seven years old. Squeezing my fingers in his strong hands, he says, "You had to run, and you did. And then you pulled off the most amazing rescue in the history of the universe. *You* did, little sis, you and these people, and you saved my life. Don't beat yourself up, because there was nothing else you could have done."

Wiping away the tears and trying to smile, I say, "Yeah, okay, you're right. You damn near threw me through that door anyway. I'm lucky you didn't break my ribs." He knows I'm just covering it up, but the important thing is that he's safe now and on the mend.

We settle into silence for a while, no sound in the room except filters drawing out the stale air. I know he still needs to rest, but I can't stop myself from asking, "How did you know what Rajcik planned to do with the Nova? And why didn't you tell me?"

He doesn't respond for several seconds. "I couldn't tell you because I didn't want you to get hurt; I figured what you didn't know couldn't be used against you."

"Dammit, David, I'm not a kid . . ."

"Yeah, I know, but it's my job, okay? You'll always be my little sister." His smirk has turned into a grimace, but not from the pain in his body. "Besides, I wasn't sure until after what happened at New Sweden. A couple of nights after Rajcik told us about the Fortress job, I was working in the wiring shaft under the com console. There was a short in my bunk's intercom and I traced it back to the panel down there. As I was finishing up, someone pinged us and then Rajcik came in and answered before I could get out of there. It was T'Kai. I was actually kind of glad to be there, to get to hear for myself what was really going on. We've both always known better than to trust Rajcik."

He shifts, trying to get a little more comfortable, and I think about ending the conversation so he can get the rest he needs. But I don't. "They argued about New Sweden. T'Kai wanted him to pick up a team of non-cits living there and use them on the job. Rajcik refused; he said he wouldn't use anyone on a job that he didn't know. T'Kai threatened him, things got ugly. I could see Rajcik's reflection in the VDU through the floor—I thought the whole deal was about to get blown, the way he reacted. But then he relaxed and gave in. A few days later, right before we were supposed to get there, he asked me about security around Tunis City, wanting to know how to get clearance, how to get close to the Capitol building. I kind of laughed, you know, because it's *impossible* to get in the Capitol's air space. I told Rajcik that a ship, a known ship like the *Temptation*, had no chance. The closest we'd ever get to Obal 10 would be one of its port moons, and then we'd still probably be shot down. It made me really uneasy, Aly. And that's when I started to think he had other plans for the Nova."

"So I got us out of the deal at New Sweden. I thought T'Kai might change his mind and set up an ambush, but I never thought Rajcik would do what he did. Jesus, how could we work for a man like that? When he killed all those people, I realized he was tying up loose ends. He wasn't going to let anything come between the plans he had, not even T'Kai. Whatever excuse he gave T'Kai must have worked, or maybe T'Kai was desperate, I don't know. But I knew it was time for us to cut loose too."

His breathing has sped up and I can see the effort hurts his wounded ribs, so I try to end the conversation. "Forget it. You need to take it easy. We can talk about it later, if you want."

He ignores me. "So after New Sweden, I told him you and I were getting out after the Admin paid up and we got our cut. I thought he'd try to convince us to stay, or threaten to kill us, something. But he acted as if it didn't matter. It was what he said that convinced me he was never planning on selling it. 'You and your sister do what you want, David. After we get that bomb, there won't be anyone left to stop you.' It wasn't hard to guess what he meant.

"The only thing more important to Rajcik than money is destroying the Admin. If he had the Nova, he finally had the opportunity to really hurt them. I couldn't kill him, not with Thompson and Fedchenko in the way, so I waited until we were on Obal 3 and tried to get away."

"You should have told me."

"I know that now. But I was so concerned with protecting you, I didn't know if you'd believe me. And I didn't want anyone else to know I suspected what Rajcik was planning. Maybe they were in on it too, I didn't know. Maybe Ortiz could have been trusted, but there wasn't enough time. The most important thing was getting away from Rajcik as soon as we could. I never thought we'd pull off the assault on the Fortress anyway." He'd sat up on his elbows while relaying the story. Now he eases back down to his pillow with a strained expression. "I'm glad I was wrong about that part, little sis. I mean, he probably had help infiltrating the station from T'Kai, but if you hadn't figured out a way to get in and outmaneuver their security, I wouldn't be here right now." His voice trails off and his eyes close again.

I want to tell him that it's time for him to stop treating me like the little sister who used to come crying to him whenever I skinned an elbow or took another hammering from Dad. But I know it won't do any good. So I don't say anything and watch as he drifts back to sleep.

Two more weeks pass and not a sign of Rajcik. People are beginning to move topside again, but no one takes any needless chances. The colony's radars are watched night and day. I'm stronger now, but Vitruzzi hasn't let me leave the infirmary yet—more because there's nowhere else for me to sleep than because of my injuries. David still has tunnel vision, but his sight is returning.

I'm standing next to the infirmary counter, my weapons broken down and the pieces laid out in neat rows, when the familiar sound of Strahan's boots approach from down the hallway. I catch myself smiling and put the Sinbad's barrel up to my eye before he notices. Staring intently down the barrel, I examine it for any excess carbon.

"Need help with those?"

Lowering the barrel, I see him grinning at me. He holds out his hand, revealing a round, ripe grapefruit. The yellow-pink skin shines with droplets of glistening oil, making it look like the roundest, juiciest, most appealing piece of candy ever made. "I saved you one."

"I haven't seen a grapefruit since I was a kid. Thanks. Someday you're going to have to show me how you manage to grow these things." Saliva begins trickling into my mouth. I've only been back on solid food for a few days, and the dehydrated nutritional bars I'm so used to eating aren't putting a dent in my appetite. I take the fruit and begin to peel the thick skin off, relishing the sweet smell, and drop the peelings onto my work rag.

"If you stick around, I will."

I don't look at him, but I know he catches the way my hands pause for a moment. "Sure."

"Aly, listen." He reaches out and gently wraps a callused hand around one of my wrists, urging me to stop and look at him. "You are staying, right?"

I gently retrieve my wrist and put the grapefruit down on the rag. "I don't know. I mean, Agate Beach doesn't really need more people, and the kind of trouble David and I could bring—it's not really worth it. Not for you guys, anyway."

His brows wrinkle in a look that says he's not buying my bullshit. "Who are you trying to convince? You know you're not protecting us by leaving, so don't act like you think you are. We bought our troubles, and we can deal with them. And what would you and David do anyway? Where would you go?" He finishes matter-of-factly, "Your friends are here."

I look intently into his sepia eyes, trying for the first time to imagine what it would be like not to be on the run. To belong somewhere with people who actually care about each other, about me.

"Aly, we want you to stay." He pauses. "*I* want you to stay."

I draw a quick, almost nervous breath and realize: this is what it feels like to be home.

AFTERWORD

Follow Aly and David on their vendetta against the Admin in the next book in the Spectras Arise Series, CONTRACT OF BETRAYAL.

Thanks for reading! If you enjoyed this story, please consider leaving a quick and honest review on the retailer site of your choice. Reviews are critical in helping authors get their books in front of more readers. And the more people who buy our books, the more caffeine us wordnerds are able to soak in and continue to entertain you. (And, let's be honest, ourselves as well.) Don't forget to join my newsletter at www.tammysalyer.com/newsletter to stay up to date on new releases and receive a free collection of stories. Cheers!

ALSO BY TAMMY SALYER

SPECTRAS ARISE SERIES

When all other options run out, never let go of your gun.

In a few hundred years, the Algol system becomes humanity's new home.
The question is: Is it a better one?

THE SHACKLED VERITIES SERIES

In a Cosmos-wide war between celestials, humans are as expendable as
pawns. Until Ulfric Aldinhuus, leader of the Knights Corporealis, uses the
celestials' weapons to fight back.

OTHERWORLD OUTLAWS SERIES

A sawbones fae with a supernatural-sized grudge, a necromancer gnome
obsessed with pixie dust, and a hoodoo cowgirl with a Sharps buffalo rifle
and damn good aim—the Tuatha Dé Danann will never know what hit 'em.

COLLECTIONS

A Scorpion's Heart: Four Twisted Tales of Love and Lust

SHORT STORIES

Artificial Fate * Creepers * No Suede Soles in Hell

Visit my website to see if anything new has been released since this
publication.

www.tammysalyer.com

ABOUT THE AUTHOR

Tammy is an inveterate verbarian, who spends her days surrounded by the written word, both hers and others'. As an ex-paratrooper with the 82nd Airborne Division, her stories are often as gritty as a grunt's pile of three-week-old field gear. Her military science fiction Spectras Arise series debuted to acclaim in 2012, and her epic fantasy adventure series The Shackled Verities was launched in 2020. She's currently five books deep in a Weird West series called Otherworld Outlaws, featuring half-fae sawbones, a necromancer gnome, and a hoodoo cowgirl galavanting into mischief in the Old West.

When not hunched like a Morlock over her writing desk, Tammy runs and bikes silly miles with her super-cool weirdo partner in the Pacific Northwest playground and spends an inappropriate amount of time watching Henry Rollins videos on YouTube. Contrary to whatever ideas her last name might conjure, she's never really been much of a Slayer fan.

Fantasy, space opera, satire, and snark fans will feel right at home with Tammy. Learn more about her and her books by visiting www. tammysalyer.com. She hopes you enjoy reading her works and welcomes your reviews.